I0761409

MILO'S RECKONING

ALSO BY JOSEPH OLSHAN

Black Diamond Fall

Cloudland

The Conversion

In Clara's Hands

Vanitas

Nightswimmer

The Sound of Heaven

The Waterline

A Warmer Season

Clara's Heart

Milo's Reckoning

a novel

Joseph Olshan

GREEN CITY
BOOKS

Green City Books

For more information, contact Green City Books:
editors@greencitybooks.com
Published 2025
Published in the United States of America
ISBN: 978-1-963101-08-9
Hardcover $27.99 US | $37.99 CAD

First Edition
designed by Isaac Peterson
cover art by Isaac Peterson
Library of Congress Cataloging-in-Publication Data has been applied for.

For Todd

"There are few reasons for telling the truth,
but for lying the number is infinite."

—Carlos Ruiz Zafón, *The Shadow of the Wind*

Part One

1994

1.

"Call me tomorrow when you get to your office," was the last thing Lenny D'Ambrosio had ever said to Milo, who never got a chance to make the call. Early the following morning, his phone rang, and a detective explained that Lenny, Milo's friend and mentor, had been found hanging from a bedsheet tied to a rafter in his apartment.

The crazy, unforeseen news pierced Milo like a shard of glass. The pain was jagged and radiant, and with the phone jammed to his ear, he collapsed into a chair at his kitchen table and began shivering.

It was seven o'clock in the morning, and he'd answered the suspiciously early call as he was about to tie the laces on his running shoes for his typical morning jog along the West Side Highway in Manhattan. "Are you still there?" the detective had to ask several times before Milo at last managed to reply.

"Yes. I am here. So, is this . . ." Milo took a deep breath and forced himself to say, "So you're saying he committed suicide?"

"That's how it appears. But we won't know until the coroner—" The detective paused. "—makes a preliminary ruling. Anyway, he apparently told his sister you were going to be there last night."

"I *was* there. He had a few people over. But I was the last to leave." The fact of Lenny being dead was refusing to sink in, let alone the idea of him committing suicide.

"So can you get up here? We'd like to talk to you in person."

Milo didn't know how to respond. He glanced at his watch. "I'm supposed to start teaching in two hours."

"Can somebody cover your class?"

Not on such short notice, he told the detective. But did it really matter? There was no way he'd be able to teach; he couldn't possibly face the students in his Italian 4 class. Another breaker of shock hit him, and he began sweating. He'd call the department and tell them to put a note on his door: Class cancelled due to family emergency.

Amidst his brewing thoughts, he could hear the detective persist. "If you take the train, we're only two blocks from the station."

"I know where you are," he managed to reply. "I can walk to my mother's house from where you are."

"I thought you grew up here, but I wasn't sure." Milo now heard somebody speaking to the detective. "Okay, the coroner wants me. I gotta motor."

"Wait, wait! Before you go, can I just ask: Who found him?"

The detective grunted. "The neighbor below him. She went upstairs to check. Because she heard commotion. His door was unlocked."

"Commotion?"

"How about we talk about that when you get here?" The detective signed off without a further word.

Standing there in his apartment cluttered with syllabus pages and language primers and large, bilingual dictionaries, Milo reflected that Lenny had seemed perfectly content the evening before, not morose, certainly not preoccupied. And yet, somehow, in some way he'd gone to an extreme. What could have propelled him to stop the motion of his life, to just shut it down? In his state of agitated bewilderment, Milo convinced himself that going for his morning run might help him gain some perspective, some way to begin comprehending what he'd just heard. He stared down at his running shoes and at last began tying them, thinking to himself that this simple daily act of tying shoelaces was something that Lenny D'Ambrosio would never do again.

He left his apartment, took the elevator down to the street, and setting out along Ninth Street, jogged toward the Hudson River, beginning to scroll through the events of the previous evening, when he'd taken the Metro-North train up to Mamaroneck to Lenny's. And then he remembered something.

It had been a typical evening. Lenny had prepared a pasta ragù with (he bragged) two kinds of pancetta that he'd learned to make from one of his aunts who lived in Parma. Milo and two much older women, former colleagues of Lenny's at Columbia, had dined with *Aida* playing in the background at low volume. When they were done, Milo made an attempt to clear the table, but Lenny sprang up from his seat, grabbed the plates, and hurried them into his large, well-equipped kitchen.

When he came back into the dining room, he placed both of his hands on the back of his chair and leaned on it. He scrutinized Milo and said in the patronizing way of a mentor, "You've been eating too much?" The women laughed.

Milo was affronted. "What do you mean?"

"I don't know." Lenny raised his bony shoulders. "You look . . . bigger. Doesn't he?" he asked the other guests.

"Oh, leave him alone," one of them said.

Milo glanced down at his stomach and then shook his head. "I'm just bulkier." He reminded Lenny that at NYU, the gym was free for faculty. "You taught there. You should know."

"I would not know. Because, as you know, I am not a gym person," Lenny reminded him. And in his reminder was a slight note of disdain, as though going to the gym were anti-intellectual.

Indeed, Lenny had been unathletically slim. He'd had one of those finely structured Northern Italian faces that you'd see in Milan, a face that hinted of Teutonic influence, of which there was a great deal in Lombardy, especially in the regions that bordered Switzerland and the provinces of Trentino and Veneto. He'd looked very much like his sister, Maria, only her eyes were a watery gray. His fashionable clothing fit him handsomely, and while he'd worn his hair long and slightly disheveled, he'd spent quite a bit of money in a New York City hair salon, keeping it cut precisely in that unstudied way.

When the evening was winding down and Lenny's former colleagues were getting ready to leave, Lenny asked Milo if he could stay a bit longer. Glancing at his watch,

Milo had agreed but told Lenny he'd have to make the 11:20 train back to Manhattan.

"Fine. I'll drive you."

After the other dinner guests had departed, Lenny sat down again and refilled his glass of red wine. He leaned back in his chair and said, "So how's *it* going?" *It* meaning Milo's dissertation.

Lenny had convinced Milo to write about the late work of Natalia Ginzburg, an Italian novelist who lived and wrote about fascism and World War II. "I haven't had much time lately, to be honest."

Lenny hectored him. "You don't have *time* or you're still stuck?"

"I'm not stuck, Lenny, I just don't agree with you."

Milo was referring to the shopworn dispute between them about Ginzburg's exclusive use of the first person in her writing, something that Lenny believed elevated her work and that Milo felt diminished it: that she avoided third person for personal reasons, perhaps that she feared writing in a larger dimension. Milo was still trying to divine and prove what these reasons were, and his own uncertainty had caused him to lose his step in his dissertation. "Is this why you asked me to stay?" He forced himself to laugh.

"No it isn't."

Itching to change the subject, Milo said, "Okay, but before I forget . . . my mom asked me to thank you for the card. You're the only person who sends her a card every year. Religiously," Milo deliberately added, the use of the word ironic in light of the fact that Lenny was no longer a practicing Catholic.

"Well, I know how difficult that anniversary always is for her," Lenny said with feeling.

He had been referring to the anniversary of the death of Milo's brother, Carlo. A senior at Iona College in New Rochelle, Carlo had been driving home for a meal their mother had prepared for him when his car was broadsided by a hit-and-run driver who ran a red light. Carlo suffered a brain injury and also a great deal of internal bleeding by the time paramedics arrived at the scene. He remained unconscious for most of his brief hospitalization, but right before he died, he opened his eyes and gazed at Milo with a look of sadness and resignation. His brother's basilisk gaze seemed to telegraph, *I'm dying, so better take good care of Mom!*—who already happened to be a widow: their father had died of a heart attack when Milo was eight years old and Carlo was ten.

Lenny asked, "Does it even feel like six years?" and glanced at Milo's left forearm, which, even in winter, he always kept exposed to exhibit his memorial tattoo: *Carlo 7/1/67—3/4/88*, a tattoo his mother had begged him not to get.

Milo shook his head, weathering a familiar breaker of misery. "No, it feels more recent."

Lenny nodded. "That's how I feel about the death of Primo Levi." Milo knew what was coming. "Not even a year before your brother."

"But a chosen death. A death by suicide." Milo always felt he needed to remind Lenny of this about the Italian writer; after all, Carlo had had no control over his own demise.

"Well, that actually has never been proven."

Lenny reminded Milo that modern apartment complexes in Italian cities were often built around circular staircases that spiraled up several stories and that these buildings, constructed right after the Second World War, didn't have elevators. On April 11, 1987, Primo Levi, who was living with his mother, came home from grocery shopping, climbed five long flights up to his apartment, and, setting down two full bags, either fell or jumped to his death. He'd been suffering from depression. He'd recently gone on medication for the condition, and that might have affected his balance as well as his state of mind.

Milo had looked around Lenny's apartment, where among his jam-packed bookshelves and his fine collection of Murano glass, one or another of Primo Levi's books in their original Italian was always lying out on some table, perpetually in view, ready at a moment's notice to be cracked open. Lenny had often referred to the fact that even though Primo Levi survived Auschwitz, part of his identity had remained there. That the camp was a constant shadow on his life; he'd had persistent survivor's guilt.

"The thing I've never been able to work out," Milo said, "is why Primo Levi would have gone grocery shopping right before he jumped."

His eyes glistening with emotion, Lenny softly replied, "He was probably buying his mother enough staples so she'd be set for a while. So she wouldn't have to leave the apartment. So she wouldn't have to look down to where he landed."

Remembering this part of the discussion just as he was rounding a corner on West Tenth Street and began heading south toward Chinatown and the looming World Trade towers that dwarfed everything in his direct path, Milo reflected that Lenny never did broach whatever he'd planned to discuss. "So what did you want to tell me?" Milo had queried him while they were driving to the train station, looking over at Lenny, who seemed about to explain and then faltered. "Let's talk about it in the morning. Call me when you get to your office." If Lenny had been contemplating suicide, why would he have asked Milo to call him the following morning knowing full well that he would never answer the phone?

2.

"You were his Italian student at Mercy, isn't that right?" asked the detective who'd contacted Milo, now sitting opposite him along with another detective at the Harrison police station. Detective Delzio was fair-haired and broadly built, with piercing blue eyes.

"I went to his lectures during high school. But they were at NYU, not Mercy."

"But you met him *at* Mercy," said the other detective, a lanky Latino man called Rodriguez who'd been introduced to Milo and explained that he'd been assigned to the case in the event that the coroner ruled in homicide.

"I met him at Mercy, but never studied with him at Mercy," Milo explained.

"What sort of lectures at NYU?" asked Rodriguez.

Milo explained that he was sixteen when he'd audited his first class: Italian literature translated into English. He'd read everything in the original Italian.

"And now you're getting your PhD?" Delzio asked.

Milo nodded and explained that he was writing his dissertation.

Rodriguez frowned. "What got you so interested in the Italian language?"

He explained that his mother's sister lived in Italy, that he'd spent every summer there, pretty much until college.

"And before my brother went to college, he spent every summer there, too."

"Sorry for your loss," Delzio murmured, clearly aware of what had happened to Carlo.

Wanting to anchor the edgy awkwardness, Milo found himself saying to Delzio, "Not that it really matters, but I think you knew my father."

The detective looked skeptical. "Your *father*? Who's your father?"

"*He's* dead, too." Milo laughed nervously. "Jack Rossi."

Delzio looked flabbergasted. "*What?* You're Jack Rossi's son? Jack-the-scratch Rossi?"

"That would be him," Milo said grimly.

"Damn . . . He was a *great* golfer," Delzio said with what sounded like grudging approval. "I played him once or twice."

"Yeah, you did. I actually remember him telling my brother and me you played him. And how you gave him a run for his money. When you called me this morning your name sounded familiar. Then when I was on the train, I remembered my father mentioning you."

"I know your dad was pretty young when he died. May I ask what the cause was?"

"Heart failure."

Delzio softly whistled. "Wow, you've been through a lot for a twenty-five-year-old kid."

Milo shrugged and explained that his father had died a long time ago—like another lifetime. "My brother's death was a lot more recent. And that's been—well, really hard on my mother and me."

Delzio nodded. "Of course."

Seeming impatient, Rodriguez resumed, "So back to Lenny D'Ambrosio . . . Mrs. Colicchio, the downstairs neighbor who found him, says late night/early morning she heard a loud engine like a sports car starting up and driving away . . . and that's basically why I'm here. In case somebody else was there, in case somebody else was involved." The detective glanced meaningfully at Milo. "How did you get to his place last night?"

Wondering who could have been visiting Lenny so late at night, Milo explained that he'd taken a train up from the city. "Just like I did today." He'd taken a taxi to Lenny's apartment from the train station.

"And what time did you actually leave his place to go home?" Delzio asked.

"Around eleven p.m."

"*Around* eleven?" Rodriguez repeated.

"Okay, precisely *at* eleven p.m. He drove me to the train station in Mamaroneck, and I caught the 11:22 back to the city."

"And what about your ticket back to the city?" Delzio said.

"I bought it at the station."

"Do you have any record of it?

"They take the entire ticket when you get on the train. But I have a receipt from the taxi that I took to my apartment."

"Good. We'll need to see that," Rodriguez said. "Just to help rule things out."

"Rule *me* out, you mean?" Milo asked tentatively.

The detectives glanced at one another. "Something like that," Rodriguez said.

"What about the two other dinner guests?"

"The sister knew who they were. They're both older ladies and they have alibis," Delzio said. "Anyway, Mrs. Colicchio, the lady downstairs who said she heard commotion . . ." He hesitated. "But here's what's complicated: Mrs. Colicchio apparently is in the early stages of dementia. So perhaps not the most reliable of sources. The commotion she claims to have heard early this morning could have been you and the professor going down the stairs last night."

"Unless somebody else went up there later on, *after* you left," Rodriguez added quietly. Milo studied the detective's face, which held no discernible expression. "And that's the main reason we wanted to speak to you. If somebody had gone up there after you, would you have any idea of who this person might have been?"

Milo shook his head. "I really don't. I mean, it could have been anybody. You have to understand that Lenny was very private. Mysteriously private."

"A lover, perhaps?" Rodriguez ventured, tapping the air with his index finger.

"*No* idea," Milo insisted. And then he wondered: Would Lenny's death be easier for him to accept if someone else were responsible for it, if there might be someone out there who wanted him to die?

Glancing at his notes, and then looking up at Milo, Delzio continued, "So, his sister says he likes to recite poetry at night."

"Yeah . . . I mean, he knew practically the whole *Divine Comedy* by heart." It felt terrible to speak of Lenny in the past tense. Poetry rhymes easily in Italian, he explained to them, and so it sounds beautiful to recite. He went on to point out that Lenny had few people with whom he could speak Italian. That he looked down on his colleagues at Mercy College because he'd started his career teaching at Columbia.

"There's a story behind that," Delzio said, "isn't there? Why he left Columbia."

Milo nodded and said there was.

"Do you happen to know about it?"

"Not as much as I should, to be frank." Lenny had always been circumspect whenever he referred to the situation. "But here's what I do know. Apparently, there was a misunderstanding between him and a graduate student, and it escalated to the head of the Romance languages department and beyond, but Lenny never gave many details."

"But he *did* tell you about the disagreement?" Rodriguez said.

"Yes. In a roundabout sort of way. I knew better than to ask him too much about it."

In the midst of Milo's ongoing state of shock, the realization of Lenny ceasing to exist suddenly slammed him, made his eyes smart with tears. But he managed to continue. "He didn't like it when anybody tried to pry. So, I didn't . . . pry." Milo always assumed Lenny had given him the bare details of what had happened only because he figured that Milo probably would hear about it one way or another. "And the sense I got was that he felt ashamed of whatever happened.

He probably developed feelings for her. If you want to know more, you should probably ask his sister."

"How well do you know *her*?" Delzio asked.

"Not too well. I've been in her presence maybe a half dozen times."

At this, Delzio pivoted his thick torso and nodded to Rodriguez, who continued.

"Preliminary forensics suggest that besides the neck contusions, there were no other obvious signs of a struggle. The marks on his neck are consistent with suicide by hanging." This matter-of-fact discussion of what Lenny's dead body revealed to a coroner was a bit much for Milo, who started feeling dizzy. How could this possibly be happening?

Delzio was watching him. "You okay?"

"Fine," Milo said without conviction.

The detectives respectfully waited a few moments. Then Rodriguez continued, "When we went through the apartment, there was no note that we could find. But . . . let me put it this way: statistically, most people who commit suicide don't leave notes. A fairly high percentage of suicides happen without—they actually happen on the spur of the moment. No warning, no written explanation left behind. Sometimes the people do it because they're . . . just overwhelmed by some event or circumstance. While others—" He hesitated. "Let's say the people close to *them* insist there is no real reason that they know of. *More* important here is that a third of these suicides hang themselves. In fact, a larger percentage of people on the East Coast hang themselves than people on the West Coast."

"Okay, but the last thing Lenny said was, 'Call me tomorrow morning.' So I keep wondering: Would a person about to commit suicide do that?"

"You'd be surprised," Rodriguez said.

And then Milo relayed the previous evening's discussion about Primo Levi.

Both detectives found this intriguing. Delzio said, "But you say talking like this for him wasn't so out of character, right?"

"No, not really," Milo said.

"Anyway," Delzio went on, "with the medical examiner's prelim, right now we *will* provisionally rule his death a suicide."

He glanced at Rodriguez, who said, "But we're not completely convinced it *was* suicide." And therefore they'd probably do some more investigation. "There's just one thing," Rodriguez said. Milo dreaded what was to come next. "Somebody hanging themselves has to get up on a chair to do it. Nine times out of ten, they kick the chair out of the way and then the chair turns over. But not in this case. The chair was still upright and several feet away from the body. Almost like somebody had positioned it there."

"Wait. So then you're saying that somebody *could* have been there?"

"Certainly possible," Delzio said.

"But why?"

"*Why?* Any number of reasons *why*, but clearly the person would have had some serious beef with him," Rodriguez said.

Milo told them that Lenny was fairly self-contained, inordinately respectful of other people, not the sort to make enemies, much less get in arguments with people he didn't know. The only time he'd ever get heated would be in discussions about politics and literature.

Milo suddenly felt nauseated. "I'm sorry," he told them. "I don't think I can talk about this anymore."

"That's okay, we're pretty much done here anyway," Delzio said, fixing Milo with his unsettling, penetrating, pale-eyed gaze. "Like I said, we're still strongly leaning toward suicide."

3.

As he left the police headquarters, Milo's heart was hammering, and he felt light-headed.

I just can't believe this is happening, he kept thinking as he walked down Harrison Avenue, passing Rizzoli's Restaurant, famous for its homemade lasagna; then Butler Brothers, the grocery store that delivered to the wealthier precincts in town; then La Vigna's Garage, whose owner always had a thing for Milo's mother, who, when she became an animal rights advocate, sold the guy's wife her beaver coat.

He kept thinking, *If Lenny was planning on killing himself, surely I would have gotten some inkling. Some warning sign.* It was hard to imagine Lenny taking his own life on the spur of the moment in the way Rodriguez described.

And then he wondered: When Delzio and Rodriquez mentioned the chair that managed to remain upright, were they withholding information that, for the moment at least, they were reluctant to share with him?

Milo made a right turn onto Locust Avenue and began passing clapboard Victorian-style homes packed tightly together, many of them two-family residences, one of which belonged to Lenny's sister, Maria.

The house was painted a deep red with gray shingles. A well-dressed elderly couple was just then walking inside—he guessed they were family members who'd rushed up from

Brooklyn or Staten Island to comfort her. Milo couldn't imagine what Maria was going through at that very moment. The wind picked up and blew a lock of his soft, curly hair over his large, coal-dark eyes. He stopped and thought about knocking on the door, but that would probably mean getting into an involved, very emotional conversation that he felt he wasn't quite ready for. Besides, he knew that his mother was waiting for him.

It was actually his mother who'd orchestrated his friendship with Lenny—right after he'd returned from Italy at the end of the summer before eleventh grade. Milo had been abroad for three months, and one day, overhearing him speaking in Italian to her sister's boyfriend during a transatlantic telephone call to Tuscany, Rose Marie decided that Milo needed to keep his Italian going during the school year and insisted that he take a high-level class at nearby Mercy College. Maria D'Ambrosio was already an acquaintance of hers from church, and she'd heard that Maria's brother, Lenny, was teaching there. Carlo, then a freshman studying science at Iona College, had stopped spending his summers in Italy and never had any interest in improving his Italian, which, despite the amount of time he'd spent in Italy, had remained rudimentary.

During the first class at Mercy, when Professor D'Ambrosio asked a question, Milo answered it fluidly and then delivered a snarky remark, which caused Lenny to turn to him and say in English, "Do me a favor, shut up for the rest of the hour." Then he pointed an accusing finger. "And come and see me afterward."

"Is this some kind of joke?" he asked when Milo finally approached him. "Did somebody send you in here to make a mockery of me?"

"My mother."

"Your mother?"

"Rose Marie Rossi."

Lenny's severe expression softened. "Ah, Rose Marie Rossi."

Then Milo explained about spending every summer in Tuscany.

"All well and good, but I can't have you in this class," Lenny said. Switching to Italian, he told Milo that, at his level, he should be studying Italian *literature*, not Italian language.

Lenny was now conversing in a faster, cultured, melodious Italian that instantly reminded Milo of the Italian spoken by an art history professor, a scholar of the mosaics in Saint Mark's Basilica in Venice who'd once invited him to a lecture.

He told Lenny that his Italian reminded him of Professor Pollaco's Italian.

"Was Pollaco Jewish?" Lenny asked him with a calculating look on his face.

Milo, whose paternal grandfather happened to be Jewish, found the question suspicious and surprising. "He *was* as a matter of fact. Why?"

"Because Jewish Italian intellectuals tend to speak with this sort of intonation. Clipped, measured. I was a student of one of them. In Perugia. And what you're hearing is the influence of the five years I spent learning to speak like him."

At this, Lenny began gathering his books and papers on his desk, and then a thought occurred to him. "Like I said, I can't have you in this class. But I have an idea. One day a week down at NYU, I teach a seminar on Primo Levi, Giuseppe Lampedusa, and Alberto Moravia. My course is in English, but you seem to have enough Italian to read the texts in the original. Come to the class, and if you'd like, from time to time, we can meet and discuss the books in the language they're meant to be read in."

And so, with his mother's enthusiastic approval, Milo began attending the NYU lectures. This was how he became Lenny's protégé.

4.

At last arriving at his childhood home, Milo went inside to a gloomy kitchen. He looked for the gleam of pots, the stove simmering with sauce, the yeasty smell of fresh bread warming in the oven, a frying pan sizzling with breaded cutlets—his mother always automatically started cooking whenever she knew he'd be arriving. But there was nothing on the stove. He found her sitting in the shadows at the kitchen table. "What are you doing?" he asked.

She looked up at him, her large, doleful dark eyes replicas of his. "Waiting for you to get home." Her hennaed hair was cut short and waved into crescents around her gaunt, sun-freckled face. She was nervous by nature and, in Milo's opinion, far too thin. Besides what she cooked for him, she concocted large meals for her church's soup kitchen, but ate little of what she made. "I didn't know when you'd arrive. I thought maybe you'd stop by and see Maria on the way here."

Milo shook his head. "You're my number one," he told Rose Marie. "I had to check in with you first."

He sat down at the table. Rose Marie slid her hands toward him; he took them and bent over and put his forehead on them. And then, unexpectedly, the tears came. As he sobbed, he realized the tears were for more than just the death of Lenny. His tears were also for Carlo; they were for any premature ending to a life of promise. When he finally stopped, wiped his eyes, and looked at his mother, he could see that she, too, had gotten tearful.

"I know Lenny was family to you. Like a father figure," his mother said.

"Well, not quite a father figure," he disagreed. "I don't need a father figure."

"You don't know what you need," his mother insisted.

This annoyed him, but for the moment he kept that to himself. Milo knew his mother wanted to promote the idea of a father figure simply because she and his father had become antagonistic in their marriage, and after his father's death, she'd always hoped that Milo would find a surrogate. "Speaking of father figures, I somehow remembered that Dad and Delzio, the detective I just met with, played golf together. I remembered it on the train up here."

"You remember that?" His mother was incredulous. After all, Milo was eight when his father died.

"I just remember Dad saying Delzio was a great golfer."

Rose Marie asked what had happened at the police station, and Milo filled her in, saying that other than the contusion areas around Lenny's neck that presumably came from hanging, the rest of his body had shown no sign of a struggle. And that therefore the presumption was suicide.

His mother looked down at the table, shaking her head. Then she looked up at him. "But Milo, you saw him last night. Did he strike you as somebody who *wanted* to end his life?"

And then Milo was enraged by the inexplicable act of violence of his friend's death. "He didn't seem like it, Mom, but how can I know for sure? Last night he appeared to be perfectly himself: giving me shit about my dissertation, *complaining* about teaching, *complaining* about how dumb his students were, and then, like always, reciting Dante at the kitchen table . . . But then pointed out one thing."

"Which was?"

"Lenny brought up the death of Primo Levi. It wasn't the first time he'd done that—and we discussed whether or not it was suicide."

His mother looked afraid. "Really?"

"Then he asked me to call him in the morning. Said he had something to tell me."

She glowered at him and then demanded, "Why didn't you ask him right then and there what he wanted to tell you?"

"Because I had a train to catch," he replied with impatience. "And it seemed like whatever he wanted to say needed more time than what we had."

His mother fell silent, trying to assimilate this, her brow furrowed. At last, she said, "So they're saying somebody *maybe* could have forced him to hang himself?"

"They're saying it's possible."

"But why would anyone want to do something like that to such a kind, gentle man?"

"Precisely my question. I mean, he was a college professor, not a mobster."

She nodded. "Okay, so . . . then what's your theory? You have to have some theory!" she pressed him.

Milo shrugged. "I wish I did. The downstairs neighbor found him. She says she heard a struggle going on above her.

But apparently, she isn't reliable because she's gaga. I mean, he was my mentor, he was my friend, but as I've told you many times, he never really *confided* in me."

Rose Marie considered the matter for a few moments and then said, "Okay, let's say somebody else *was* involved. Why would they *want* Lenny to die? Why would they *want* to make it look like he killed himself?"

"*That's* the million-dollar question."

Rose Marie looked a bit discomfited. "Did you ever think he might have been into men, or—" She hesitated, peering at him fixedly. "Boys?"

"No, Mom!" Milo was emphatic. "I never got any impression like that."

"Well, he didn't exactly strike me as heterosexual either. Maybe asexual?"

"No! He always talked about women, about women he desired." About women Lenny had once been in love with, about women who'd rejected him.

Rose Marie shuddered. "Have you spoken to Maria?"

"I'm about to call her."

"When you do, can you find out when the wake is?"

"Okay, Mom. I will."

There was a phone extension in Milo's bedroom, which up until Carlo's death, he'd shared with his older brother. Rose Marie had insisted that Carlo's effects be left where they were—so nothing in the room had much changed since then. Carlo's college textbooks on genetics and biology still lined the shelves above his alcove desk, and his colored pens and highlighters spiked out of a round leather vessel. His electric pencil sharpener carefully lined up next to a neat stack of *Popular Mechanics*. All Carlo's clothing still hung in his side of their closet: pressed Oxford shirts, maroon sweatshirts with the yellow Iona insignia, a shoe tree filled with loafers and clunky sneakers and a highly polished pair of black Doc Martens. Among these belongings there was only one item of sentimental value: their father's prized golfing putter that had been tailor-made for him and which he'd given to Carlo, the only other golfer in the family. The putter was now leaning against a corner of the room. Milo had repeatedly tried to convince his mother to clear Carlo's belongings from the room, but she stubbornly insisted that she needed the room to remain as it had been during his short lifetime.

Although he obviously could never confirm it, Milo assumed that when she was alone in the house, which was most of the time, Rose Marie came and sat in this room, immersing herself in the remnants of her departed son's life. She would say that she felt him in every breath she took, his presence in every waking moment when she wasn't plunged in the distraction of an activity: cooking the church's meals for the needy; keeping her house maniacally tidy; baking bread and Italian cookies for relatives who lived in far-flung boroughs. She always said it was easier for her to think about Carlo constantly rather than less frequently; by doing this she claimed she was keeping him alive for herself and for Milo whom she knew had his own life and career to be concerned about.

And yet after the car accident, Milo found it really difficult to get used to the fact that Carlo's life presided so heavily over his uninhabited side of their shared bedroom space—but eventually, slowly, he got used to living under the spectral shadow of his brother. When Carlo died, Milo was already a freshman at Boston College. Then he went to graduate school at NYU, so for quite a few years now he'd spent very little time in the room the two of them grew up in.

He'd never been all that close to Carlo whose reticence was immediately apparent to anyone who met him. But it was an agitated sort of reticence, arguably the result of some mysterious, unarticulated inner conflict. It ended up creating a barrier between the brothers, and whenever Milo tried to break through that barrier, Carlo quietly but persistently brushed him off.

Milo remembered one incident shortly before his death when Carlo, then in his third year at Iona, was home for the weekend, and Milo had come down from Boston College. Even though Iona was only eight miles away, Carlo, in fierce opposition to Rose Marie, had insisted on living in student housing adjacent to the college. They were both in their room when a call came through from a woman who'd wanted to speak to Carlo. When Milo handed him the phone, his brother jammed it against his chest and said tightly, "Can you leave now? Go downstairs or something." Six foot three, long-limbed, and awkward, Carlo was huddling over the phone like a praying mantis, and as Milo left, he couldn't help noticing that his brother looked angry.

"Who *was* that?" he asked later on after dinner when the two brothers were alone again.

"A girl from my chemistry lab. She needs my help."

"Is she sweet?" Milo asked.

Carlo smiled tightly. "She is. But she's also very . . . I don't know, needy I guess is the word, and it gets under my skin."

"So, you're not interested in dating her?"

"No, not really."

One thing that Carlo and Lenny had in common was they each fiercely guarded their private lives. "Well, is there *anyone* you're interested in?"

Carlo shook his head. "I don't have time." And then said quietly, "I'm not like you. I don't need to be dating someone all the time. I don't need to rely on anyone."

Milo thought better to ask, "And why is that?"

With a weary tone, Carlo said, "It's just not my style."

"What *is* your style?" Milo pressed.

"My style is to make sure I'm left alone," Carlo had said. "So I can study."

You're always studying, Milo wanted to say. *But what exactly are you studying for?* But he didn't ask for clarification, because he knew that Carlo was undoubtedly referring to his dream of becoming a research biologist specializing in genetics. Milo always wondered if his brother had been so fatigued from studying late into the evening the night before the accident, that early the following morning he just didn't have the reflexes to avoid the reckless driver. And with that thought in mind, he reached for the telephone and dialed Maria D'Ambrosio.

5.

An older woman answered the phone. When Milo announced himself, she didn't recognize his name and seemed reluctant to pass the call along. "Can you please just tell her it's Milo Rossi?"

This time his name carried through the receiver, and he heard, "Oh, Fran, just give me the phone, will you? I'm sorry, Milo," Maria said when she came on the line. "Aunt Francesca is protecting me. Newspapers have been calling. I'm glad to hear from you."

"I've been wanting to call you all day. I'm—well, I'm just so confused, shocked. Trying to get my head around this. Around what happened . . . so I can at least say something—"

"Milo, we're *all* in shock. What can you or any of us say? I don't know how my brother seemed to you, but he sounded just fine on the phone with me."

"Yes, but don't forget that I was in his company when you telephoned. He always puts on *la bella figura*." Milo felt obligated to relay the conversation about Primo Levi's death, and as did so, he heard Maria begin weeping. Then, of course, he regretted telling her.

At last, she sighed and said, "Well, then I don't know what to think. They asked me—and I suppose they asked you—if I could think of anybody else who could have been visiting him last night. And I said I couldn't."

Milo said he couldn't either.

"Anyway, more immediately, I have a major problem on my hands. I have a letter that Lenny wrote me ten years ago . . . saying if anything should happen to him, he didn't want a Catholic funeral. That he wanted to be cremated."

Milo knew what was coming next.

"The family is horrified. Aunt Fran is insisting that no matter what, we do it the Catholic way and bury him. But I don't feel that I can . . . because he became such a rabid atheist."

"Well, it's your decision, not hers." Milo went on to say that, on more than one occasion, Lenny had said to him that anyone who believed in God could not possibly have a first-rate mind.

Maria actually laughed when he told her this. "I know. He said that to me, too. And yet he loved going into churches. *And* sitting through Mass, but only in the cathedrals that had high art he could look at during the liturgy."

Milo told her that, ironically, he and Lenny were about to enter a church in Rome when Lenny elaborated on his atheism. "I'd known him for four years by then. It was something I thought he would have discussed with me, long before then."

Maria now told him that Lenny had been reluctant to discuss his atheism with her, assuming that either she wouldn't understand or she would condemn him for it. "Anyway, are you staying the night or going back into the city?"

Milo wasn't teaching the following day. "I haven't thought that far."

"Well, if you do stay over, come and see me tomorrow morning, will you? I'm swamped with aunts and uncles and cousins coming in and out for the rest of today."

Milo told her that he would, but more than likely he'd end up going back to his apartment in Manhattan.

6.

Lenny had discussed his atheism with Milo during the summer of his junior year at Boston College, when Milo had gone to study at the American University of Rome. Lenny came down by train from Orvieto where he'd been visiting one of his aunts. In the high heat of a summer afternoon, they decided to meet outside the small fifth-century church, San Lorenzo fuori le Mura. When Milo arrived, Lenny scrutinized him harshly, and with firm patience, said in Italian, "You can't visit a church dressed like this. It's a disgrace. It's disrespectful." Milo looked down at his baggy cargo shorts. "Go back and change," Lenny now ordered him in English.

Milo was perplexed. "You want me to go all the way back to the *campo* and change? It will take almost an hour to get there. And then another hour to return."

"Yes, I want you to go back to the *campo*. You've spent enough time in Italy to know how to dress before going into a church," Lenny chided him. "Look at me, for example."

On that broiling Roman day, Lenny was wearing a three-piece herringbone suit, hewing to the style of many Italian intellectuals who, despite punishing heat, wore suits to almost any occasion, including sightseeing. "Look at me," he repeated, "and I no longer believe in God. So . . . vai!" he ordered Milo.

"And you're just going to sit here until I get back?"

Lenny held up a book of Eugenio Montale's poetry published in an edition that said *Premio Nobel* (Nobel Prize). "I'll be in good company," he said, smiling. "Montale and I."

And so, Milo crossed the chaotic city and back at his hostel, changed into a long-sleeve button-down shirt and the only pair of slacks he'd brought with him that weren't blue jeans. By the time he got back to San Lorenzo fuori le Mura, he had large sweat circles under his arms. Absorbed in Montale's poetry, Lenny looked up through his reading glasses that magnified his brooding eyes and framed his long, elegantly cut hair. When Milo pointed to his sweat stains, Lenny remarked, "Human bodily function. The Catholic religion understands that."

"But *not* sex before marriage."

Lenny chuckled at this, but then with dismissive-sounding sarcasm said, "Don't be so clever!"

He led the way inside the nearly empty church and soon they were standing below a huge quadrant of vibrant, restored frescoes that depicted the Hebrews' flight from Egypt. Below the frescoes, a carved marble vessel sat on top of a marble tombstone. "By the way, that's Saint Lawrence buried down there," Lenny said, pointing to the slab. "Did you know they grilled him to death?"

"Grilled?"

"*Alla griglia*," he replied in Italian, and Milo felt the sultry air invaded by a sepulchral chill. "And when they finally promoted him to sainthood, guess what he became the saint of?"

"You got me."

"Patron saint of cooks," Lenny said, and laughed delightedly. The Catholic Church has a sardonic sense of humor, you have to give it that."

"I guess I have to," Milo said.

When they were outside again, Milo asked why, being an atheist, Lenny still loved visiting churches. Lenny reminded him that seventy-five percent of the world's high art was in Italy, much of it ecclesiastical, and that one could say what one wanted about the politics and dictates of the Catholic Church, but at least the religion itself inspired some of the great art of humanity.

"Were you an atheist when you went to Catholic school?" Milo asked, referring to Stepinac, the Jesuit high school Lenny attended.

"No. And by the way, I got a great education at Stepinac. Besides religion, they certainly promoted literature and art." Milo pondered this for a moment, and then Lenny asked him, "I assume you're a believer?"

"Honestly, I haven't made up my mind . . . yet, whether or not I'm a believer."

Lenny stopped to look for something in the leather book bag he was carrying. Whatever it was, he couldn't find it. Then he said, "When I was your age, the existence of God didn't matter so much to me. It did later on. It mattered after I got broken a few times, after I saw such misery in other people. And then . . . the question of whether there was a God began to nag at me."

"What do you mean exactly by *broken*?"

"Failure in love. That sort of thing."

It seemed to Milo that Lenny's idea of being broken was a universal affliction that happened to nearly everybody at one time or another. Therefore, the question of the existence of God didn't naturally follow. However, Milo decided (for the moment, anyway) not to argue the point.

Brushing his long locks of hair out of his eyes, Lenny continued, "But back to your original question. I stopped believing for the same reason most people stop believing. Can one accept the gross inequity between those who really suffer and die in poverty and harsh conditions—no food, no water—and those who are continually blessed and pampered by wealth and good fortune? Realizing this, if one can still believe in God, then I suppose one can practice religion." With that, he began steering them toward the busy thoroughfare.

The Roman boulevard was clogged with traffic that seemed to be flowing in from all directions. As they stood waiting to cross, Lenny took the opportunity to slip the paperback of Montale's poetry into his book bag. Looking at him, Milo continued to be amazed that, wearing such a beautifully tailored three-piece suit, Lenny wasn't drenched in perspiration. Nodding at the confusion of traffic, Lenny grabbed Milo's arm and said, "You have to jump right into it with confidence, and they'll stop," and rushed him into the middle of the automotive madness. The sun was beating down, and in a state of momentary panic, Milo felt swallowed up by a molten sea of glinting enamel and petulant car horns.

Once they managed to cross through the chaos and enter the calm realm of a street lined with tailor shops,

Lenny said, "I stopped believing the summer after I finished college."

He had been doing three months of postgraduate summer study at an Italian language institute in Umbertide, a small non-touristic town in central Umbria, twenty-five miles from where one of his aunts lived. Leaving a grocery store, he'd been approached by an extremely thin, undernourished-looking man, a Libyan refugee who, two years before, had arrived by boat to Sicily, the only place in Europe that was regularly accepting undocumented immigrants. "The man came up to me and started speaking in English," Lenny recounted. "At first, I thought he pegged me as an American and was after a handout, but then I realized that, besides his native tongue, English was his only other adequate language—that he probably had very little Italian. Anyway, we began to talk, and he told me his story."

The thirty-two-year-old man had quarreled with his father, who'd kicked him out of the family house. He worked until he saved enough for a passage to Italy on an overcrowded boat that took ten days to go three hundred and twenty-eight miles. He watched half the passengers get sick and die, their bodies thrown overboard. Once he landed in Italy, he felt lucky; he felt saved. But then he began wandering from city to city, cadging odd jobs here and there, mostly in landscaping, without a place to live, hoping to get a leg up, hoping to at least become financially stable. "When we met, he'd been in the country struggling for five years. He still had no permanent job, no security, no place to live.

"He was lonely. He was desperate. I ended up giving him the cheese and milk and fresh bread that I bought plus most of the money I had on me. And I thought to myself: Here is a brave man who crossed the sea in treacherous conditions, only to encounter more misery. And once again I asked myself: With this kind of inequity in the world, how can I possibly believe in the existence of God?"

"I see your point," Milo said.

Then, Lenny said, "I often think about this man. I often wonder what ever happened to him. I often wonder if he's even still alive."

7.

At the funeral home, a long line of mourners were waiting to pay their respects to Maria D'Ambrosio. As Milo and Rose Marie joined the line, he noticed on the far side of the room a cluster of what looked to him like college students dressed in tattered jeans and wrinkled button-down shirts, some of the girls in short skirts. *What's with these kids?* Milo often thought the same thing about his own students at NYU, when they showed up in class wearing crop tops (both men and women), tight jeans, and lots of décolletage. He figured the motley gathering was made up of Lenny's Italian-language students at Mercy, about whom Lenny always used to bitterly complain.

Maria smiled crookedly when she noticed Milo and Rose Marie. "You go first, Mom," Milo said, ushering his mother forward.

"I'm so pained for you," Rose Marie said as she took both of Maria's hands. "I've been praying for him and for you ever since we heard."

Maria drew Rose Marie into a tight hug and thanked her. Once the embrace was broken, she said, "I'm hoping that you and Milo can at least comfort each other."

"He's my rock," Rose Marie said, leaning into Milo, who stood only a few inches behind her.

Then Maria said to her, "Of all the people here, you're probably the only one who really understands what I'm going through." And then tears began meandering down her face—Milo was amazed that, for her part, his mother was able to maintain her own composure. Maria made a half-hearted attempt to wipe her cheeks; then some attentive person standing nearby handed her a cluster of tissues. With a glance toward the dark mahogany casket (that he knew Lenny would have condemned) surrounded by tall sprays of white lilies, Milo leaned forward and embraced her. He could feel her delicate bones, her fragility.

Even under these circumstances, as Milo took a step backward, he couldn't help remarking on how lovely Maria D'Ambrosio was, particularly in her state of mourning—the delicate planes of her face, her limpid eyes. Then he noticed, standing just off to the side, two elderly women in loose, black shapeless dresses gawking at him. He figured that one of them was probably Aunt Francesca.

Glancing at the long line of mourners waiting to pay their respects to her, Milo whispered to Maria, "People are waiting to see you."

"Come by when you can," she requested. "There are things I need to tell you. Things to discuss. Promise me?" she said.

"Of course," Milo assured her. "Tomorrow is Sunday." He'd already told his mother he'd spend the night. "I'll still be here."

Milo and Rose Marie remained at the wake a while longer, milling among the other mourners and ended up speaking to a few townspeople they knew. "Look at that expensive coffin," she pointed out. "I guess the family got what they wanted. To bury him. I can't imagine *that* will be going to a crematorium."

"Being buried is not what Lenny would have wanted," Milo insisted.

"Well, what he would have wanted is a shame."

"That's narrow-minded thinking!" he told her.

They were on the verge of departing when a local priest appeared at the door of the viewing room and immediately commanded everyone's attention with, "If you all could sit down for a few moments, I'd like to pay some respect to Professor Leonard D'Ambrosio." The priest, who had a florid, jowly face, pattered over to a podium to the left of the riser that was set up next to the coffin. There were perhaps thirty foldable chairs gathered around this podium, and they were quickly occupied by some of the more elderly mourners in the room. Milo and his mother went and sat in the second row.

The priest began with a thumbnail of Lenny's life: how he grew up in Portchester, went to Stepinac, then Kenyon College, then Columbia, and spoke of him in merely biographical, not personal or anecdotal, terms. It quickly became clear that this cleric had never met the person whom he was making a half-hearted attempt to eulogize. As the priest burbled on, it occurred to Milo that there was actually something not right about this fellow, who soon began to rant against, of all things, the E. J. Korvette department store in Portchester, inveighing that it was a notorious hangout for high school kids who went there to smoke cigarettes and marijuana and be generally rowdy.

"Oh my God, he's *soused*," Rose Marie whispered to him. "This is not good."

"Well, we just have to put up with it," Milo whispered back to her.

"No, we don't!"

And before Milo could say or do anything else, Rose Marie sprang out of her chair and clapped her hands together loudly. "Okay! Enough! Amen!" The priest recoiled and stopped stammering. Shortly thereafter, he stepped down from the podium and made his wobbly way toward the door.

Milo was horrified. "Did you have to?"

"Yes, I had to," Rose Marie insisted. "Look at him. That drunk! I don't know why they didn't ask Father Flannery to come in."

Milo glanced over to see Maria's reaction and was surprised to see her chuckling through her tears.

As they made their way outside the funeral home, several people they knew approached Rose Marie and thanked her for intervening. And to a group of them, she said, "I know I was rude, but that priest is on the sauce." She glanced at her watch, and then dismissively said, "You don't hit the bottle and then go speak at somebody's wake at eleven o'clock in the morning. If he'd shown up to speak like that at our *Carlo's* wake, I would have strangled him."

"Okay, enough now," Milo told her quietly.

To outsiders, Rose Marie Rossi would constantly refer to Carlo, to keep his dwindled light aflame. She didn't do it to elicit sympathy—if anything her insistence on bringing him up would elicit discomfort—but rather to let people know that she was determined to keep him in this world by talking about him, by writing notes and signing them from herself, Milo, and Carlo with a halo above his name. She attended Mass nearly every day to pray for his soul and his salvation—she'd even attended Mass the day after she and Milo had buried him. When Father Flannery noticed her in the pews that day, he approached and said, "Dear Rose Marie. You just buried your son. Why are you here today?"

"Where else would I go?" had been his mother's answer.

8.

They were walking down the street, each steeped in their own thoughts when they heard a male voice from behind say, "Uh, 'scuse me." They pivoted around to find Detective Delzio, who introduced himself to Rose Marie as he reached out to shake her hand. "I think I met you once before," he said. "When your late husband and I were playing golf, you picked him up at the golf course."

Rose Marie leaned slightly forward, squinting at Delzio. "Well, *I* don't recognize *you*."

"I didn't think you would," Delzio said bashfully. Glancing Milo's way and flicking his finger at him, he said, "This one, on the other hand . . . unfortunately, I'm going to have to take him into custody."

The words froze in Milo's ear, and he felt the blood in his body plummeting toward his feet. He and Rose Marie stared at Delzio, dumbfounded. "What?" he squawked, and the detective immediately started laughing.

"I'm just kidding with him."

"Kidding with him?" Rose Marie said crossly. "Can't you see we just left a wake?"

Delzio flushed with embarrassment and for once seemed unsure of himself. "You're right. I apologize."

"*Baccalà*!" Rose Marie used a southern Italian expression that, though it literally meant "salted cod," was used to call somebody thoughtless, or a blockhead.

"That's what my mother used to call me," Delzio told her with a tight grin. Then he laid a heavy hand on Milo's shoulder. "But I actually do need Milo. I need him to look at a few photographs. For a possible ID."

"Wait a minute, wait a minute," Milo spoke up. "What do you mean possible ID? I told you I didn't see anyone at Lenny's apartment."

"Understood," Delzio said. "But I'd still like to know if you recognize somebody."

"Recognize who?" Rose Marie demanded.

"If I identify the person now, then Milo can't be objective," Delzio explained.

"But if my son just told you he didn't see anybody, why does he have to look at photographs?"

His full attention on her and now careful to be deferential, Delzio said, "We just need Milo for a half hour. You're welcome to come with him if you'd like."

"*Me*? Come with *him*? Why would I want to come to a police station? I have better things to do," Rose Marie said.

Delzio shrugged as if to say, I can't blame you there.

"Let me just walk my mother home and I'll be right over," Milo said and Delzio strolled away. "You're really on a tear today, aren't you?" he remarked to Rose Marie as they continued walking.

"Look," she said. "Somebody we love just died. First, we have to listen to some screwball priest, and then you have this detective acting like a clown." She turned to him.

"Surely he knows how important this man was to you. So why joke about any of it?"

An hour later at the police station, Milo was led to a room with a long table and four office-style swivel chairs. One of the walls was taken up by a thick, tinted-glass mirror. He cupped his hands against the glass and, staring through it, said aloud to himself, "This must be a two-way mirror. Looks like there's a space out there, but it's too dark to tell."

"That's for lineups," said Detective Rodriguez, who'd quietly entered the room.

Then Delzio came in, greeted him more officiously than he did on the street, and asking him to sit down at the conference table, slid an eight-by-ten black-and-white photograph toward him. "Recognize this guy?"

The man staring directly out of the photograph looked to be around thirty, with a rough complexion, blond spiky hair, and a sizable diamond chip in his left ear. He was wearing a jean jacket covered with sewn-on patches, most prominent among them a skull and crossbones affixed to the left breast pocket. It could have been the black-and-white photo, but the man in it looked pale and unwell.

"Do I recognize him? No, not really," Milo said.

"Are you certain?" Rodriguez pressed him.

Milo looked up and met Delzio's keen gaze. "Is this a trick question?"

Delzio said, "Does the name Matteo Cipolla mean anything to you?"

"Of course it does; he was one of my brother Carlo's closest friends at Iona."

"That's what the records office at Iona College told us. Apparently, they were roommates for a while." Milo nodded and said this was accurate. Rodriguez pointed to the photo. "Well, that's the older brother, Valentino."

Milo was shocked. "*I* know Val." Looking back at the photo, he said, "If this is Val, it's a shit picture of him."

Rodriguez said, "Sorry it doesn't meet your standards."

"No, what I'm saying is: unless this guy has really changed, this makes him look like he's lost a lot of weight and is no longer lifting. But I also haven't seen him in a while."

"It *could* be a shit photo," Delzio conceded, "but it's the only photo of him we have."

"Okay, so what does any of this have to do with Lenny?"

"We're getting there," Rodriguez said, crossing his arms on his chest.

Delzio paused, took a deep breath, and then said, "I need to switch gears for a moment. I need to tell you what we found in Lenny D'Ambrosio's apartment." He paused, looked down at the sheaf of papers that he'd brought with him into the office, and finally resumed. "A large stash of sadomasochistic pornography. A cardboard box of photos and around three dozen videos—all sadomasochistic. Some of this shit is really racy, very hard to . . . procure. And a lot of it is made in Europe with undocumented actors, sex workers trafficked in from places like Russia and the Ukraine." Jabbing the photo with his index finger, he said, "This guy Valentino distributes it. And we think that your professor bought most if not all of the illegal porn from Cipolla's company."

Bewildered, his head buzzing, Milo had to ask Delzio to repeat some of what he'd said.

"Of the videotapes we found, many of them were being stored in their original mailing packages. All mailed from the same post office, in Italy. "

Rodriguez chimed in. "There's a database that the FBI has. They're cracking down on the distribution of these films that are made with undocumented people. The address came up."

In the midst of his confusion, Milo had the presence of mind to say, "You talk about sadomasochistic porn, what exactly do you mean by that?"

Rodriguez explained that people got roughed up on camera, beaten, women often the victims. He paused. "But not in this particular case." He paused and then continued. "In the videos our guy looked at, the men were actually the victims."

"Men?"

"With women manhandling them," Rodriguez added. "Punishing them for things they've done. Pretty much garden variety sado-porn."

"So you're saying these films are illegal because they're made with undocumented actors?"

"Refugees," Rodriguez said. "Refugees from repressive countries who arrive in places like Italy, desperate for work. Promised a career in movies but then terribly compensated and forced to live on top of one another in flophouses. With no other means of supporting themselves."

"Anyway," Delzio went on, "here in the U.S., distributing a sex video made illegally with unregistered or undocumented actors is a felony. And this guy . . ." He flicked the eight-by-ten photograph with his index finger. "Val Cipolla, from what we've learned, purveys it."

Milo was desperately trying to imagine Valentino Cipollo involved in the distribution of pornography. "But why would he of all people be in this kind of business? I mean, the guy got a scholarship to Amherst. My brother used to call him effortlessly smart."

"Well, it's a joint brotherly business," Rodriguez informed him with a hint of sarcasm.

But then Milo remembered something: that shortly before he died, Carlo actually made a wisecrack about Val's brother, Matteo, having a lurid interest in the buying and selling of pornography but Milo hadn't really taken the idea very seriously. He mentioned this now and then asked, "So will you arrest Val for being a distributor?"

Delzio said, "We'd have to find the films in his possession and then prove the actors were illegal and undocumented. It'd be a hard sell."

"And getting proof would have to be done in Europe," Rodriguez said. "So out of jurisdiction, anyway."

Delzio said, "My question is: Do you think D'Ambrosio and Cipolla actually knew one another?"

Milo thought about this. Lenny, who'd often been to dinner at the Rossis', obviously had known Carlo and, Milo reasoned, probably had at least heard about Matteo. "I don't know how or where they would have met though."

Then Delzio said, "Have you've been in touch with him at all?"

"With Matteo?" Milo asked.

"With either of them."

"Why would *I* be in touch with them?" Milo then explained that Matteo had attended Carlo's funeral but he'd not heard from or seen him since.

The detectives glanced at one another and then Rodriguez said, "Did you ever hang out at Cooks?"

Milo screwed up his face as he gazed back at them. "Cooks? Not since maybe sophomore year in college. Why?"

"That's where Valentino Cipolla apparently likes to go," Rodriguez said, indicating the photo. "On Saturday nights."

"*Val* does?" Milo asked, incredulous. "By now the guy must be like thirty years old." Why would he want to hang out at a place like Cooks, a diner that catered to predominantly high school and college students?

With a tight, knowing smile, Delzio said, "Well, let's just say he likes his women on the younger side: early college, for example. Anyway, when we found there was a connection between you and the Cipollas, we figured we'd ask if you knew anything. Or if you knew about an acquaintance between them and D'Ambrosio."

"I would have had to ask."

Rodriguez continued. "Anyway, I've pretty much signed off on the case. We're now pretty convinced it's suicide. If anything comes up, talk to him." He indicated Delzio with a tilt of his head.

But Milo now felt he just couldn't accept this, that it was suicide.

9.

Rose Marie was in the kitchen making one of her health drinks, throwing all sorts of fruits and yogurt into a blender. The main ingredient was derived from a plastic tub on which the word *MUD* was boldly printed.

"You're not really putting mud in that drink, are you?" Milo asked her.

"It's not mud," his mother said loftily. It's a health meal in a drink formula."

"Is this some kind of new fad?"

"It increases energy levels."

"As if you need that," Milo said.

"Shut up you, you always say I don't eat enough," Rose Marie said.

"You don't!"

She waved him off as she reached into the tub, took out a clear plastic scoop, and measured out two equal portions of MUD into her blender. After carefully dusting the powder from her hands, she said, "I went to a nutritionist and this stuff is what they suggested I do to gain calories. It's really not bad." She dusted the remnants of the protein powder from her hands. "So were you able to identify that person in the photograph?"

Milo told her that he had and who it was.

She frowned, confused. "Hold on, hold on. Do I *know* these brothers? Did we see them at the wake?"

"*I* remember seeing Matteo at Carlo's funeral, but I don't think either of them came to the wake."

"But if Matteo was at the funeral, I'd remember him, right?" Rose Marie insisted quietly.

"Not necessarily, Mom. You know how it was," Milo said, referring to the convergence of relatives and family friends on the drab, rainy April day; the strain of having to greet everyone, to acknowledge awkward outpourings of grief for what he and Rose Marie were going through; the sensory overload of shock and anguish; the church crowded to the rafters, bearing the gleaming coffin from the street to the nave and then back to the hearse; thinking of his brother lying still just above his shoulders; and the slick heads of his male cousins from Brooklyn, conscripted by his mother to help carry Carlo—cousins Milo hardly knew.

"But beyond all that, why wouldn't I know this Matteo?" Rose Marie pressed. "If he was a close friend of Carlo's at Iona?"

How many of Carlo's friends from Iona—or from anywhere for that matter—had they ever met? "I don't remember him bringing anybody home. You know how guarded he was."

Rose Marie had to concede that this was true. "Maybe he didn't bring friends home to meet us, but he certainly talked about friends. And I don't remember him mentioning this Matteo."

"He did, Mom. They were roommates for a while."

Intending to keep the news about the brothers' pornography distribution to himself, Milo relayed to his mother what Delzio and Rodriguez had revealed to him about Lenny's collection of videotapes, figuring it would be a distraction.

She challenged him. "I thought you said he was always reading."

"He always seemed to be reading . . . whenever I was there."

Shaking her head, she crossed to the refrigerator, took out a plastic tray of ice and twisted it, aiming half the contents at the blender. Then she started adding the rest of what she'd prepared on the counter: a sliced apple, a bag of frozen blueberries, and nonfat yogurt. She glanced at Milo wearily and then turned the blender on, and it screamed and crunched and did its work with a heavy thrumming. Once she was through, she said, "So what do these brothers have to do with Lenny dying?"

It was an obvious question that he was obliged to answer and he did: that the brothers distributed pornography and that Delzio suspected Lenny had procured it from them.

Rose Marie received the news with a guarded glance, but then she surprised him. "You don't think Carlo was working with these guys, selling whatever . . . they were selling, do you?"

This was something Milo hadn't even considered. "I can't imagine that. You know how strait-laced he was. What makes you ask?"

Shaking her head and sighing, Rose Marie poured the contents of her blended drink into two glasses, both of which she put in the refrigerator. Then she began rinsing the blender and wiping down the kitchen counter.

"Mom, what is it? You okay?"

She waved him off and didn't respond immediately. "Breathe in, breathe out," she muttered. "Got to keep telling myself that. Because I lose . . . my breath sometimes when we talk about Carlo."

"Why don't you sit down," Milo suggested.

"I'll be okay. Give me a few seconds."

"Mom, sometimes I don't know what to do or say. Because you always tell me we should talk about him—"

"It's not what you think," she interrupted him. And then explained. Four years ago, when she was going through Carlo's effects, the ones that Milo had brought back from Iona College, she'd found a video cassette. "I didn't like the looks of it," she remarked.

"What did you do with it?"

Rose Marie looked desolate. "What did I do with it? I threw it out is what I did with it."

"Why did you do that? You haven't thrown out anything else of his!"

She flicked her hand at him. "I threw it out because I figured what was in it was up to no good. I had a bad feeling, so I got rid of it."

"Couldn't it have been a video for his studies at school?"

She shook her head. "No. I remember it had an address on it. From a post office in Lucca."

"*Lucca*?" Milo cried out. Lucca was where Rose Marie's sister, Lara, lived and where he'd spent many of his summers. The once close relationship between the two sisters had grown strained after Lara had made a rather unconvincing excuse for not flying back to America to attend Carlo's funeral.

"Yes, Lucca," she said. "I thought maybe he . . . got it over there when you both were visiting in the summer maybe, and then he brought it home."

Milo was intrigued: What videotape could his brother possibly have procured in Italy? Maybe it *was* pornography.

Rose Marie said, "Do you think your brother had girlfriends and just never told us?"

"Hard to say," Milo told her. "Carlo was only twenty-one when he died. Some people are just late bloomers."

She nodded grimly. "Not you. You got a little ahead of yourself in high school with that nineteen-year-old girl, if you want my opinion," she said, referring to an older girlfriend that Milo had dated when he was sixteen.

"Yeah, Mom, you've given me your opinion on that more than once," he told her. "Anyway, this video you found could have been any video. Not necessarily pornography."

Rose Marie looked at him warily.

10.

Milo kept scrolling through his memory for any outward clues of a substantial pornography stash in Lenny's apartment. On his way to visit Maria, he suddenly remembered one curious thing that happened in Rome on the evening of the day Lenny had confessed to his atheism—outside the church of San Lorenzo fuori le Mura. After seeing the church, Milo had gone back to his hostel and, once there, realized he was coming down with something; despite the great Roman heat, he felt chilled and febrile and lay down on his bed in the narrow room that a century before had been a monk's cell. He managed to fall asleep and dreamed of being in an overcrowded boat crossing the sea, wedged in with passengers who were praying for safe arrival in Sicily, when he woke up sharply to the scream of, "*Minchia!*"—slang for "fuck."

Lightheaded, he managed to get up and go to the window and look down on several bands of clamoring children, who couldn't have been more than ten years old and who were screaming obscenities at one another.

He and Lenny had planned to meet up that evening to attend a private viewing of the recent restoration of the ceiling of the Sistine Chapel; Lenny belonged to a Roman organization called Il Circolo Italiano, whose members were allowed to visit the sites of great art off-hours, to wander through museums and churches before or after public viewing time. When they met in front of the Vatican Museum and he told Lenny he felt unwell, Lenny scrutinized him and remarked, "Maybe you picked up Roman fever."

"What's that?"

"Read 'Roman Fever' by Edith Wharton," was his reply. Typically unsympathetic to illnesses, Lenny told him to suck it up, that few people outside the inner circles of Roman society would ever be granted such a glorious opportunity to view the Sistine ceiling in such a small gathering.

There were no chairs set up in the chapel, and so they and the other guests sat on the travertine floor next to one another, their backs against a cold stone wall, and craned their heads to look up at the ceiling. The lecturer spotlighted the restoration in each section, then superimposed upon it a slide of that part of the ceiling in its original tarnished state, before work began. So you could see, for example, how the fresco of God parting the waters had been emboldened and made vivid, as had the parable of the great flood that Noah survived. Milo forgot himself and the incoming malaise and later would vaguely wonder if the raw sensation of illness intensified the experience of viewing the chapel, where he got to witness two miracles: Michelangelo's original creation and the faithful, mindful restoration of the painter's work hundreds of years later.

When the lecture was over and they were standing outside among all the well-heeled, well-coiffed Romans who attended it, Milo still feeling feverish and uncomfortably lightheaded, a young man in a black robe and a white clerical collar approached Lenny and tapped him on the shoulder.

The man was holding a slim folder, which he offered in a surreptitious manner. Lenny refused the man with a violent hand gesture. The priest reacted with surprise and seeming offense but remained standing where he was.

"Excuse me for a moment," Lenny said. He took the priest roughly by the arm and walked him several feet away and argued with him in low tones for a minute or so. When he rejoined Milo, he looked unnerved, and Milo naturally asked who the man was and what he was holding.

Still flustered, Lenny said, "He's collecting money . . . for a relief fund."

"But the folder—"

"Disturbing pictures of suffering people I'd rather not see. I told him now was not the time."

Milo noticed the priest had crossed to the other side of the square and was regarding them with unbridled curiosity. He was struck by the man's face, which looked just like one of the youthful nudes on the Sistine ceiling, and particularly in the panel *Separation of Light from Darkness.*

"Anyway," Milo resumed, "when you see that kind of beauty—"

"What kind of beauty?" Lenny interrupted him.

"The chapel's kind of beauty," Milo clarified, "and recognize one man's ability to create it, don't you think there just might be some kind of God?"

"No, I don't," Lenny said definitively, and with a hint of impatience.

Maria D'Ambrosio's two-family house was a split-level structure that characterized many homes in Westchester

County. For a number of years, her parents had rented out the top floor to some second cousins on their mother's side who'd relocated from Staten Island. In the wake of the death of both D'Ambrosio parents, the cousins had eventually vacated, and Maria now lived in the house entirely on her own, enduring frequent visits by her domineering maternal aunt, Francesca.

Dressed in a shapeless floral housecoat, Aunt Francesca was a stout, dour-looking woman with noticeably large earlobes and small, dark, glittering eyes. When she answered the door, she stood there glowering at Milo for a moment, without even a greeting. She was clearly Maria's first line of defense against ghoulish neighbors coming by with casseroles and homemade biscotti, newspaper reporters trying to preempt their competition for clues about Lenny D'Ambrosio's death. And in fact, when Milo said he was there to see Maria, Aunt Francesca asked defensively, "Are you from the *Reporter Dispatch* or the *Daily Item*?"

"Neither. I'm Milo Rossi. Don't you recognize me from the wake?"

The grimacing woman smiled thinly and said, "Not really. Is Maria expecting you?"

"Yes." Milo considered throwing out a phrase of Italian but then reminded himself that, like most sixty-year-old Italian Americans, Aunt Francesca was probably at least second-generation and therefore would have no substantial knowledge of the language. In general, Milo made the aunts and uncles and grandparents of his friends nervous whenever he tried to speak to them in Italian. At last, Aunt

Francesca stood aside to allow him into the foyer of a house redolent of the sweet burning smell of scented candles.

The place was crammed with dark, heavy-limbed furniture that gave the impression that the belongings of two dwellings had been herded together—perhaps the cousins vacating the upstairs had left behind their more cumbersome belongings? Beyond this density of worn-looking sofas and armchairs, there were numerous crucifixes nailed to the walls, as well as some religious-looking ceramic reliefs and a large number of crudely executed oil paintings of what clearly were Italian maritime provinces, but northern ones like Portofino and Lerici. He noticed two matching rocking chairs painted in glossy red enamel, and when entering the kitchen, spied yet another one of these garish matching rocking chairs pulled up to the golden-flecked linoleum counter, which matched the golden-flecked linoleum floor. He couldn't imagine Lenny wanting to spend time in a house so saturated with religious imagery.

Wearing a black caftan, Maria sat at one end of the kitchen table covered in an oily cloth, hunched over the letter she was writing, her face pinched with thought. Milo was once again struck by how lovely she was. Blessed with the same fineness of features that graced her late brother, Maria had the light-olive complexion and pale eyes of people you see in Veneto and Friuli. The impression Milo had had of her at the wake revived itself: There was something naturally sensual about her. Detecting his presence in the doorway, she looked up, smiled kindly, and told him to come and sit down next to her. As he did, he noticed a neat pile of perhaps fifteen letters, all notecard size, addressed in a careful flowing hand—the result of the strict primary school instruction of nuns, he concluded. Acknowledging the letters, Maria explained that she was replying to some of the people who'd written such beautiful things about her brother. "Have you ever been to this house before?" she asked him with a quizzical frown.

He shook his head.

Momentarily tamed into cordiality, Aunt Francesca entered the kitchen to offer Milo a cup of tea, and after pouring it from a ceramic teapot hewn in the shape of a US mailbox, she brought it to him and left the room.

Seeming more nervous now, Maria asked how his teaching gig at NYU was going. He explained that he was still teaching undergraduate Italian language classes; however, in his more advanced sections, he had introduced more accessible works of literature: the slim novels of Cesare Pavese and even small sections of Primo Levi's *Survival in Auschwitz.*

"My brother loved that book," Maria remarked.

"He thought it was the greatest work of the mid-twentieth century. He insisted that I read it when I was in high school."

"Reading it the first time, how did you find it?"

"Not too difficult. Levi has a very clear, straightforward style."

Maria nodded thoughtfully, and in the brief silence, Milo could hear a hair dryer blaring upstairs. At last, she said, "Did Lenny ever show you any of his translations?"

"The Primo Levi ones?"

"Those, or any others."

Milo shook his head. "I asked him many times. I asked him, for example, if I could read the unpublished Natalia Ginzburg he was working on, and he refused. He seemed afraid that I'd find it inadequate against the original. Or worse, unfaithful to it."

"He was *very* hard on himself," Maria pointed out with a sigh. "Didn't you spend your summers in Italy? I think Lenny told me that." Milo said that he had. "Well, Lenny began studying Italian when he was eighteen."

Milo assured Maria that Lenny's Italian was nearly perfect. "He certainly spoke it way better than I do."

Maria shrugged. "On the one hand, he was hard on himself, but on the other hand, he was very self-indulgent." Her face collapsed into a miserable mask. She bowed her head, and Milo could see a few tears falling into her lap, making wet stains like sudden raindrops on her caftan. "A brilliant man," she resumed, "who really looked after me. But an enigma." The last words were uttered with a hint of bitterness.

Milo leaned toward Maria and said, "So Delzio told you about what they found?"

Looking grim, she nodded. "He did, yes."

"Did you have any idea that he had this kind of . . ." Wanting to be delicate, Milo thought for a moment and at last said, "hobby?"

She hesitated and raised her eyes to meet his. "I went to his apartment two weeks ago. He was away. I needed something—a fan that had belonged to our mother for a party I was going to. It was in a safe along with some other valuable things, heirlooms that belonged to both of us. I've always had a key to his apartment. *And* the combination to the safe. I asked him if I could let myself in. He may not have realized I'd be opening the safe."

"I know about the safe. But I don't think I've ever seen it."

"It's . . ." Maria hesitated, "hidden. You wouldn't have seen it. Anyway, when I opened the safe, I saw a stack of video cassettes that looked homemade. They had white labels with handwriting on them. Titles in Italian and dates. I suspected they were pornography."

Milo leaned back in his chair and placed the ankle of one leg on the knee of the other.

"Did you ask ever him about them?"

She shook her head. "No, and why would I? It's his private business."

Milo digested this for a moment. "I guess I'm trying to understand why he would like pornography where men are the victims of women."

Maria fixed her sad, watery eyes on him. "I've been thinking about this since I got the phone call . . . from Delzio. My only explanation is that my brother very much wanted to have a long-term relationship and get married. But all his relationships were, for one reason or another, disasters. He always claimed women were cruel and unkind to him. But I've always wondered: Maybe he instigated it, their cruelty and unkindness?" She hesitated and looked meaningfully at Milo. "I think you get where I'm going with this?"

What she perhaps didn't want to say was that her brother eroticized what he considered to be his ill treatment by women.

Maria continued, "Watching pornography, no matter what kind of pornography, Lenny was doing something safer than taking a risk with another person and perhaps having another disappointment." She began shifting uncomfortably in her chair and then resumed. "I don't suppose Lenny ever told you there was an accusation against him?"

"An accusation?" Milo repeated.

"By one of his Columbia grad students."

"He never used the word *accusation*." He went on to explain that Lenny had made this so-called accusation sound more like an altercation that escalated to the point where the Romance languages department had to be brought into it.

Maria shook her head. "No, in fact, he was accused of inappropriately touching a student."

Milo was flabbergasted. "Did he admit to it?"

Maria shook her head. "No, he never did. But his denial—to me—didn't sound all that convincing."

"Then again, I suppose admitting to it would have completely derailed his career," Milo pointed out.

"Would have? You don't think it did?" Maria exclaimed. "I mean, because of the woman's accusation, after the semester was over, he was denied tenure and couldn't find another teaching job anywhere. Except for third-rate Mercy College." Maria had clearly co-opted her brother's high-handed dismissal of the small, perfectly adequate Catholic college.

"So, with the Columbia student, it was basically he said, she said?"

"That's pretty much the impression I got. For all I know, there very well could have been other accusations against him."

"Delzio certainly would know about them, though, wouldn't he?"

Maria looked wary. "If Delzio knows anything more, who says he's bound to tell *us* about it?"

She had a point there. "I'm just having trouble imagining Lenny putting his hands on anybody without an invitation," Milo said. "He was very proper, very formal."

Maria sat there, pensive for a few moments, staring down at her pile of handwritten notes. Then she looked up at him and said, "Surely you realize that in private people can behave in ways that are completely contrary to their outward demeanor."

She looked so incredibly forlorn that Milo hesitated to ask the question that was burning through him but felt he had to. "Do you think," he began quietly, "do you believe that Lenny actually took his own life?"

Maria looked startled and bewildered and didn't reply for a moment. "What other explanation is there?" she said at last.

"That somebody was there, somebody made him do it. Someone who knew him?"

"Like a lover?" Maria said.

"I don't know. Maybe?"

The detectives had mentioned this to her. But who would it be? Lenny had always been very private; however, if he were having an important relationship Maria figured somehow he would have let her know, that it would have come out in some way. "And anyway, he was a gentleman. Caring. Why would anyone want to do such a thing to him?"

Why, indeed, Milo agreed.

11.

Lenny's death, was it now inextricably linked to his secret collection of pornography that exploited immigrants and refugees? Refugees like the Libyan man whose plight affected Lenny so much that he severed his tenuous ties to Catholicism? It was a paradox. It made absolutely no sense.

On the train back to Manhattan, Milo tried to get his head around the idea of Lenny watching films in which the actors committed sexual violence against one another. He just couldn't square this obsession with anything about the Lenny that he thought he knew.

Sitting by the train window in a state of agitated numbness, gazing out at the urban stretches of Mount Vernon and the Bronx that struck him like grim foothills leading to the steel and concrete mountain range of Manhattan, he kept trying to recall if Lenny had ever made even an oblique reference to the *real* events that upended his teaching stint at Columbia University. He'd given Milo the distinct impression of a student disputing a final grade with a professor, the dispute morphing into a roiling argument when perhaps Lenny, who had a short fuse, ended up saying something withering and caustic, forcing the student to lodge a formal complaint. And perhaps, as a newly minted academic, he quickly got the reputation of being volatile—that had been Milo's previous assumption as to why Lenny's teaching career at Columbia had come to an abrupt end. But it wasn't this at all, but rather an incident involving physical contact with a graduate student who'd then accused him of sexual impropriety.

Who was she? Was she still at Columbia? And why would a handsome, highly intelligent man brimming with self-confidence and kindness—yes, he was a kind man who volunteered at homeless shelters, a man who gave to charities in the names of people in lieu of birthday and Christmas gifts—have behaved so recklessly? Whatever the reason, he certainly took pains to hide this dark corridor of his personal history, probably fearing that Milo would blame him, think less of him, lose faith in him.

But then, as the train began to slow in anticipation of the station at 125th Street, and Milo was afforded a view of the slate-gray doldrum that had fallen on the narrow inlet of the East River, he thought about what his mother had said to him when he was leaving to walk to the train station. In the midst of making a sauce for a food drive put on by her church, she waved a wooden spoon covered with bits of tomato and said, "Painful personal history, it can really twist up people's behavior. And you've always said Lenny had a lot of anger."

"Yes, but the anger was toward himself. For his own failings. I never heard him blaming anyone else for anything."

Rose Marie had nodded. And then, in a burst of wisdom said, "By the way, Milo, watching pornography can be an addiction like any other addiction, like drinking or smoking."

Of course. But the disconcerting fact was that it was pornography that centered around abusive acts. Try as he might, Milo could hardly imagine the gentle soul he knew watching it, thrilling at it. As far as he knew, Lenny had watched little or no television; the profusion of books on shelves and in stacks everywhere in his apartment attested to his thoughts prevailing primarily in the world of the printed word.

Later that day, after he finished teaching his last class, Milo headed over to the Bobst Library at NYU, whose Escher-like floor design had garnered a reputation of mesmerizing students looking down on it from above, to the point where a few lost souls had actually jumped to their deaths on the hard, brittle, unforgiving black-and-white tiles.

He headed to a familiar corner of the library: the home of current Italian newspapers on wooden racks, as well as the microfiche archive of issues dating back ten years—the place he'd go to relax into the journalism of a language far more lyrical than English. He often turned to Italian newspapers as a way to get another perspective on the world order, in particular, the state of affairs in the U.S. Because Italy had several popular national newspapers that competed against one another with varying points of view, he convinced himself that he was getting a more nuanced account of world politics and economics than perhaps he would in the U.S., where reporting in newspapers like the *New York Times* and the *Washington Post* was unassailable, unless they were countered by a competing opinion in a global newspaper like the *Wall Street Journal.*

It didn't take much searching to find several articles published during the last twenty-four months: one in the

Corriere della Sera, another in *la Repubblica*, and, coincidentally, two in *Il Terreno*, the local Tuscan newspaper read by his aunt Lara, who lived just outside of Lucca where, coincidentally, there was a post office box that served as a return address for the videos found in Lenny D'Ambrosio's apartment. All the articles cited a refugee population exponentially growing due to the fact that, of all the countries in Europe, Italy found it far more difficult to turn away foreigners seeking asylum, searching for a better life. Many of the refugees—like the Libyan man Lenny had met in Umbria—lived from hand to mouth and had trouble assimilating, and this was responsible for an alarming uptick in crime, as well as a growing industry of pornography that employed these refugees. Milo tried to convince himself that if the pornography were made in Italy, the filmmakers could not be Italian, but rather foreigners taking advantage of Italy's open-door policy, exploiting refugees on Italian soil because it would be too expensive to transport them elsewhere.

He left the library just before seven p.m. and walked the four blocks back to his apartment at Ninth Street and Broadway. It was a small western-facing, one-bedroom flat overlooking other buildings and their water towers and filled with light only in the late afternoons. Milo's biggest investment was having built-in bookshelves made by the same guy who'd constructed the bookshelves in Lenny's apartment—an aged, dour Sicilian man whose English was limited and whose dialect of Italian Milo had trouble understanding. The man had worked slowly but had done a beautiful job, creating enough shelf space in Milo's living room that he was able to organize his books, including the language primers, workbooks, and dictionaries he used to teach his language classes. A number of the books were in French, a language he began studying in high school and continued studying in college. French had been fairly easy for him to learn—due to the fact that it was characterized by the same grammar that ruled Italian.

He dropped his overnight bag by the door and, knowing there was very little food in the refrigerator, headed into the kitchen to take a survey of what he might need to pick up at D'Agostino, the grocery store down the block.

When he opened the refrigerator door, the first thing he saw was a white plastic container filled with lowfat apricot yogurt, left there by the last woman he'd been with: a grad student in anthropology, whom he'd dated and split up from three weeks before when she confessed to still being hung up on her previous boyfriend. One thing Milo couldn't abide was ambivalence. In this way, he was very much like his mother. He grabbed a Granny Smith apple and a knife and sat down on his sofa and began cutting it into neat quadrants. The fact that Lenny was permanently gone slammed into him, and he felt lonely and bereft.

And then Maria D'Ambrosio flashed through his mind.

He remembered the first time he'd ever met her. She'd stopped by Lenny's apartment carrying their recently deceased mother's wedding silver to keep in his safe (the safe that Milo had never seen). Brother and sister were both superstitious and had decided that Maria should postpone using the silver until she herself was married. Lenny had already told Milo that his sister was quite beautiful, so it was hardly a surprise for him to meet a woman who had her brother's fine nobility of features, the olive skin and pale eyes.

He knew it was probably wishful thinking, but Milo could have sworn something flashed between them on that first meeting—wishful thinking because at the time, five years ago, he was twenty and she was thirty, and in his mind, he wondered, *Why would a thirty-year-old woman have any interest in somebody like myself?* And yet he'd felt the same frisson again when he'd gone to see her earlier in the day. He tried to pinpoint what exactly it was: her hand touching and lingering on his as they both spoke of Lenny? As Carlo and his mother always liked to point out, Milo's first girlfriend was nineteen when he was sixteen, and after that, he always felt drawn to older women.

12.

After hearing about him from Delzio and Rodriguez, suspecting that his brother might have possessed one of the videos they described, Milo decided he wanted to make contact with Valentino Cipolla, and also perhaps find out if he'd been acquainted with Lenny D'Ambrosio. And so, a week later, remembering Rodriguez saying that Cipolla liked to hang out at Cooks on Saturday nights, he took the train from Grand Central up to New Rochelle with the idea of stopping in at the diner. He went in the company of his weekend guest, a professional soccer player (who played for ACF Fiorentina) whom he knew from all the summers he'd spent in Lucca. Paolo was playing a bunch of matches in the U.S. and had taken advantage of a three-day break in his schedule to spend time with Milo in New York City. Paolo was up for any adventure, and Milo told him that at Cooks he'd be able to see some beautiful American girls, albeit seventeen- and eighteen-year-olds. At twenty-three, Paolo was two years younger than Milo.

The train from Grand Central to New Rochelle was rather crowded: families with squawking children who kept darting into the aisles, well-dressed couples returning from a day of shopping or theater-going in Manhattan, groups of punk-looking teenagers who glared at anyone who bothered to look at them. All of this local color, however, hardly registered with Paolo who instead was preoccupied by the slow speed of the train. "What is wrong with this, anyway? Is it broken?" he asked shortly after the train's departure, when it finally emerged from the tunnel beneath Manhattan. They were conversing in Italian.

"Nothing is wrong with it. This is what trains are like here."

Paolo, who had the same combination of dark hair and light eyes that graced Maria D'Ambrosio, was a bit shorter than Milo, and the way he walked and moved attested to his power and balance and agility. He was a top-notch player, blessed with plenty of sportswear endorsements from companies that profited from his joviality, his dazzling smile, but most of all his charming, humble self-effacement that Milo, who'd been Paolo's friend since they were ten and twelve respectively, knew was genuine. "How many times have I told you that train travel in America is nothing like it is in Italy?"

"Yes, but this is the worst I've seen it."

"That's because your team gets chauffeured around in those cushy buses."

"Believe me, the buses that take us, they are not so great," Paolo said, leaning forward as though he was about to stand up. "Where's the toilet, I need a quick one."

"There's a toilet at the end of the car, but I advise not to use it," Milo told him. "Wait until we get to where we're going."

"Because the toilet is dirty?" Paolo asked with a bit of alarm.

"Uninhabitably dirty," Milo told him.

"Oh, you Americans are really so filthy," Paolo opined, and Milo laughed, knowing his friend was mainly referring to the fact that bidets in America were few and far between.

"Trains like this one are not for 'a quick one,'" Milo insisted. "However, the trains that go longer distances—"

"The Amtrak?" Paolo asked.

"Yes, those have better bathrooms."

"We took the Amtrak to New Haven," Paolo said. "That one took two hours to go a distance that in Italy would be maybe thirty minutes."

"Like I've said, America has a weak transportation infrastructure."

"Stop using those big words," Paolo said. "You know how badly educated I am."

This was hardly the case. Paolo was quite sharp, and he was also a good judge of character. At this point, the conductor came by to collect their tickets. Turning to Paolo, Milo said in English, "Go ahead and do this . . . for us."

Shooting him an exasperated glance, Paolo said to the conductor, "Okay, we don't buy our—" he turned to Milo. "How do you say *biglietti*, again?"

"Tickets," Milo said, smiling at the conductor, a strongly built Latina woman with long glossy curls who'd crossed her arms over her chest and was looking at them, already amused.

"We lose time buy our tickets on Grand Central."

"Then you have to pay more now, honey," she said, winking at Milo.

"How much? Round trips?" Paolo persisted.

"Twenty-five dollars," said the woman.

"*Cazzo*, so expensive for so little ride," Paolo said in Italian.

"Just pay and shut up," Milo told him. And then to the conductor, "Sorry, I'm giving him some immersion."

Paolo looked at him quizzically, and Milo explained what he'd said.

Milo had provided Paolo with only a thumbnail of the events of the past few weeks and few details about Lenny's collection of rough-trade, illegally made porn. Interestingly, Paolo knew something about the porn business and said he believed these kinds of films were actually shot in Tuscany. Milo hated hearing this because he held Tuscany to a higher standard than he did other parts of Italy. Even though they were postmarked from Lucca, he'd just assumed the films Lenny watched were made in the south, south of Rome.

As they were walking along the main drag of Mamaroneck, Paolo nodded and commented, "This village is so cute and quaint."

"Maybe to an Italian it is. To me, it's a pretty generic suburban town."

Paolo turned to him and squeezed his shoulder. "You say this because you grew up in a place like this. Just the way I feel about Montecatini, which you think is quaint, too, don't you?"

"Well . . ."

"Whereas I think Montecatini is a bore." And then Paolo put his arm around Milo as they walked, and Milo couldn't help but squirm. This sort of open affection between men, with which he felt entirely comfortable while in Italy, was unusual in the U.S., and yet he was reluctant to discourage

Paolo's gesture. Often, when they were having conversations, Paolo spoke to Milo with his face only inches away; indeed, one of things Paolo immediately noticed in New York, arguably one of the more demonstrative American cities, was the distance Americans generally kept from one another during conversation, the prime example being the soccer players on the teams they competed against.

Milo had explained to Paolo that Cooks was probably the only watering hole in Westchester County where all the different high schools and colleges within a twenty-mile radius converged and mingled. Mingled until somebody, usually from one of the high schools, picked a fight: often one football player taunting another from a rival team. Whenever this happened, the elderly, bushy-mustached Greek owner of the restaurant didn't come out screaming as one would expect. He preferred to let people duke it out, and this is perhaps why all the food was served on paper plates and all the tables were riveted to the ground. The plastic chairs were solid, the sort you could throw out of a window and would bounce down a sidewalk and never break into pieces.

When Milo and Paolo strolled in, they were nearly blinded by the network of bright fluorescent tubes of lighting above them.

Paolo turned to him. "Why these lights? I feel like I'm in an operating theater. We don't have this lighting in our stores and restaurants in Italy."

"What are you talking about? The Esselunga on San Concordio in Lucca is lit exactly the same way."

Paolo wagged his finger at Milo, tutted while simultaneously raising his eyes. "No, not so bright."

"Uh, Paolo, when was the last time you went into a big Italian supermarket?" Milo challenged, reminding Paolo that he still lived at home, waited on hand and foot by his doting mother, who did all the shopping and cooking.

Paolo shrugged. "Well, if you say so, then I suppose I should believe you."

With a glance Milo could tell that most of the customers were high schoolers: tightly knit groups of nattering kids in acid-washed jeans and varsity jackets with white sleeves who were looking at them suspiciously, clearly noting the fact that they were older.

"How about a good old-fashioned American hamburger?" Milo suggested.

"Great. I've been hoping for one."

They joined a relatively short line of kids waiting to order. "Don't expect to get beer here," Milo said.

Paolo turned to him, "And why not?"

"The drinking age is twenty-one. None of the kids who normally come here are twenty-one."

"*Twenty-one*? To drink? This is also American-crazy," Paolo said.

"I don't agree with you. People drink and drive here in a way they don't over there."

"Ah, yes," Paolo said, knowing that Milo was referring to the hit-and-run driver who killed his brother and whom the police had strongly suspected was a drunk driver.

At just that moment a skirmish broke out on the far side of the crowded restaurant. A tall, skinny kid from one group had rushed over to another shorter, beefier kid with a bad complexion and shoved him so hard he fell off his chair. The second kid scrambled to his feet with his fists clenched, and this led to the inevitable chanting of "Fight, fight, fight, fight!" from the high schoolers surrounding them.

Paolo was both fascinated and horrified. "Always looking for some kind of battle to prove yourselves, you Americans, aren't you?"

"Yeah, unfortunately we are," Milo agreed at the precise moment that a tall man in a black bomber jacket breezed into the crowded restaurant, flanked by two girls who wore little makeup and looked rather plain, clean-cut, and preppy in comparison to some of the war-painted girls who were surrounding the two kids going at it. Milo pegged the women as college freshmen.

Without even breaking stride, the man stalked over to the group of kids and injected himself. "This is over," he boomed.

"Why do you even come here?" asked a sharp-featured girl wearing a baggy pair of acid-washed jeans.

"Because I like to come here," the man said with disdainful authority.

"You just like 'em young," she quipped.

"You got a problem with that? Because if you do, lodge a complaint over there." He indicated the Greek owner of the restaurant, who was standing at a cash register gaping at them and shaking his head in disgust.

"You don't own this place," the girl persisted.

"True. But if there's a fight here, I'm going to break it up," the man said, glancing back at the older man. "Because he can't."

"Okay, Mr. Policeman," said the larger of the two combatants, who was not nearly as big or tall as the man in the bomber jacket. When the guy turned around, Milo could see it was Valentino Cipolla.

"That's our man," he murmured to Paolo.

"Kick the shit out of me," Paolo managed to say in English.

In person, Val Cipolla looked nothing like the sleazy photo that Delzio had flicked across the conference table—no wonder Milo hadn't recognized him in it. In fact, Val had well-cut, longish dirty-blond hair and strong, square, Scandinavian-looking features, and seeing him in his black jeans and black nylon bomber jacket, you could tell he was anything but slight. His left ear glinted with the diamond chip that Milo had noticed in the photograph.

Lowering his voice, Paolo said, "Madonna, but those girls he's with are sweet."

"Agreed."

"So, you're wanting to talk to him?"

"Just waiting to catch his eye." Which Milo did a moment later and waved nonchalantly when Val had started heading back in their direction.

Val stiffened and looked confused, as though he knew he should recognize Milo but just couldn't quite do so. Milo got up and approached him, stuck out his hand and said, "Hi. Val, I'm Carlo Rossi's brother, Milo."

Val slapped himself in the forehead. "Of course you are, I'm sorry. You looked familiar but—"

"It's been six years and . . . we didn't meet so many times."

"Yes, true, but still—"

"Really, don't worry about it. Nice to see you."

Nodding, and with a cursory glance around the restaurant, Val said, "Are you here alone?"

Milo explained he was with Paolo, whom Val waved to, and then explained how he knew Paolo and why Paolo was in America.

"Really?" Turning to the two women still flanking him, who were now looking bored, he announced, "I'll be right back," and walked over to Paolo with his hand outstretched, "Hello, I'm Val."

"Nice to meet you, Val."

"Milo just told me you play for Fiorentina?"

"Yes? Do you know it?"

"Do I know it? Of course I know it. I watch your games whenever I can. Whenever they're televised, that is. Which, unfortunately, is not so often."

Val dug a small pocket-size notebook that had a pen affixed to it out of his jacket pocket. "What's your last name?" he asked. Paolo squinted at him, clearly not quite understanding. "*Cognome*," Val said.

"Ah, you speak Italian," Paolo said. "Good, because my brain is getting tired by English. My surname is Zaccarelli."

Val jotted this down and then looked up. Continuing in Italian, he said, "I'm speaking for the moment, but soon I'll probably fall off a cliff." Paolo threw back his head and laughed. Then Val said, "I studied it in college."

"But somebody obviously taught you that expression," Milo said in English.

Val smiled. "Yes. My brother Matteo taught me."

"Where *is* Matteo?"

"*Matteo* actually now lives in Pistoia. He's the one who got me into watching Fiorentina."

"*Pistoia*?" Milo was incredulous. "*Matteo* lives in Italy?"

"He does."

"We were just mentioning Pistoia," Paolo said. "I was born right next to Pistoia. In Montecatini."

"Why does Matteo live in Pistoia?" Milo asked.

"Well, why not?" Paolo said. "At least they have bidets in Pistoia."

Milo explained his friend's preoccupation, and Val nodded. "Right?" he said to no one in particular.

Milo noticed that the women who had come in with Cipolla had gravitated over to a table of younger kids whom they presumably knew and were chatting with them.

"Why don't we all sit down together," Val suggested. Indicating the girls with a tilt of his head, he said, "They'll join us . . . eventually."

Milo and Paolo's hamburgers were done before Val's order of fried chicken and French fries, and they found a table and had a few minutes alone.

Milo said, "It makes no sense, somebody like him hanging out in a place like this. He's got to be thirty."

"But they told you he likes them young."

"But he just came in with two young women."

"Maybe he's their chaperone."

"Doubtful."

When Val finally arrived at the table and set down his flimsy tray of greasy-looking fried chicken and large sizzling fries, he surprised Milo by asking, "So how's your mother doing?"

Milo was a bit taken aback at this question and managed to answer, "She's hanging in there. She's got to. Have you ever met her?"

Val shook his head. "No. I actually haven't."

"Did Matteo?"

Val hesitated and said, "Yes, briefly after the funeral. Carlo, however, met *my* mother several times when he came home with Matteo."

"But Matteo never came to our house?"

"No, he never did," Val confirmed.

After a nervous silence, Milo asked, "So why is he living in Pistoia?"

"He wanted to get away from here. From New York. And Florence is too expensive."

Paolo, who understood this much said, in Italian, "Yes, Florence costs an eye."

Milo asked where the girls were from and Val said, "They're both at Vassar. I tutored them at Rye Country Day."

"Ah, makes sense. That's why they look so preppy."

Val shook his head and seemed to bristle at this remark. "By the way," he said, "what *is* 'preppy' in Italian?"

Milo thought for a moment. "You know, I don't think the equivalent exists. But let's ask the expert. Turning to Paolo, who was trying to listen to the conversation, he asked about the word *preppy*.

"I don't want to leave him out," Val said. "You can continue in Italian. I can follow pretty well. I studied it. I'll rely on English to reply."

"We use actually *preppy*," Paolo said. "No translation. But not so often."

Val said, "I think in France they call it BCBG. Bon chic, bon genre . . . I went to college with a couple of French kids. They taught me a lot of expressions."

"Amherst, right?" Milo asked.

Val nodded. "Yeah," he said, "the real Amherst. Not UMass, Amherst."

The real Amherst had turned Milo down flat. "I knew that. Ever visit the Emily Dickinson house?"

Val smiled. "I was actually one of the student docents at the Emily Dickinson house," he explained. "Don't know if you know this, but most of her significant stuff, her important papers and diaries, went to Harvard."

Milo felt dazzled and gripped the side of his plastic, contoured chair. Could Delzio have all this wrong? It was hard to reconcile that a former docent at the Emily Dickinson house in Amherst, Massachusetts, might be a dealer of illegally made pornography in Westchester County, New York, less than thirty miles from midtown Manhattan. The parts of Val Cipolla he was now seeing just didn't fit together.

Paolo was tucking into his hamburger. "Ah *cazzo*, this is so delicious. This is one thing I wish we had better in Italy. Pizza I could live without." This made Val laugh.

They continued eating in relative silence. Milo knew he needed to ask the question lingering on the tip of his tongue. "Believe it or not," he said at last, "Matteo crossed my mind lately. Related to Carlo. Who said something to me once that I've always wondered about." He hoped that he sounded convincing, and then realized that so far, he'd been telling the truth, because he *had* thought of Matteo lately and, with Detective Delzio's prompting, *had* remembered something Carlo had said.

"What's that?" Val asked blithely as he took a long swig of a tall plastic vessel of Coca-Cola.

"That you guys had a business that distributes and sells pretty extreme pornographic videos. And I think my brother may have owned one of them."

Val's face darkened. There was a menacing glare in his eyes, and he looked formidable. "Why would I discuss any of that with you?" he said with annoyance.

Why, indeed, thought Milo. At just that moment, the two former Rye Country Day girls approached the table, and turning to them, Val dug into his pocket for a set of keys that were attached to what looked like a silver tablet and handed them to one girl, very politely saying, "Could I ask you and Patty to wait for me in the car? I need to speak to these . . . guys." He glanced shrewdly at Milo. "It's probably going to be mostly in Italian." He looked at his watch and said, "It's almost time for me to get you both home, anyway."

Milo wondered if the parents of these girls knew who they were spending time with. He glanced at his watch. It was 9:45. Once the girls left he said, "Don't tell me they have a curfew?"

"*I* do," Val said. "I'm in bed by ten every night. In college, I used to go to bed at nine."

"No partying?"

"I find partying boring," Cipolla said. "And I *don't* like to talk about what I do for a living."

"Well, I just remember Carlo mentioning—"

"Well, they were arguing, my brother and your brother late the night before your brother died."

Startled, Milo didn't respond at first and could feel his face prickling with heat. Noticing this discomfort, Paolo rested his hand on Milo's shoulder. At last, Milo said, "I didn't know about any of this. But how *would* I know? Carlo never made it home the following morning."

Val's face crumpled and he shook his head, as though realizing he was being inadvertently insensitive. "You're right," he said. "I guess you wouldn't know. But okay, they went out drinking together and got into an argument."

"My brother did NOT drink!" Milo countered tersely.

"Well, he did that night. I happened to know . . . because there was a blowup."

"A blowup?" Milo asked, incredulous.

Val kept his eyes on Milo. "I didn't get details. But it was about our business."

"The porn distribution business," Milo interjected.

"Whatever you want to call it."

"Okay, but just so you know, the autopsy reported zero alcohol in his blood."

Val was looking at him sadly. And then, he noticed the tattoo on Milo's forearm: *Carlo 7/1/67—3/4/88*. "When did you get that?"

"Three months after he died."

Val impulsively reached over and gently ran his rough fingers over the design. Milo normally would have pulled his arm away, not wanting to be touched by a relative stranger. But for some reason, he didn't. And in a strange sort of way, the physical contact with Val Cipolla made him feel momentarily comforted, less agitated, and he didn't quite know why.

"This tattoo of his, it really upsets my mother," Paolo now told Val. "She told me that whenever she sees it, she feels like weeping. And she doesn't understand why he would have it to remind himself all the time."

"I *want* to be reminded," Milo told them. "All the time." It was hard to explain that he and Rose Marie felt that Carlo's life, his existence, had to be kept close, tactile, so that he'd never for a moment be forgotten.

Val said, "Your brother once told me he didn't have a lot of close friends."

"Yeah, so?" Milo said defensively.

"He told me that girls found him geeky. This is something I can relate to."

And how is that? You, geeky? Milo wanted to ask.

Val went on. "When I was a kid, I used to be really skinny. I got bullied a lot. So I started hitting the gym when I was fourteen. But no matter how big I got, I always felt scrawny." Milo said nothing in reply, so Val went on. "Anyway, you may not know, but your brother's friendship was very important to my brother and, I believe, vice versa."

"I knew they were pretty good friends. But I don't know much more than that. I don't believe either of you came to Carlo's wake."

"My brother was afraid of losing it completely and upsetting your mother. We both went to the funeral. Matteo went up to your mother afterward. They'd never met before that, and so he introduced himself."

Milo almost said ***she** told me they **never** met.* And then realized, for obvious reasons, that would be the wrong thing to say.

13.

Thumbtacked to the walls of Delzio's small office were pastoral posters of the top-rated golf courses, one of them with an ocean view that Milo recognized as Pebble Beach, California. Leaning against the wall opposite the detective's desk was a line of golf clubs: a driving wood and some irons—suggesting that Delzio practiced his swing during his downtime.

The detective had been leaning back in his swivel chair, listening to the report of Milo's conversation with Val Cipolla and how Rose Marie, four years before, had probably found one of the videos imported by the Cipollas among Carlo's belongings.

"Did you ask Cipolla about his business?"

"Yeah. He didn't deny it."

"How about if he knew Lenny?"

"I didn't get a chance."

Delzio looked at him dismissively. "That was a miss."

"I know. I know. Don't rub it in. I got distracted by something Val told me." That his brother and Matteo apparently had quarreled fiercely the last night of Carlo's life.

"Sounds like it was about the porn business."

"But I wanted to ask. When you originally said that someone *might* have been involved in Lenny's death, could it possibly have been Val?"

The detective leaned forward in his chair, planting his massive forearms on his ink blotter. "What would motivate Val Cipolla to kill Lenny D'Ambrosio, who if anything was just a customer?"

Milo considered this. By the way, Val and I exchanged phone numbers."

"Good. Since we're no longer investigating, if I were you I'd try to find out more about his business and if he knew Lenny D'Ambrosio."

"That's my intention," Milo told Delzio, "but what about that Columbia student who accused Lenny of assault? I mean, shouldn't she be questioned?"

Delzio waved at him dismissively. "We spoke to her right away. When we were putting everything together." The detective reached for a half-finished paper cup of black coffee and took a large swig. Fixing his intense eyes on Milo, he said, "Unfortunately, this graduate student gave us very little. She had a lawyer with her who kept trying to shut us down. And in fact, she played down his 'inappropriate behavior.' She seemed—it almost seemed like she'd forgiven him and didn't want to make a big deal out of it."

"I see," Milo said, disappointed.

"Point is, we didn't get any impression that she (or anyone associated with her, like a parent or sibling) would have built up enough animosity or resentment to try to get back at D'Ambrosio . . . for what happened. I mean, think about it. It would be a very risky proposition to go to somebody's apartment, hold them up at gunpoint (or knifepoint), and force them to get up on a chair, put a bedsheet around their neck, and then step off that chair into a choking death."

"Do you have to be so graphic?" Milo complained.

"Yeah, I do to make my point," Delzio said. "Because so many things could go wrong in that scenario. Like being seen or heard by a downstairs neighbor."

"A *batty* downstairs neighbor," Milo amended.

Neither said anything for a few moments, Delzio peering at him with curious intention. At last he said, "Did Maria tell you about the videos she found in his safe? Before he died?"

Milo nodded. "Yeah."

"Did she happen to tell you that once we unsealed the apartment, she went over to check on a few things and went into the safe. And that apparently, the videos were no longer there?"

Milo was stunned into silence and his knee-jerk response was, "No. But do we believe her?"

"I was going to ask *you* that."

"I hardly know her. But then why would she make up a story? Or have anything to hide?"

"Why, indeed," Delzio said with a smirk. He raised a stubby finger. "When we were searching the apartment originally, she never told us about the safe. And maybe didn't—or doesn't—want us to find those particular videos."

Milo pointed out that the videos could have been taken out of the safe at any time between when Maria first saw them up until Lenny's death. "Okay, but let's say somebody other than Maria wanted those videos and took them. Why?"

Delzio turned up both his palms. "Maybe this person appeared in them?"

"But you said the videos were made abroad?"

"They probably were. But we never got to examine the ones that went missing." Delzio was tapping his fingers on the desk. "I just had a thought."

"What's that?"

"*Somebody* has got to be retrieving D'Ambrosio's mail."

"I would imagine Maria is."

"Just wondering if since his death if he's received any more of these videos."

"I guess we can ask her."

Delzio made a move to get up from his desk.

"Wait, one more thing," Milo said. "On a totally different subject."

Delzio settled back in his chair. "What's that?"

Milo started to feel breathless. "It's about my father."

Delzio frowned and said quietly, "What about your father?"

"Well, like I told you, I was eight when he died. And like I said, he told me that he played golf with you."

"Right, and?"

"How many times did you guys play golf together, would you say?"

"I don't know. Several. Why?"

"I've just been wondering: How did he strike you, my father?"

"How did he strike me?" Delzio repeated, looking momentarily perplexed. "You mean as a person?"

"That's what I mean, yeah."

The detective reflected for a moment, and of course Milo wondered if what was forthcoming would be filtered.

"Well, he was kind of a quiet guy. A brooding kind of guy." More like Carlo, Milo had long since concluded to himself. "He was also quite tall." Delzio looked at Milo appraisingly. "You certainly didn't inherit his height."

"My brother did."

"Maybe so, but otherwise you're a dead ringer for him, for your dad. Every time I see you, you remind me of him. Looks certainly, but mannerisms *and* the way your brain seems to work."

"Some people have said that we're very much alike." But this was indiscernible in photographs. His mother's relatives always insisted he looked a lot like her—he did, after all, have her large brown eyes. But these relations, of course, were biased.

Delzio continued, "By the way, I just remembered another thing about him, about your father. He had a putter—whenever I saw it, I drooled. He'd had it made: It was one of the first 'ping' putters I'd ever seen."

For some mysterious reason, hearing about Delzio's envy for his father's golf club was painful. "Before he died, my dad actually gave that putter to my brother. He didn't care what happened to the rest of his clubs, but he wanted Carlo to keep the putter because Carlo was the only one in the family who played golf. Long story, but Carlo eventually gave the putter to me because he decided he didn't want it." Milo, who didn't play golf, momentarily considered offering the golfing putter to Delzio, but then reconsidered.

14.

Maria was looking unusually pale and had a delicate air of agitation about her. They were sitting at her kitchen table that, since his last visit, had had its oily tablecloth removed. Milo couldn't help but note this aloud, and Maria said, "I know that tablecloth is hideous. Aunt Francesca always puts it on, and I really should insist I don't want it there."

"She seems kind of willful," Milo remarked. "Not to mention overly vigilant. I'm actually surprised that she didn't answer the door."

"She's not here at the moment."

Aunt Fran had gone to visit family in Friuli, which, apparently she did every year at Christmastime. "The fact that I haven't bothered to put another tablecloth down tells you how depressed I've been," Maria now admitted. "But to answer your question, I got those."

She was referring to two battered-looking padded brown packages that looked like small coffins. Gazing at him sadly, she said, "When I collected his mail and saw them, I just mentally put them aside."

"What did you make of the fact that the videos in the safe were missing?"

She shrugged. "He could've moved them. He was always reorganizing."

Her response was at once glib and brusque, and Milo got the impression that Maria perhaps wasn't telling him all she knew. But his momentary suspicion got sidetracked when he picked up one of the packages; the first thing that jumped out was the handwritten return address: *I Films, Via Antonio Vallisneri*. It was a post office within the walls of the city of Lucca, which Milo knew from having spent so many of his childhood and adolescent summers with Aunt Lara. The next thing was even more eye-opening: the packages, battle-weary from crossing the Atlantic, bore Lenny's correct Mamaroneck address but the wrong recipient: Fabrizio del Dongo. This was a grim reckoning for Milo—why had Lenny decided to use *this* name for a protective pseudonym, a name that would, if pressed, presumably allow him to deny the videos were meant for him? Fabrizio del Dongo was the name of the main character in *The Charterhouse of Parma*. He mentioned this, and Maria seemed surprised, obviously not recognizing the character's name.

"Lenny loved that book," she said with quiet bitterness.

"That was another book he had me read while I was in high school. But in the original. My French at the time just wasn't good enough to get much out of it." He went on to explain that he'd read the book again during his junior year at college.

"So you studied French in college as well as Italian?" Maria asked.

Milo explained that his official degree was in Romance languages and that he'd taken quite a few courses in French as well as Italian.

Milo couldn't help noting the irony that Lenny's Italian-language library, filled with some of the most erudite writers in the world, also extended to his crude collection of Italian-made pornography.

"Well, I wasn't planning on doing anything with them," Maria now told him, indicating the packaged videos. "But if you want to . . . watch them."

"I don't want to watch them. But maybe I should try to have a look at them. To try to understand . . . what this fascination of his was."

"If you think that's necessary," she said.

"I do, kind of."

"Well, if you decide to watch them, I want you to tell me about the content, no matter what it is."

Milo studied her face, which was now looking impassive. "Are you sure you want to know?"

She nodded slowly and said she did.

They both fell quiet, and the peaceful house reminded Milo that Aunt Francesca had a kind of brash, clanging presence. He admitted to himself that he was glad she (who didn't seem to like him) was in Friuli. "When is your aunt coming back from the Friuli?" Milo asked.

Maria looked perplexed. "For some reason she doesn't like you."

"I was just thinking the same thing. I'm glad it's not paranoia. Why do you think she doesn't like me?"

"I think because you were close to my brother, who became an atheist. Maybe she assumes you're an atheist and that you likely encouraged him to be one also."

Influencing Lenny about anything would have been impossible. "Did she *know* your brother at all—"

"Clearly not very well."

"Anyway, you *could've* gone with her to Friuli. Just to get away."

"She *did* invite me. But visiting family in Italy after what's happened? Do you really think that would be relaxing? They'd smother me."

"Ah, yes. Good point."

She smiled at him, brushed her hand over his arm and said, "But you're sweet to worry about me."

Her touch was electric, and Milo could feel his face flushing. Despite this, he managed to say, "I know Lenny would want me to worry about you."

This seemed to unsettle Maria, who rose quickly from the kitchen table, moved to the stove, retrieved a kettle, and went to the sink to fill it with water. The pale-blue silk dress she was wearing hugged the lovely curves of her body. Once the tea kettle was back on the stove, she remained there, facing away from him. And then Milo noticed her shoulders beginning to shake. She turned around, her head bent, her eyes flooded with tears. Without even thinking, he jumped up and went to comfort her; the moment they embraced, his whole body began to burn.

"Sit down," she said. "I need to tell you something."

Her tone was ominous, and Milo obeyed as a shudder went through him. "What?" he said.

She continued standing, now looking down on him. "A few days before Lenny died, he transferred a substantial sum of money into a bank account that we shared, a joint bank account."

"Really?" Milo said, considering this for a moment. "I guess you could say the timing was . . . either curious or deliberate?"

Maria nodded. "Yeah, I guess you could say that." She was staring at the floor. "I haven't even told Aunt Francesca. I haven't told her or anyone what I am about to tell you." She now looked at Milo, tears still misting her eyes, and quietly said, "The amount that he transferred into the account was 1.5 million dollars."

Milo was stunned. He didn't know what to say except, *How did Lenny, who earned a very modest living as a professor of Italian at Mercy College, come upon all that money?* But (for the moment) he kept that to himself.

Maria went on. "He always told me he wanted to make sure I was taken care of, should anything happen to him. Normal for an older brother, though, right?"

"Certainly," Milo managed to say.

Maria went on. "So I guess the first question I have is, Why did he put the money into the joint account right before he died? And the second more obvious question is, How and why did he have such a large amount of money?"

"Well, if he did this right before he died, it had to be . . . strategic."

"Presumably."

"But let me ask you this. It's been almost a month. Did you mention anything about the money to Detective Delzio?"

She looked irritated. "Why would I do that? There's no longer an investigation."

"You told him about the missing videos."

Maria explained that she'd made the mistake of telling Aunt Francesca about the videos and Aunt Francesca would not stop hounding her to report this and the fact that there was a hidden safe to the police. "Aunt Fran assumed they were stolen from the safe and the police should therefore know about it. When my brother first died, I didn't mention the safe because there are personal and private things in there and when they were investigating and looking for clues, I didn't want these things disturbed or looked at."

"So what about this money that he deposited in your bank account?" Milo asked.

Maria shrugged. "One thing you might not know about my brother: He sometimes liked to gamble in the stock market. However, the estate attorney can't find a brokerage account or, for that matter, a bank account besides our joint account that held any substantial sum of money."

"But a huge deposit like that has to be traceable?"

"Oh, they were able to trace the deposit. It came from a bank in Belize."

"Belize?" Milo cried. "This does not sound good."

"Exactly. So I'm really afraid that the money, one way or another, is not legitimate."

"Don't you think you should report this?"

"Report it to whom?" she asked curtly.

"I don't know. Again, maybe Delzio?"

"Milo, once again, he's not investigating anything anymore. And this is a transaction from a foreign country that would have to be followed up. A local cop wouldn't be involved in that."

"The FBI would, I guess, right?" Milo asked.

"Probably," Maria said. "But why should I contact them? I don't want to stir something up. Clearly, Lenny obviously deposited that money in my account because he was planning on taking his own life."

"Could he have been afraid somebody was going to try and kill him?" Milo asked. "And made the deposit first?"

Maria's brow furrowed and she shook her head. "That's your scenario. You're the only one who thinks it's a possibility."

"So you don't even consider—"

"I don't," she interrupted him. "I don't!" she emphasized. "But I *do* think, I *do* feel something specific drove him to suicide. And I just can't figure out what that could possibly be."

Part Two

15.

The film's quality was grainy, its colors muted, its English subtitles crude and poorly superimposed and unidiomatically translated. Before he pressed forward, Milo coached himself to try to look at whatever appeared with numbed interest, not to believe whatever was portrayed had actually occurred. But his resolve dwindled almost immediately due to the home movie–like documentary quality—and that was the point, wasn't it? To make fiction look like fact, to make film look like reality? He pressed pause.

Milo did not have a VCR at his apartment in Manhattan, but there was an outdated color television and video player in his and Carlo's childhood bedroom. So after leaving Maria's, on impulse he'd stopped by his mother's house, greeted Rose Marie, and told her he needed to go upstairs and watch a video for one of his classes. Now, with a glance up at his brother's bookshelves, thick tomes of biology and genetics that were maintained and dusted regularly by Rose Marie, he pressed play again.

The narrative starts simply enough, with the silhouetted profile of a woman standing at the entrance of a motorway. In the distance behind her, the uniformly characteristic architecture of an Autogrill—Italy's version of the food-and-gas franchises that are built on the side of American highways. A much higher end establishment than its American counterpart, however, Autogrills are a combination of fueling station, restaurant, bar (Americans have troubling believing that, in Italy, there are full bars on the side of the highway and that people customarily stop in for a cocktail), and grocery store that sells an impressive quality of meats, cheeses, dried pastas, and other premium canned and bottled goods. As to which autostrada or Autogrill is anyone's guess; Autogrills are prolific throughout Italy, from the toe of the boot to the elegantly stitched borders of Switzerland and Austria.

The hitchhiking woman in silhouette becomes more visible: a towheaded blond woman with light eyes framed widely by broad features that look distinctively Eastern European. Girlishly flat-chested, she wears an orange tube top, showing bare midriff, and a short denim skirt that rides on the tops of her thighs. She looks remarkably young—Milo wondered if she might be even younger than eighteen.

Wanting to look at her more closely, he grabbed the video remote and froze the frame. Heavily mascaraed eyes stared back at him with an unmistakable glint of sadness, of resignation. For a moment, he imagined a whole jagged and desperate history: that she spent every last cent clawing her way to Italy, and then maybe met someone who knew someone else and got caught up in the sex trade, assured by some predator that she was soon to be a film star? He looked at the woman again. She appeared incredibly young and, he couldn't help remarking, seemed like the sort of woman Val would be interested in.

He restarted the film. A man driving a car, a man with an impressive head of salt-and-pepper hair, his shirt unbuttoned to reveal a smooth, muscled, hairless chest, leaving the parking lot of the Autogrill, maneuvering at a very slow pace toward the hitchhiking woman. Either an Alfa Romeo or a souped-up Fiat, the car passes the woman, screeching to a halt, and she jumps in without hesitation. It occurred to Milo that, without any sort of pretext, a woman jumping into a car like this strained credulity. What woman with any sense would do this? Then again, he realized that in his limited experience watching pornography, one often found the same narrative disregard for believability.

The man's accent identifies him as Southern Italian; however, the woman's Italian, though perfectly adequate, is a heavily accented foreigner's Italian. Milo strained to identify it and ultimately guessed she might be Romanian. Or maybe, just maybe, Albanian.

Now a passenger in the sports car, the woman's denim skirt hikes up; she is wearing no underwear. Driving fast on the autostrada, the man keeps glancing over at her exposed genitals and at last pulls up her skirt to get a better look, then reaches over and proprietarily begins caressing her, but in a very gentle, almost loving way. She, in turn, pulls aside one of the flaps of his shirt and runs an exploratory hand over one of his nipples. Her touch sends a jolt through him.

Multitasking while driving, so Italian, Milo remarked to himself.

He told himself that so far nothing out of the ordinary had happened and found himself responding to what initially seemed like real tenderness between them, something completely unexpected, something he'd never seen even in traditional pornography.

All at once, the film's scenery changes: a long shot of the same car driving in the countryside. It passes a train station that Milo believes he recognizes as Spello, a town in central Umbria that ironically tends to attract a lot of wealthy Americans.

Then to a cheap motel, the woman lying on a bed with a red coverlet, still dressed, her skirt hiked up. The man, now shirtless but still wearing his pants, is on his knees next to her, running his hands over her body, again with a sort of proprietary gentleness, and then, with a jolt to the viewer, she grabs his hand like a vice, which causes him to cry out. She slowly twists his arm until she has him begging to be released and forces him to lie on the bed; the change from tenderness to brutality is shocking.

There are two metal rings protruding from the walls on either side of the bed; reaching under the bed, she grabs two pieces of rope, orders the man to grab the rings and soon the man's arms are stretched out and completely restrained. With one of her diminutive fists she begins punching him in the biceps, which immediately turned red from the abuse. Milo thought he'd seen enough of the video and turned it off.

He sat there in the bedroom of the house that he'd grown up in, the place where he and Carlo had lived and sometimes, as moody adolescents, argued ridiculously, the place where Carlo mostly had kept his distance, conveying little of what he was thinking or feeling and where, after his mysterious death, Milo grieved inconsolably, guiltily. He glanced once again at the television screen, almost expecting that, despite being turned off, it would have a mind of its own and continue playing the video that wasn't shocking so much as it was disheartening and perhaps would have been less so if he hadn't originally observed an almost touching benevolence between the two actors. The screen remained blank, cooling into a deeper, darker blue.

Lenny had always complained about being ill-treated by women, but watching the video, Milo could only wonder if his dear friend's only way of dealing with rejection was watching some sort of perversion of it.

Yes, of course people were different in their private downtime, but it was hard not to wonder if Lenny had engaged in amorous activities similar to those Milo had just witnessed.

And then his eyes alighted on his brother's desk, where there was, propped up, a vintage postcard that advertised the film *La Dolce Vita.*

La Dolce Vita happened to be one of Lenny's favorite films, Fellini's narrative a far cry from this bewildering, depressing stab at moviemaking.

When he finally headed back downstairs, Rose Marie immediately could detect something amiss. "What did you have to watch?" she asked him with noticeable suspicion and grew even more wary when he stalled in his response. "What's going on in your head?" she asked him nervously.

He suddenly felt ashamed and realized that he just could not lie to her. "Okay, I was watching one of those videos that belonged to Lenny." She looked confused. "Maria had one. I just wanted to see what it was all about."

Reaching toward him with one hand, Rose Marie said, "Let me have a look at this video?"

Instinctively clutching his book bag to his chest, Milo asked, "Why? For what purpose?"

"I just want to see if it looks like the one I found in your brother's things?"

"How can you possibly remember what it looked like?"

Rose Marie sighed. "Because it was peculiar, that's how."

Still reluctant, Milo pulled out the video and handed it to his mother.

Whenever she got nervous, Rose Marie's left eye sharpened a bit more than her right eye, which then looked droopy. She examined the cassette closely, turned it over, and then noticed something. Handing the video back to Milo, she said flatly, "Yes, it's the same kind . . . I remember this insignia on this corner?" She pointed to a small yellow decal of sorts. Milo took the video, scrutinized it, and then things turned surreal. He looked up at his mother, whose face was pinched with concern.

"This is really weird, Mom. I didn't notice this. But I actually recognize the insignia. It's the likeness of a funerary sculpture in the cathedral in Lucca. You and I have seen this sculpture before, in fact. It's that marble carving by della Quercia of a woman called Ilaria del Carretto, who died young—her dog is at her feet."

"Oh, *that* one," Rose Marie said. "I remember the little dog. Your aunt Lara once said to me that the dog is gazing at her for all eternity."

The sculpture was arguably Lucca's most important artifact; people came from all over the world to see it. That the image of Ilaria had been coopted to a porn film insignia repulsed him.

And then Milo remembered the Lucca post office address on the package the video came in and specifically *I Films*. He wondered if the *I* stood for Ilaria. Bizarre, ridiculous name for a porn film company. Now he wished he'd pressed Val about the company he clearly owned. Beyond this, the insignia based on the famous sculpture suggested yet another connection to the small, walled Italian city where, in his twenty-five years, he'd spent most of his summers. And then it occurred to him: If Matteo lived in Pistoia, which was around twenty-eight miles from Lucca, why were the videos being mailed from Lucca rather than from Pistoia?

Milo noticed that his mother was now staring at him with a blank expression.

"Can you look this guy up and ask him about it?"

"Ask . . . ?"

"Val, isn't that his name?"

"What would I ask him?"

"Why your brother had one of his videos?"

"What does it matter now?"

"Because I want to understand."

Milo hesitated and then explained that he'd actually spoken to Val.

"What do you mean you spoke to him?"

Milo explained about going to Cooks when Paolo was in town and running into Val and what he'd said about the argument between Carlo and Matteo the night before Carlo died.

Rose Marie wrung her hands together. "Why didn't you tell me about any of this?"

"Why? Because I didn't want to upset you."

"But what could they have been arguing about?"

"He seemed to suggest it was about their video business?"

"Why would they argue about that?"

"I honestly don't know."

"So can you get in touch with him? Can you call him and find out exactly what his brother and Carlo were arguing about?"

Now Milo was getting frustrated. "Mom," he said, "does it really matter what they were arguing about?"

"Of course it matters. Who knows, it could have something to do—"

"Mom—"

"Maybe they were arguing about something that had to do with Carlo's car accident."

"No, Mom. The car accident was caused by a drunk driver who plowed into Carlo's car. A hit-and-run driver who is out there in the world living his worthless life. A criminal living off our grief!"

Rose Marie jammed her fingers in her ears. "I can't hear that. Please don't say it. Father Flannery told me I have to give the other driver the benefit of the doubt, that he or she didn't mean what they did. That will help me deal with my grief."

"You give this priest way too much leeway, you swallow hook, line, and sinker everything he says."

Holding both her hands up for him to stop, she said, "Milo," more quietly now, more resolute. "You may not need it or want it and that's up to you. But *I need* my religion," she told him.

He thought it best not to press the subject of the car accident any further.

16.

The ride on the number seven subway from Grand Central to Whitestone took around fifty minutes. Milo figured that Val probably lived in or close to Whitestone, which, although it possessed some lovely turn-of-the-century architecture, was not the sort of place that would normally draw a culinary tourist looking for a memorable meal. The name of the restaurant was La Caviglia ("the ankle")—Rose Marie thought it was the most ridiculous name for a restaurant she'd ever heard. But Milo wanted to give the place a fair shake.

He had never actually visited the town of Whitestone, except when passing through it when he and Carlo were children in the back of their parents' car, driving over the Whitestone Bridge, whose lofty cables looked like they rose all the way up into the empyrean, the ascending view of them so stupefying that even now, in his adult life, he still had dreams of driving over the bridge to Long Island—most of them involving a catastrophe: the bridge collapsing into the East River, the green lights at the top fizzling into the cold currents as the tall girders sank and drowned.

La Caviglia was located on Clintonville Street; Clintonville, Milo knew, was the incorporated area of Queens, whose original name came from DeWitt Clinton, the governor of New York state in the late 1700s, and it happened to share the name of the high school in the Bronx that his father had attended.

Already seated and waiting inside La Caviglia, a restaurant he'd highly recommended, Val Cipolla was wearing a pair of skintight cargo pants; a black T-shirt under a black windbreaker, which was open; and a red bandanna, neatly folded and tied across his forehead. When Milo first saw the bandanna, he thought, despite the fact that it was fashionable, something about it looked contrived. But he then reasoned that Val's fair hair was rather thick and longish like Björn Borg's, so maybe he needed the headband to keep it from becoming unruly. As soon as Milo sat down, Val took off his jacket. His bare arms popped with veins and looked powerful.

A middle-aged waiter dressed entirely in black, with bulging eyes and stringy hair combed across the dome of his head, appeared at the table and poured out a mixture of ice cubes and water into their tall glasses. The sound of the ice rattling was bone hollow. The waiter said something unintelligible in low tones to Val, and Val answered the man in pretty good Italian. And then fixed a merciless gaze on Milo, as though to say, *Did you check that out?*

Milo said, "I guess you studied Italian at Amherst?"

And in Italian, Val said, "Well, what actually happened was one night I went to bed, and when I woke up the next morning, I was speaking Italian."

"Yeah, right. Matteo probably taught you how to say that."

Val grinned. "No. I actually spent six months in Italy right after college."

"Did you study Italian in high school?" Milo asked.

Val nodded. "Yeah, three years in high school. And then in college. But in college I still majored in econ."

"Most high schools don't teach Italian anymore," Milo remarked, wistful.

"I went to a Catholic school in Mineola, and the school was run by a Florentine."

"*Chaminade*?" Milo asked.

"Yeah. You know it? You know Chaminade?"

"Fancy-schmancy Chaminade. Did they offer Latin, too?"

"They did. I took both."

"God! I'm jealous. I didn't get either."

"What do you expect from public school?"

"I didn't go to public school. I also went to Catholic high school."

"Stepinac?"

Interesting. That was Lenny's school. "No, Thornton Donovan." He went on to explain that at Thornton Donovan, interest in Latin was so minimal that the discipline had been phased out. "Anyway, my aunt Lara, my mother's sister who lives in Italy, has been after me to study Latin, especially now that I've completed everything but my dissertation and I'm teaching Italian. She says knowing Latin will greatly improve my Italian."

"*Suus 'sera numquam*," Val said.

"Alright, stop trying to impress. So, are you Italian on both sides?" Milo asked.

Val shook his head. "Nope. My mom is Polish."

"Then where's your father's family from?"

"Genoa."

"Really? Cipolla doesn't sound like a Northern Italian name."

"What are you, some kind of a *Nordista*?" Val said with a canny smile on his face.

Ignoring this jibe, Milo said, "From my experience, Slavic people have an aptitude for learning other languages," thinking of the young woman in the porn video. Every time he remembered it, the woman punching the man's biceps, he got a bottomed-out feeling in his stomach.

"Well, there's a particular reason I learned Italian," Val told him. "I was emulating my older brother."

With an obvious note of sadness, he began relaying his family history. He was born when his mother was close to forty; his brother Matteo was born four years later. However, his older brother whom they'd never known, had had a tragic accident at the age of eighteen. A star athlete and a model student, his brother had gone off to Jones Beach with a friend one day in the middle of July. "You know those weird gas stations they have in the middle of the Grand Central Parkway? Right in the median between the east- and westbound traffic? They stopped to get gas, my brother pumping it, and some old lady lost control of her car and drove right into the filling station." Val hesitated a moment, staring blankly at Milo, who was holding his breath. "Her car crushed my brother into the gas pumps. He was dead within five minutes." All this was delivered quietly and, oddly, matter-of-factly.

Milo was staring at Val in horror. The silence between them seemed to last for several minutes. "So, you lost your brother, too?" he uttered at last, his voice in a rasp.

Gently, Val said, "I suppose you could say that, but it's really not the same. *My* brother died before I was born. So, I never knew him. Whereas you *knew* your brother. However, *my* mother and *your* mother have something in common, for sure."

Milo asked if Val's family had sued the woman who'd killed his older brother. Val shook his head and said there was no point. That she'd had some kind of stroke and passed out at the wheel. "She went into a depression after that, clearly felt awful about causing the death of an eighteen-year-old kid. My parents didn't have the heart to make her life any worse. They just insisted that her family forbid her from driving anymore. And as far as we know, they did." He paused and then, as an afterthought, said, "Suing her wasn't going to bring my brother back.

"Anyway, my mother immediately tried to get pregnant again. But it took her four very tough years before she was able to . . . get pregnant with me." Then Val let out a sigh. "Then, when I was born, she insisted on calling me by my older brother's name."

Milo blurted out, "Your dead brother's name was *also* Valentino?"

Val nodded. "Yep. It actually was."

"I've never heard of anything like this."

Val looked bored. "Well, now you have. So," he continued, "even though Matteo and I never knew my brother—Val One, we call him—my mom held him up to us: according to her, he was perfect; he was beyond reproach. That meant Matteo and I had a lot to live up to. Val One studied Italian at Chaminade, so I ended up studying it at Chaminade to be like him. He was a straight A student, so I buckled down and studied hard and got accepted to Amherst. Matteo, however, responded differently. He resented Mom's pressure. He could have done a lot better in high school but didn't apply himself." Shaking his head, Val said, "And for him, college was even worse. He even says it was basically a waste of time *and* money." Gazing sadly at Milo, Val said, "So maybe you can understand how cut up my brother was when *your* brother got killed. It was like a car accident killing a family member all over again."

Milo nodded and momentarily was unable to respond.

The waiter arrived with dishes of antipasto: sliced prosciutto, provolone, and caponata. "I ordered for us," Val said when he noticed the look of confusion on Milo's face. "I know what's good here. Too bad your mom couldn't come."

Glad for a change in subject, Milo responded, "It's not that she couldn't come. She didn't want to come. She distrusts Italian restaurants in New York. She actually gets aggravated by most of them."

Val chuckled and shook his head. "Italian-American culture is really such a matriarchy, isn't it? At the end of the day, the mothers rule the roost. At least mine did. And yours probably still does."

"Does your mom live anywhere near here?"

Val shook his head. "Nope, she moved to Arizona. With this guy who's in the witness protection program. I'm pretty sure he was Mafia—cliché as that might sound. She and I aren't really in touch. We don't get along anymore."

"Sorry to hear that."

"I actually really like *him*, though. Sweetheart of a guy. You'd never know he was once a Mafia dude. Interesting thing about my mother. She's a wing nut, but her taste in men is fairly okay. My real father, unfortunately, is a bit of a drunk. Which is why *I* really don't like to drink. He's in Staten Island. I see him fairly regularly."

Remembering Val's admonition of the two girls he was with that night at Cooks, that partying in college was not all it was reported to be, Milo tasted the caponata. "This is excellent!"

"Did you doubt this was a good place?" Val asked him with frowning skepticism, just as the waiter passed by the table.

Turning to the man, Milo said in Italian, "Is this your own caponata?"

"Certainly," the man said. "We make it every day."

Feeling pretty certain he recognized the man's accent, Milo politely inquired if he was from Naples. The waiter nodded his head and said, "I am. Do you know it?"

"My aunt took me there once," he said and explained that they'd traveled from Tuscany—all because Aunt Lara had wanted him to see it: the street life, the art, the churches. "But I haven't been there since."

Val nodded. "I've also been. Definitely worth the trip. By the way, your Italian is pretty darn good."

"My Italian is supposed to be okay—good. I *am* getting my PhD in it, after all."

"You said you're working on your dissertation?"

"Supposedly."

"What's the subject matter?"

"A writer called Natalia Ginzburg. She's not that well known."

"I know who she is," Val said. "I think she wrote about World War II."

"Of course you know who she is," Milo said sarcastically.

"So how's it going? Are you still researching or are you now writing?"

Milo sighed and shook his head.

"Tough question?" Val persisted.

"I'm pretty much stuck."

"How so?" Val seemed authentically interested.

Milo explained that Ginzburg wrote mostly in the first person and he was scrutinizing what made her avoid writing in the third person and that his suspicion was that she felt incapable of using the third-person technique.

"Does it really make a difference what her narrative choices were?"

Milo explained that the critics thought so because writing in the first person could be limiting. "The thing is, I'm having trouble finding anything she might have written to anyone that discusses this idea in any great detail. So I think I might have made the wrong choice."

Val seemed to grow fidgety and for some reason looked impatient. "How'd you get the idea for that particular writer to begin with?"

Here was Milo's opening. "From my friend, Lenny D'Ambrosio, who died recently. It was his idea, he pressed it on me," Milo said, carefully watching for some sort of reaction on Val's face, some indication that the two men knew one another. But he detected no discernible flicker of recognition.

"There's something I need to ask you," he said to Val.

"About?"

"About your mail-order business."

Val's face flushed, and then he looked peeved.

"This guy I just mentioned, Lenny D'Ambrosio, does that name ring a bell?"

Val slowly shook his head. "I don't think so. Why?"

"Well, he owned a lot of hardcore and what seems to be illegally made pornography. Probably made with undocumented actors in Europe."

Val crossed his arms over his chest protectively and leaned back in his chair. "And?"

"I guess I was wondering if maybe he bought any of his videos from your company."

"Lots of people sell this stuff, you know. And lots of people buy from us. Where does this guy live?" Milo told him and explained that Lenny had taught Italian at Mercy College in White Plains.

"That I would remember, somebody I met who taught Italian. But you got to understand, our business is entirely mail order. Pure and simple. So if there were even a customer in my area . . . I wouldn't come into contact with them directly."

"I brought one of the videos with me," Milo said, patting the cassette, which managed to fit in the pocket of his coat that was now hanging from the back of his chair. "Would you mind having a look at it?"

Initially reluctant, Val at last relented. "Okay, sure."

Milo turned around, reached for his coat, dug out the video—still in its packaging—and placed it carefully on the table, like a domino.

Val frowned at the name written on the package. "Fabrizio del Dongo," he noted smirking, "well that guy has been dead for at least a hundred years." Val recognized the name of the protagonist in *The Charterhouse of Parma*. He pulled the black cassette out of the packaging. Blinking a few times, he turned it over and brought it closer to his eyes. Pointing to the small yellow holographic decal on the flip side of the cassette, he said, "Yup, it's one of ours. The image is of Ilaria del Carretto. By Jacopo della Quercia. She—"

"I know the sculpture," Milo interrupted, finding it difficult to conceal his indignation. He explained that Lucca was where he'd spent many of his summers. "I've been to see the sculpture in the cathedral at least a dozen times." Val looked chastened by this.

"I Films. Was that your idea?"

"It was, actually," Val said.

Feeling bolder now, Milo said, "I think it's kind of perverse to use this poor virginal woman, who died at the age of twenty-five or whatever as a logo for pornography."

"*Virginal?* What are you talking about?" Val shot back. "She was married!"

"Briefly. The relationship (probably) was never even consummated."

Val laughed at him. "You think people held back in those days? She lost her virginity on her wedding night, like everybody else. And don't get all wrapped up in an icon. Like I said, this is a business, pure and simple."

"A business that sells an illegally made product," Milo emphasized.

Val shook his head in exasperation. "The only thing that's illegally made is child porn. And obviously my brother and I wouldn't touch that with a ten foot pole."

"So you have some degree of porn morality."

Val held up both his hands. "Look, I don't need your judgment here."

"I've done my research on these films and most of them are made with actors that have entered Italy illegally."

"You can do all the research you want. But you have no proof of where these actors come from."

"Okay, well let me ask you this: Have you ever watched any of these films?"

"Not a single one, not a single frame," Val said.

"Why not?"

"Why not?" Val asked gruffly. "I have zero interest. What people want to get off on, that's their business.

"Lucrative," Milo remarked.

"It certainly pays the rent." A bit calmer now, Val tapped his fingers on the cassette on the table. "Did you watch this?"

Milo said that he'd watched several scenes.

"And?"

"I turned it off when it started to get rough."

"It *is* rough stuff. But *that*'s why people buy it. Now, can we move on?"

"Yes, but I'm just curious . . ."

Rolling his eyes and crossing his arms, Cipolla said, "You're *too* curious, that's the problem."

"Who's the customer for a video like this?"

"I'd have to ask my brother. He'd know more about who's buying." Cipolla started self-consciously toying with the strands of his shoulder-length hair.

"Look, Val, you've had a great education, you're clearly very smart, and you could probably do anything you wanted: be an economist or a civil servant or even a lawyer or a doctor. So, why this? Besides the fact that it's easy money."

Val sat there, smoldering and fidgeting. "I should have shut this conversation down ten minutes ago. But my brother was ecstatic that I ran into you, and then I told him we were having dinner together. The thought of that actually made him really happy. I'm supposed to call him tomorrow to tell him how it went." He paused. "I don't want to have to tell him that it went south."

This was a telling yet odd statement for Val to have made.

"But okay, smartass, I'll tell you exactly why I'm involved in this beyond the fact that it's extremely lucrative. It's for him, it's for my brother. I do my bit because he can't seem to do anything else for himself, for his own life. He has no ambition." Val hesitated. "Also, he loves Italy . . . just like I assume you do," he said to Milo. "Our business allows him to live there."

The main courses arrived. Milo's veal Milanese, a golden brown, was so flat and large that its continental mass extended well beyond the plate. "This is humongous!" he remarked.

"Whenever I order that, I always cut it in half. And take the rest of it home." Val grinned. "You'll be able to live on it for a few days. Get your mom to try it and see what she thinks."

"My mother told me she found one of your video cassettes among my brother's effects. I guess she and I were wondering how he might have gotten his hands on it?"

"How? I guess maybe Matteo gave him one to watch. And maybe that was the cause of the argument between them. What you don't seem to realize," Val barreled on, "is that anyone watching these videos is watching fiction, not reality. It's all staged; it's just really edgy. But so is some of the violence in mainstream films, much of it, by the way, just as graphic."

"But what I saw—the violence—it looked somehow more real," Milo said. "More real than actors in a mainstream movie."

"Like I said, I haven't watched the videos, but I know that the people who make these movies, their entire purpose is to have viewers believe they are seeing real-life domination, real-life rough sex. But does it actually happen out there when the cameras are rolling? Of course not! It's all staged. Rehearsed. Shot like any other flick. Nobody gets hurt. And let me tell you, the actors who make these films can't get any work elsewhere."

"Exactly. Which is why they're working illegally. And probably exploited."

"Exploited?" Val repeated. "That's a broad accusation. And hardly accurate. Certainly not in comparison . . . Do you have any idea of what the lives of these people are like in some of those repressive countries? How they live from hand to mouth? How close they come to starving?"

"Of course I understand. But the reading I've done suggests that people *do* get hurt and harmed when these films are being made."

Val threw up his hands. "*I* think we need to *end* this conversation and finish our dinner. End the evening on a positive note. So I can call my brother tomorrow and tell him that, all things considered, it went pretty well."

17.

Maria had gotten in touch with Milo to ask if he'd accompany her to Lenny's apartment. She needed to look for a few things—some correspondence, papers involving family genealogy—and didn't want to go on her own.

He was now sitting in her kitchen and drinking coffee, which she'd freshly made from a gold-rimmed cup. Upstairs a vacuum cleaner was roaring intermittently; Milo could hear its wheels scraping and bumping across the wooden floors. Aunt Fran was back from the Friuli.

"She's really going at it up there," he remarked.

Glancing up at the ceiling, Maria smirked and said, "I think she's taking out some frustration."

"Frustration?"

"It doesn't sound like she had a great time in Italy."

Now, taking a sip of his coffee, Milo asked, "So will she continue to stay with you?"

"She doesn't have anywhere else to stay at the moment. So I guess she'll stay for the foreseeable future. Why, is that a problem?" Maria asked, looking momentarily bemused.

"I just hope she can lighten up when I'm around."

"She's ornery, Milo. Not friendly to a lot of people. Don't take it so personally. She's been very helpful to me."

"I guess that's what matters."

Maria suddenly seemed nervous. She was staring at her slim, dainty hands, turning them over as if inspecting something. Then she looked up at Milo.

"So, I assume you watched that video."

Milo tried to sound measured when he replied, "Only part of it."

She looked skeptical. "Only part of it?"

He knew he had to at least make some attempt to explain precisely what the film was. And so, he told Maria that he was able to watch the film until it began to get violent, and that the grainy quality of the documentary only enhanced the effect of realism on the screen. What he'd found most disturbing was that there had been moments of tenderness between the actors that on a dime turned to sadism. "It was . . . unnerving."

Looking grim, Maria said, "Well, I've already given you my theory on why my brother would want to watch sadism. But then I've been asking myself: What's the point of theorizing? And the film, you said, was all in Italian?"

Yes, Milo told her. All in Italian.

After a few moments, she said with impatience, "So are you ready to go?"

Milo glanced at his watch. He'd planned on catching a train back to Manhattan and asked if Maria could drop him off at the Mamaroneck train station after they were through. "My brother used to drop you off, so why wouldn't I?" she said as she got up from the kitchen table.

Lenny's spacious one-bedroom apartment had always kept a distinct characteristic smell of garlic and dusty books;

now it reeked of lemony cleaning fluid. Despite the fact that the rooms looked pretty much the same, this marked difference in the smell of the place gave his death, which was still difficult to accept and process, a palpable resonance. Maria had unlocked the door and gone in first, and as soon as he crossed the threshold behind her, she seemed to falter, took a step back, and half leaned, half fell against him.

"You okay?" he asked, propping her up.

"No," she said, and tried to hold back a sob.

"Go ahead," Milo said to her. "Don't stand on ceremony for me."

This made her laugh, and she punched him lightly in the shoulder. "I'm okay now," she said, and walked deeper into the apartment.

It was three o'clock in the afternoon. Bars of winter sun were invading the silent, uninhabited apartment. The tarnished light made Lenny's collection of Murano glass vases glint soberly in their carefully chosen places. The low, cherrywood cabinet with sliding doors that housed his vast collection of opera recordings was open, as though he'd recently been browsing for something to listen to—perhaps an aria from Wagner that he'd wanted Milo or some of his other mentees to hear in what would end up being a doomed attempt at kindling an appreciation for the art form. And as Milo stood there, trying to gather his sad, rampant emotions, he kept asking himself, Why, even though everything looked the same, did the place feel so different? And finally realized: It was the silence. A complete and utter silence that he'd never before experienced—because Lenny was either chattering away about a book or a poet, or the apartment was swelling with some form of music: classical, operatic, even zydeco, as well as the celebratory soundtracks of Lenny's favorite movie, *Never on a Sunday*. As he walked deeper into the apartment, Milo passed a framed photograph propped upright of Lenny and himself, each holding a glass of wine at the Casa Italiana downtown on Twelfth Street.

And then in the midst of his reverie, he heard Maria say, "I just realized—I don't think you've been here since the night before . . ." She walked over to him and rested her arm on his shoulder. "How about you? Are you doing okay?"

He made a half-hearted attempt to describe his weird state of disbelief.

Nodding, Maria said that she, too, felt detached, as if she were sleepwalking through a familiar landscape.

Beyond the carefully chosen glass objects from the outer Venetian islands and the impressively equipped kitchen full of copper pans and utensils and food appliances, the apartment's obviously dominant theme was books: books everywhere, not only in the extensive network of shelves, but also left in neat stacks on the floor. On a mission-style desk that was pushed against the wall that led from the living room to the solitary bedroom was an untidy, haphazard collection of printed papers, a mix of syllabus leaves and scholarly articles. Lenny had independently told Milo and Maria that he'd been working on a critical study of Primo Levi's writings; he claimed he had an agreement with Yale University Press, something that both Maria and Milo doubted (and which neither could bear the idea of verifying), only because, for years, Lenny had been going about his research and writing with what seemed like uninspired motivation. He'd spoken to both of them about how daunting and vexing his "project" was.

Insecure about his own inability to progress on his study of Natalia Ginzburg's final novels, Milo could obviously relate to this. Glancing around the room, it occurred to him now more than ever that, despite all the time they'd spent together, despite their discussions of literature, their conversations about Milo's education and career path, he knew very little about the inner life of the pathologically private Lenny D'Ambrosio.

On an end table next to the bed, Milo noticed a book with a black sleeping mask placed on top of it. Something about that unforeseen detail jolted him: that Lenny needed an eyeshade to get proper sleep, and that the last time he probably used it was the night of his death—maybe right after reading the book on which it was perched: Bernanos's *Diary of a Country Priest.*

At that moment he felt Maria standing behind him and turned. "Have you ever read *Diary of a Country Priest*?"

"No," she said. "Should I?"

Milo explained that this was yet another book Lenny had insisted that he read in the original language—that and *Madame Bovary.* He told Maria this and said, "I liked *Diary of a Country Priest* a lot more than *Madame Bovary.* Or perhaps I should say that I somehow related more to the narrator."

Milo asked where the safe was, and she pointed to a medium-sized painting with bright, angular shapes that reminded him of a late Picasso. "It's in the wall behind that."

"What do you mean 'in the wall'?"

"You'll see."

He walked over to the painting that protruded out from the wall. He grabbed hold of it on either side of its frame and lifted it off its hook. The drywall behind it had been cut so a metal combination safe could be inserted. He leaned the painting against a nearby sofa. "Wow, that's a pretty substantial safe." He absently turned the number dial back and forth with two fingers. "Why didn't he just get a safety deposit box?"

"Lenny hated them. He said safety deposit boxes were for the bourgeois."

Milo could easily imagine Lenny's imperious tone as he uttered this.

Maria came and stood next to him, holding a small square of lined notebook paper. Squinting at it, and with a deft movement, she dutifully followed the combination and soon sprung open the safe. She grabbed a small flashlight out of the pocket of her cardigan sweater, switched it on, and shined the light inside.

And immediately began removing things. First, what she'd come to collect: a battered Manila folder, a collection of documents attesting to their family genealogy. She handed them to Milo who, with a glance, saw they were in formal-looking Italian. Then there was a heavy green rectangular box that, when she removed it, produced a clattering. "This is Mom's silver," she said, reminding him that the first time they'd met was when she had brought it to Lenny's apartment for safekeeping. There were two rolled up diplomas, one from Kenyon College, where Lenny had gone to undergrad, and the other Columbia, where he'd gotten his PhD with his much-lauded dissertation on Primo Levi, the subject that ended up bedeviling him for the rest of his short life. And indeed, in the safe, there was an original copy of this document, which Milo had already studiously read.

"By the way," he hazarded to say, "I wonder if there are any manuscript pages of the Primo Levi book he was working on."

Maria turned away from the safe and peered at him, her eyes blinking rapidly. "He wasn't writing a Primo Levi book, Milo." This was shocking to hear, but perhaps not surprising. She turned back to the safe and shined the flashlight in and continued. "Beyond his dissertation, there's certainly no manuscript in here." Milo was trying to digest this demoralizing fact when Maria said, "But wait a minute. There is something I've been wanting to ask you. This must be a first edition, right?" She turned around and handed him a book that Milo immediately recognized as a publication by Einaudi, the premier Italian publishing house. The book was Primo Levi's *Se Questo è Un Uomo* (*If This Is a Man*), the original Italian title of what in English became *Survival in Auschwitz.*

"I believe so," he replied.

The parchment-like pages were in excellent condition and their moldering scent reminded him of how Lenny's apartment used to smell. The cover had no illustration but rather simple black lettering against a white background. He gently flipped through to the opening passages, feeling sad because he'd first read the book at the age of sixteen in Lenny's Italian literature class, which he'd audited at NYU, and then again with Lenny just two years ago, in the summer.

They'd read aloud passages of the harrowing memoir to each other. Milo remembered one night in particular, a very warm night, when he was visiting Lenny, who hated air conditioning and had opened all the windows in the apartment to create a cross breeze. Facing Milo, he'd sat on the sofa right where the painting was now leaning, holding this first edition (that he must have paid a premium for) as though it were a precious artifact. They had been discussing Levi's famous observation of how one echelon of prisoner treated the one just below it with contempt and how this was powerfully illustrative of human nature, when Lenny said, "This, Milo, is the greatest work of twentieth-century Italian literature. Better than Moravia. Better than Morante. Better than Ginzburg. If you think about all the great classics of world literature, if you consider all the works that tower above the rest, you'll find that they are the books that were written in reaction to some kind of social calamity or conflict of war or political repression." Setting the book down for a moment, leaning back, and gazing at Milo with an unfathomable look of melancholy, Lenny said, "It makes me sad to think that nobody who reads this book in another language, rendered by even the most gifted translator, will really be able to calibrate its greatness . . . which is known only in Italian."

And Milo had said, "But the reader can get a strong enough flavor, if not perhaps the complete texture of it?"

Lenny had shaken his head. "But there is such a sweetness to Levi's tone, such a ring of poetry in his deceptively simple sentences. It's impossible to re-capture." He flipped over the book and gazed at the picture of the meticulously bearded Primo Levi on the back.

"Have you ever thought of giving a translation of this a go yourself?" Milo had asked him.

Lenny had smiled bleakly. "I've *tried.* Believe me I've tried and with no great success. My English words felt stilted and flat."

"Would you like me to have a look at it, your translation?" After all, Milo *had* read *Survival in Auschwitz* in its original as well as in translation; perhaps he'd be a good judge of any English-language version?

Lenny shook his head. "I'd be too mortified for you to see it."

"*Mortified*?" Milo was incredulous.

Lenny had nervously run his hand across the top of his head, gathering the long strands of his mane of hair and nervously pushing them back. "Trust me, you'd be disappointed in my lamentable effort."

"I doubt it. I doubt it precisely because I know you're always so hard on yourself."

Smiling, Lenny had said, "If you are going to be a serious thinker, if you are going to be writing critically about literature, you have to be hard on your own ideas, especially your own writing attempts. You have to question your own methods. Otherwise, you run the risk of being intellectually self-indulgent. And *then* you've really lost the battle."

Standing there now, flipping through the precious pages of the book and remembering Lenny's passionate exclamations, it occurred to Milo that Lenny's rigorous standards were left at the door of his personal and private life, in which he was anything but hard on himself and arguably was what he always railed against: self-indulgent. Recognizing this painful paradox, Milo got choked up, but then managed to grab hold of himself and tell Maria, "Lenny never said anything, but I think this *must* be a first edition. Otherwise, why would it be kept in a safe?"

Milo held the finely hewn volume out to her. "You can take it to a rare book dealer and have it evaluated. It's probably worth a lot."

She made a motion to indicate that she didn't want him to pass the book back to her and said, "Well, it won't be sold, so market value doesn't matter. However, I suggest you deal with your fears. As it's now going to belong to you."

Incredulous, Milo looked at her fixedly. "To *me*?" he managed to ask in a hoarse voice. "What are you talking about?"

She took a deep breath. "What I've been meaning to tell you and haven't told you is that the estate lawyer and I finally went through my brother's will. And he left you his entire Italian-language library."

Milo was stunned into silence. Why would a forty-year-old man be thinking so specifically about the disposition of his valued library? Maybe he would?

At last Milo said, "That was very thoughtful and generous of him. I'm honored. However—" He held up the book. "This is valuable; if this is a rare first edition. It could probably be sold for a nice price and really supplement—"

"Supplement my inheritance?" Maria interrupted to ask.

"Well, yes."

"I told you he left me enough money."

"But what if it's . . ." Milo hesitated, "ill-gotten money?"

She smiled with irony. "What if it is? What am I supposed to do, give it all away?"

"I don't know. Maybe? Some of it, at least?"

"I've actually been considering that," Maria said, then raised an index finger, conveniently reverting back to the original subject. "However, I still don't want to sell or give away his books because . . ." She paused. "Because I know he felt that if anything should happen to him, that the books go nowhere but to your library. However, if you can't or won't take all of them, I guess I could try find a good home for them at a university," she said sadly. "Maybe some school with a strong Romance language department? But not Mercy College." She couldn't help taking a dig at Lenny's final teaching gig.

Milo told her, "Don't get me wrong. I'd *love* to have his books. Not sure if I can fit all of them in my apartment. Although I do have some wonderful, handmade bookshelves, which they'd look great on."

"Okay, so then when I give up this apartment in a month or two, I'll keep whatever books you can't take to your place. And then when you have more room, you'll come and collect the rest of them."

"But where will *you* keep the books? Your walls have no space for bookshelves. They are almost completely taken up with religious paintings," Milo said, forthright and yet careful to use a measured tone. "And I don't think a rare collection of books should be stored in a basement."

"I know you think those religious paintings are hideous," she said, smiling, and they both laughed. She held up her finger again. "But they belonged to my parents. One day you'll see what I mean. You'll see how hard it is to get rid of your parents' valued possessions even when they're truly horrible."

Placing *Survival at Auschwitz* gingerly on the nearby mahogany dining table, Milo remembered one more thing Lenny had said to him about the book: that the English-language title was awful and why did the publishers have to use the name of the concentration camp? Why couldn't they have used the literal translation, *If This Is a Man*?

"I think the word *Auschwitz* is probably an attention-grabber," Milo had replied.

"A ring of hell," Lenny had muttered, and then had said something incomprehensible in Italian under his breath. "To be honest, I've never been able to convince anyone—none of my colleagues anywhere, at NYU or at Columbia—that the title is wrong and should be changed."

Maria took her small flashlight and continued to search the safe. She extracted some expired passports, a worn-looking leather wallet and two Manila folders. She began perusing one folder, which appeared to contain letters. She looked up and explained that it was a folder of correspondence, handwritten letters from a few women, including the Columbia graduate student who'd accused Lenny of inappropriate behavior.

Milo was taken aback to hear this. "Really? How extensive *was* his correspondence with her?"

Maria peered at him. "Well, they had a friendship, a dear friendship."

"*I* didn't know that."

"I thought you *did* know," she said distractedly.

"Like I told you before," Milo said, "I knew almost nothing about this woman. Did he ever discuss her with you?"

Lenny had discussed the woman only when he learned that Maria had found out about the accusation and that he was about to lose his teaching job at Columbia. At the time, Lenny had acknowledged the accusation but then denied it and said it wasn't true, and offered no more about it. "He basically shut down the conversation after that. You know how he was."

Milo was bewildered: He wished he'd had some kind of inkling that Lenny had once had a close friendship with this graduate student. If anything, that would shed some light on the dark truth that he'd forgotten himself and crossed a line.

Maria went back to perusing the letters in the first folder. "There are a bunch in Italian, which I haven't read because I really can't read them. But they seem to be from the same woman. Same handwriting." She handed Milo around ten letters housed in mailing envelopes that were designed to look like billowy cloud formations, as though perhaps to suggest air mail travel. The correspondence had a distinct patchouli-like scent. "Maybe you should read them and tell me what's in them," Maria said.

Milo felt curious enough to take one letter out of its envelope when he heard Maria gasp. He looked up to see that, in the midst of examining the contents of the second folder, she'd gone completely still, continuing to read something and then in a hoarse voice said, "I honestly haven't noticed these before. These letters. I have no idea when he could have put them in the safe. Could they have been here the last time I looked and I just didn't notice? " She glanced at Milo in bewilderment.

"What?" he said. "What are they?"

Holding up a bunch of letters that were not housed in envelopes, she said, "They're letters to Lenny . . . from your brother."

"From Carlo?" Milo yelped.

She nodded slowly and confusedly.

"Can I see them?"

She held up her hand in an almost savage gesture. "Hold on," and read further and finally gazing at him with tear-glossed eyes, said, "They're confessions!"

"What do you mean, confessions?"

"Who's Matteo Cipolla? Why is that name is familiar?"

He reminded her he was Carlo's best friend from college, the guy coincidentally whose company had supplied Lenny with his porn videos. "What about him?"

"Carlo's best friend?" she repeated.

"Are you listening to me?" Milo asked her with annoyance.

She shook her head and said, "Well . . . actually more than best friend."

18.

Back home, Milo and Rose Marie read Carlo's four letters to Lenny several times, discussing the confessional contents at great length, mystified that they knew nothing about what was described in them and that Carlo had literally in these writings become a stranger to them. Rose Marie felt certain that Val must know more about the situation between the two men and implored Milo to make an introduction. When Milo tried to remind her that the dinner he'd had with Val didn't go all that well, she said to him, "Call him and tell him I can make better food than that place."

"How do you know, Mom? You haven't even been there."

"Please ask him to come. Tell him it's for me."

"But under what pretext?"

"Just say that I've been bugging you to invite him and that I want to ask him some more questions about Carlo."

"Okay, I'll see what he says."

And so Milo called Val, who after some hesitation, agreed to come for Sunday lunch.

Val was a half-hour late. He launched into a litany of profuse apologies as he shook Milo's hand and then hugged Rose Marie, who was hardly expecting such an outpouring of affection. "Don't break her," Milo said, and Val laughed as he released Rose Marie and took a step back and sheepishly stuck his hands in his pockets.

Almost immediately, Rose Marie brought out her own homemade caponata. They sat down in the living room, Val in an armchair facing Milo and Rose Marie, who sat on the sofa.

"Go ahead, try it," Rose Marie said, and Val dutifully obeyed. His eyes sparkled. "Wow, this is amazing. I think it's even better than Caviglia's caponata."

"What a weird name for a restaurant," Rose Marie couldn't help but comment. "Italians don't eat ankles."

"It's Neapolitan," Val said. "Could they possibly eat cow or pig ankles in Southern Italy?"

Milo said to Val, "You once asked me if I was a *Nordista*. Maybe you're one, yourself."

Val grinned. "I'd like to think so," he said.

"It's not something to aspire to. It's like a Southerner calling somebody from the north an uptight, elitist Yankee."

Val held up his hand in a surrendering gesture. "I guess I wasn't aware of that. Where in Italy is your family from?" he asked them.

"Roman on my father's side," Rose Marie said. "Siena on my mother's. My parents were first generation," she added. "How about you?"

"Genoa on my father's side," he said. "My father came here as a child. His family were in shipbuilding. Milo may have mentioned that I'm Polish on my mom's side."

Milo concluded that Val, who'd been sent to a fancy private Catholic high school and a top-tier college, probably came from some means. It would occur to him much later that what his mother said next must've been propelled by her feeling nervous about Val's visit.

"I'm curious to know about your mother," Rose Marie said.

Val leaned forward in his chair, took another cracker, slathered it with caponata, and then explained about his mother living in Arizona and her boyfriend being in the witness protection program.

"She and I don't see eye to eye on most things. Every time we get together it— Well, let's say it gets ornery. So we rarely see each other anymore."

Rose Marie was horrified. "What? Oh no, that's no good. No matter what, she's your mother. No matter what she says, you can't turn your back on her. Especially because your mother and I, what do we have? We have *malafortuna*." She used the Italian word and wagged her finger. "And we had no choice in the matter. It fell on us like a brick from heaven. We'll never get to see our sons again. No one except your mother realizes how hard that is."

This brought a momentary pall down on the conversation.

Val turned to Milo. "So I guess you told her about my older brother."

"I wanted to share that with her."

Nodding, Val said, "Unfortunately, I've been living under *my* mother's *malafortuna* my whole life."

"How about we eat?" Milo suggested as a way of diverting from the turn the conversation had taken. As though released from a spring, Rose Marie jumped up and darted into the kitchen. While she was there, Milo turned to Val. "I'm sorry. I had no idea she'd launch into this."

"It's okay." Val seemed oddly composed. "Believe me, I know where it's coming from."

Milo invited Val to follow him into the dining room just as Rose Marie brought out steaming platters of food. She'd decided to make stuffed pork, Brussels sprouts, and roasted new potatoes. "I guess we should have asked if you eat meat," she said, standing behind her chair with a devilish look on her face. "But by the look of you I would assume you do."

"Don't you see 'carnivore' written all over me?" Val said. "This looks incredible," he said as he sat down and the food was passed to him.

"I could've made the typical Italian, but at the last minute I decided on the typical American." Rose Marie sat, Val on her left, Milo on her right. "After all, we're Americans, much as we all love Italy." Passing Val the roasted potatoes, she said, "Milo said your brother lives in— Where is it, Pistoia?"

"That's right."

And once again, Rose Marie began to zero in. "Milo told me about your mother naming you after this older brother. That must've been hard for you."

"*Mom!*" Milo protested.

"It's okay, it's okay," Val said with a dismissive flick of a hand and a surprising smile. "But yes, it was."

"And your father never tried to stop her from naming you after him?"

"Oh, sure he did. But like I was saying, she is stubborn to the hilt. She dug her heels in, even after relatives on both sides of the family begged her not to do it. However, as much as it was a difficult thing for me (and by extension, my brother), I now understand why she did it." He hesitated a moment, looking up at the ceiling, as though trying to find the right word. "She was desperate in her grief." This produced a sigh from Rose Marie. "And it eased her pain . . . to have another son she could call Valentino, a son who had the same name as the son she lost."

"So being able to say his name, to call his name, could somehow, in some strange way, bring him back?" Milo asked, and Val nodded.

"Of course I can understand *that*," Rose Marie said. "But I guess I'm just different: I can't imagine having another child and naming him Carlo."

"Well, but you *had* another child. You already had this one." Val leaned across the table and flicked Milo playfully on the shoulder. "For four years until I was born, my mother had nothing—no child at all."

"Ah, yes, that *is* true," Rose Marie said.

Wanting to move the conversation along, Milo said, "Speaking of children, have you been in touch with Matteo lately?"

"We spoke yesterday, as a matter of fact. I told him I was coming over today. He really wished he could be here." Pointing to the food, Val said, "In Italy, he misses this kind of home-cooked American meal."

Milo asked, "Are you in touch with him often?"

A look of suspicion flitted across Val's face, and then he fixed Milo with a probing stare. "Maybe every five days or so. Why do you ask?"

"I guess you must run up quite a phone bill."

"We don't speak for very long," Val said slowly and with a hint of sarcasm.

Rose Marie picked up the thread of conversation. "I actually found a picture of your brother among Carlo's things. I had never seen *him* before." She hadn't told Milo about finding the picture, and he was taken aback. Then she said to Val, "I've never seen you before, either. If I'd ever seen you, I would remember you. You're a good-looking man," she said with forceful candor.

"You did see my brother," Val insisted with restraint. "You probably just don't remember seeing him. It was after the funeral Mass. There were a lot of people around. He was only able to get a few moments with you."

"Mom," Milo said, "like I've told you before, a lot of that day is a blur. To both of us."

Rose Marie had eaten almost nothing. Her fork was poised in her hand as though she might use it as a weapon. Then she laid it down carefully next to her. "Okay, *that* was the funeral," she said. "But if they were such good friends, how come your brother didn't come to the wake?"

Val, who'd been eating avidly, paused to meet Rose Marie's gaze. He finished chewing and swallowing the food in his mouth and said, "Matteo and I, both of us, wanted very much to come to the wake, but we decided not to."

"And why was that?" Rose Marie probed.

And then Milo was shocked to see tears glossing Val's eyes. "For the same reason you never met Matteo while Carlo was alive." He hesitated. "Because Carlo didn't want you to meet him."

The conversation had finally arrived to where Milo and Rose Marie had steered it, and in anticipation of it, Milo actually grew breathless.

"Didn't want me to meet him?" Rose Marie repeated.

"I'll tell you why in a moment. But I need to explain something first."

Turning his attention on Milo, Val said, "I told you that they were up the night before Carlo was—" He faltered, and then said, "Carlo died."

"Yeah, and you told him Carlo was drinking and *I* know that's not true!" Rose Marie interjected.

Val turned back to her with a dismal expression. "I know you don't believe it. And I know *why* you don't believe it. Because it was uncharacteristic of Carlo to even have a drink." Glancing at Milo, he said, "I know this because when he came to my mom's house with Matteo several times, he was offered wine and beer and never took anything. And Matteo also told me that Carlo hardly ever drank."

"He went to your mother's house, but your brother never came to my house," Rose Marie pointed out.

"So I assume Milo told you they were arguing about our business in Europe?"

"Yes, he did."

"Well, in all honesty, arguing about our business was really the least of it. They were arguing about something else."

"We know what they were arguing about," Rose Marie now informed him.

Taking a deep breath and exhaling, Val turned to her and with gravity, said, "How did you find out?"

Milo now explained about letters that Carlo had written to a friend. Both he and Rose Marie had decided at least initially, not to bring up Lenny D'Ambrosio.

"Well, then I can assume you know that my brother was very much in love with your son?" Val told Rose Marie who nodded. "So the altercation they had the night before Carlo died was really more about what their relationship was or wasn't. And Matteo didn't go to the wake *only* because he knew Carlo would not have wanted him to."

There was utter silence; nobody was eating now. Several blocks away at the station, a commuter train from New Haven to Grand Central Station rambled by with a distant clatter of its wheels and a mournful gale of its horn.

"Why didn't you say something when we were at dinner in Whitestone?" Milo asked him.

"I was planning to say something. In fact, that was the real reason why I agreed to meet you. But then we got into the argument about the videos and—" Val shrugged. "I just wasn't up to it. I guess I thought you might not be sympathetic to the story."

"What?" Milo cried. "Why wouldn't I be sympathetic to something like this?"

Ignoring the question, Val asked, "So what was in the letters?"

Milo explained that the letters were confessional, Carlo expressing the fact that he couldn't handle the powerful emotions that had grown between himself and Matteo and asking their friend for guidance on what to do. "He was really struggling," he now told Val. "He just couldn't deal with it."

"Whom did he confess all this to?" Val asked.

"A family friend," Rose Marie said.

His eyes focused on her, Val said, "Well, I don't know what Carlo wrote in the letters, but I can tell you on that last night, Carlo told my brother he didn't feel the same way."

Rose Marie interjected, "He was too afraid to tell him. He was a very fearful young man. But surely Carlo would have been kind to anybody who confessed they had feelings for him. *Surely,*" she repeated, resolute.

Val shook his head. "But that's not how it was, Mrs. Rossi. And that last night, they were arguing *because* Matteo was asking to meet you, *wanting* to meet you. He knew Carlo was coming home the next day and wanted to accompany him. But Carlo kept refusing him."

"Well then I'm very sorry to learn this," Rose Marie said.

"There were plenty of times, in fact, when my brother drove Carlo home and Carlo insisted on getting dropped off a block away from . . ." with a sweep of his large hands, Val said, ". . . this house. Your house. Because he didn't want them to be seen together."

"Because then it would require some explanation?" Milo filled in. "Of who Matteo was?"

"So it seemed," Val said. "And now I need to add that until that night, the night before the accident, Matteo never asked—he was afraid to ask—Carlo what his feelings were . . ." And then Val's voice grew shaky. "But he did that last night, because I urged him to do it, because I knew how much Matteo was suffering." His shoulders slumped. "Unfortunately, Carlo told my brother, he made it clear that under no circumstances would he have wanted Matteo to meet either of you."

19.

After Val had gone home, Milo and Rose Marie sat together in the kitchen. Milo had made her a cup of tea that sat steaming on the table. Pots and pans from the meal were stacked in the sink and three dirty plates lay on the counter, crisscrossed with used silverware. It was understood that Milo would be doing the dishes, but he put that task off for the moment. Because the kitchen was redolent of cooking and garlic, Rose Marie had decided to light a scented candle to help neutralize the odors.

The last thing either of them expected was that after several years, Carlo's death would become even more enigmatic, and therefore, in its own way, more aching. Why, for example, if Carlo wasn't exactly a friend of Lenny D'Ambrosio, did he confide in him so profoundly? Had Carlo turned to Lenny because he was in some ways like an honorary member of the family, close to Milo but distant enough so that his opinion or reaction perhaps wouldn't be so threatening?

Rose Marie said, "So I guess he was hiding it all along, the fact that he was struggling with . . . his sexuality?"

"Struggling I guess in his case means hiding," Milo pointed out, reminding her that Carlo had only been twenty and that lots of twenty-year-old men were still coming to terms with their sexuality, particularly if they were attracted to members of the same sex. "And by the way, why would introducing Matteo to us be such a big deal if Carlo felt nothing but friendship for him?"

Clearly agitated, Rose Marie was gripping the sides of the kitchen table. Looking squarely at his mother, Milo could tell that it had been a while since she'd gone to the hairdresser. Her highlights had grown out and looked brassy. "So you're saying you had your suspicions about Carlo all along?"

And Milo reminded her that during his very brief life, Carlo had, as far as either of them knew, never dated anyone. "Maybe that was the telltale sign."

Rose Marie nodded as she stared down at her cup of tea.

He waited until her eyes raised to meet his. "How come you didn't tell me about the photograph you found? Of the two of them together?"

"I did tell you," she said, "eventually."

"Don't be coy, Mom. Explain to me why."

She smirked. "It was my own little tactic. I kept it to myself thinking it might provoke something."

Milo was frustrated. "I thought I was doing the talking."

Rose Marie dragged her fingertips from her throat to her chin as though to make a dismissive gesture.

Momentarily exasperated and deciding not to press her farther on this, Milo continued, "One way of looking at this: If Carlo did have romantic feelings for Matteo, isn't that on some level a relief? Because at least he went out of this world caring for somebody. I'll be honest, I used to worry that he never had any romantic interest in anyone."

And then Milo remembered when he'd been a junior in high school, the parents of the girl he'd been dating had gone had out of town unexpectedly. She was an only child and had the house to herself on a Saturday night. In his second year at Iona, Carlo had happened to be home the night Milo was planning to spend out. He'd made Carlo promise to back up his assertion that he was spending the night at a friend's house. When he returned home the following morning, not only did he refrain from asking how Milo's night was, but Carlo also seemed agitated.

"Did Mom ask you anything?" Milo had inquired after he arrived upstairs.

Studying at his desk, Carlo glanced up at him. "Why would she have asked anything? You lied precisely so she wouldn't ask," he'd said as he cracked open a thick organic chemistry textbook.

"Can you talk to me just for one second?" Milo had pleaded, feeling deflated by his brother's dismissive attitude toward him.

"Sure," Carlo said, marking his page with a finger and closing the book on it. "But be brief. I have a lot of orgo to get through before Monday. I really need to study."

"That's what you always say whenever you don't want to talk to me about something . . . personal," Milo pointed out.

Carlo needed reading glasses, and when he glanced up from his textbook, his eyes, a lighter brown than Milo's, were magnified by the lenses, his glance as penetrating as an owl's. "Okay, so talk to me," he said somewhat stiffly. "Here I am. What do you want to tell me? You spent the night with your girlfriend when her parents were out of town. I assume you took advantage of the opportunity."

"Of course I did," Milo said.

"Well, then lucky you," Carlo said with no inflection at all.

It sounds like it bothers you, Milo almost said—one of many things he almost but never said. "I don't know if I'd call it lucky as much as what happens when you're sixteen and have a girlfriend whose parents go out of town." The moment the words "when you're sixteen" left his mouth, he realized it had been the wrong thing to say. That it made it seem like he was patronizing his older brother who, in retrospect, must have felt diminished.

"Speak for yourself," Carlo said dismissively, now glaring at him. With that, he got up out of his desk chair, walked quickly across the room, and grabbed the golfing putter that his father had given him shortly before he died. Turning to Milo, he said, "I don't really want this. I never wanted it. I actually hate golf. I hate everything golf stands for. So I'm giving this to you," he'd said, handing the club to Milo. "It should be yours anyway, since *you're* the real man of the family."

Totally bewildered and speechless, Milo stood there holding the club.

Carlo went and sat down again at his desk, riveting his eyes to his organic chemistry book. "Now I *really* have to get this done."

His mother interrupted his reverie. "I think I need to speak to this Matteo."

"For what purpose?"

"I want to ask him myself about his last night with Carlo."

"But what more do you think you can learn other than what Val has already told us?"

"Val told you part of the story about them when you were at the restaurant and *then* more of the story today. How do we know he told us everything? He could be holding something back."

"Actually, Mom, that's an excellent point."

"I want to see this Matteo with my own two eyes. To remind myself." She pointed to them with her index and middle finger. "I want to see him, and I want to ask him my own questions and see what he says in reply."

"Well, that's not going to happen unless you go to Italy."

Rose Marie shrugged and said unconvincingly, "Well, then maybe *we* could go."

"Mom, come on, when was the last time you went to visit Aunt Lara?" Milo said. "It's got to be more than ten years. You're afraid of flying." He referred to a specific incident when Rose Marie was coming back from Italy. Crossing the Atlantic, her airplane had developed engine trouble, with black smoke and orange flames visible from the passenger windows. The plane was forced to make an emergency landing in Newfoundland. She'd told Milo that for a nearly unendurable half hour, before the plane descended onto a runway in barren, forbidding-looking Saint John's, she felt certain she was going to die. She'd never boarded a plane since.

Rose Marie said, "Maybe Matteo might come back here to visit?"

"He hasn't been back in years. He's also involved in a questionable business. So I don't think he's coming home any time soon."

She nodded grimly. "I suppose not."

"How about this," Milo said. "I have spring break coming up in two weeks. I could probably get a last-minute flight, go and visit Aunt Lara and then Pistoia to see Matteo. Then I can ask him whatever you want me to ask him."

"That might be good," Rose Marie said, sounding a bit brighter. Then she looked at Milo hopefully. "But would you really do that? Go to Italy just for me?"

"I'm due for my yearly visit anyway."

"My sister will certainly be pleased." Rose Marie finally took a sip of her tea. "I will say, it makes me very sad to think that Carlo never felt he could bring Matteo home to meet me. But I guess you're right: We should be glad that he cared for somebody and that person cared for him at the end of his life."

20.

Milo picked up the grainy photograph of a woman taken from behind as she was striding away from Lenny's apartment building. She was wearing a royal blue woolen hat pulled down over her ears and a dark coat that fell to her ankles. Despite the dim glow, he could tell it was Lenny's street because he recognized his white Honda Civic. He was startled to see that the woman's long, wavy hair suggested she might be Maria. But it was hard to tell definitively.

Milo looked up at Delzio. "Where did this come from?"

The detective grunted. "The downstairs neighbor, Mrs. Colicchio, took it."

"And you're finding out about this *now*?"

Delzio explained that Mrs. Colicchio had only just mentioned to her daughter that she'd taken it.

Milo scrutinized the photo. "There's no time stamp."

"Correct," Delzio said. "But we got our hands on the original roll of film from the place where it was developed—her daughter took it in for her—and one of my guys was able to tell it was taken fairly recently."

"Fairly recently isn't necessarily the day of," Milo pointed out.

"True enough," Delzio said with a grimace. "Now you're sounding like someone else we know."

"Who's that?"

"Rodriguez, who doesn't think this is enough to reopen an investigation. *However,* look at this." Delzio pointed to the space above head of the woman in the photograph, the glass pane of the door's transom. "See the color of the sky?"

"Okay, early morning, I got that," Milo said, noticing that Delzio's stray golf clubs were no longer perched in the corner of the room; in their place was a pair of thirty-five-pound dumbbells, which were positioned upright and had made twin dents in the flimsy sheet-rocked wall. It was February, so Milo was doubtful Delzio was still going out to play; maybe he was doing seated arm curls in his spare time.

"Just hear me out," Delzio continued. "When I went to speak to Mrs. Colicchio, I asked how she could've heard commotion so early in the morning and have the time to grab a camera and take a picture of somebody leaving the building. She told me she never sleeps past four a.m., so she was wide awake and up at five. She says she heard commotion upstairs, people arguing, something scraping against the floor—like a chair—and cracked her door to listen. Apparently, she'd heard this sort of commotion and arguing before from up there, but this time she armed her camera. Waited until she heard someone pass her door and the door leading to the outside. Then came out and nabbed the photograph. Maybe an hour later, she thought to herself maybe go upstairs. And found his door ajar. And the rest you already know."

Intrigued by these new details, Milo nevertheless said, "But this doesn't really track. She positions herself and then waits for just the right moment to take the photograph?

That's very precise reasoning *and* timing for somebody who is supposed to be dotty. To me the story sounds fabricated."

Delzio shrugged his massive shoulders. "Exactly what Rodriguez said." He raised a thick finger. "However, if she was able to explain all of this to me, every single step, how dotty could she really be?"

"But who's to say that Mrs. Colicchio even took that photograph? Couldn't it have been somebody else?"

"With her camera? Like who?"

"Like her *daughter*?"

Delzio made a screwed-up face. "Her daughter doesn't live there. And as soon as the daughter found out about it, she came to me."

Milo pivoted to face him squarely. "What would motivate Mrs. Colicchio to lie in wait and take a photograph of somebody leaving an apartment?"

"Come on, Milo," Delzio said. "We both know the type. Italian-American mother lives alone, lives down the street from her kids with *a lot* of time on her hands. The kind of neighbor constantly eavesdropping on other peoples' lives—obviously her favorite pastime was eavesdropping and snooping on Lenny D'Ambrosio."

Milo went quiet. "So what are you trying to tell me—that *she*, that *Maria*, might have had something to do with her brother's death?"

Delzio tapped his broad fingers rhythmically on the photograph. "Well that's the thing. Not necessarily . . . probably unlikely. What reason would she have to do in her brother? They had a close relationship. But that still doesn't explain why there's a photograph of somebody exiting

Lenny's apartment building in the early morning who, at least from behind, looks a lot like her."

21.

Maria was in the act of writing a bunch of notecards that were carefully arranged fanlike on the kitchen table that Aunt Francesca had refitted with yet another garish, oily tablecloth. Milo couldn't help wondering why Maria, opinionated and willful, would allow her aunt total dominion over the look of the household.

When she saw Milo glancing at the table, she assumed he was taking notice of what she was endeavoring to write. "Easter cards," she told him.

"I can't believe it's nearly that time of year," he replied.

She nodded and seemed to be gathering her thoughts before saying, "So, were you planning on telling me that you met with Delzio?"

"In fact, that's the main reason I stopped by to see you." Which of course was not quite the truth.

Maria began intertwining her hands, the gold bangles on her right wrist making a gentle clatter as she flicked her pen aside. "So this Mrs. Colicchio swears up and down that the person in the photograph (who at least from behind appears to look like me) ran down my brother's stairs at five o'clock in the morning on the day he died."

"Her story hasn't changed. She just presented a bit of evidence to that effect," Milo replied. "Anyway, it's a bit blurry, the photograph," he pointed out.

Maria went on to say that she'd gone down to the police station to have a look at the photograph. She now leaned forward in her chair and placed her elbows on the kitchen table. "So, for the record . . . I wasn't anywhere near my brother's apartment the night or the morning he died. I was here, asleep. I told Delzio that.

"And anyway, what purpose would bring me to my brother's apartment at five in the morning? The only motivation would be that I was after something of value." She went on to say since she'd already had access to the safe, she could've taken anything at any time without Lenny's permission when he wasn't at home, when she knew, for example, he was teaching his class at Mercy. "And let's not forget he transferred all that money into our joint bank account before he died . . . He was always generous with me," she added. "So why would I lie about being at his apartment?"

"Well, that's what I was going to ask you."

Incredulous, she cried out, "So you really think I did harm to my brother?"

"No, of course I don't!" And he really didn't. "But I just wish you had some kind of back-up."

"Oh, please, Milo! Don't insult me."

"Was Aunt Francesca here the night he died?" he asked, thinking that, if necessary, she could corroborate Maria's assertion.

"No, she wasn't here! She came in from Long Island the next day, *after* I called and told her what had happened.

"So I guess the question is: *Was* there a woman with him overnight?"

"Until I saw that photograph I would have said no."

"But what do you say to the fact that the photograph looks like you from behind?"

Maria smiled grimly and Milo could tell that she had anticipated this question from him. And so, she began, "I really don't like saying this because it actually sounds kind of unhealthy. But some of the women Lenny got involved with . . ." She hesitated. "Well, they looked somewhat like me to be honest, especially the hair. The graduate student, Emma Stein, for example. I've seen pictures of her. We have the same color and type of wavy hair and we have the same sort of figure, and maybe we're the same height, but that's where it ends. She has a broader face . . . She is Jewish of Eastern European background whereas I, as you can see, have a narrower Italian, I suppose it is, face. Because the photograph shows a woman from behind, I'm sure you agree that it's hard to pin an identity on anybody."

"So maybe it *was* her. The graduate student. Maybe she *did* come to the apartment. Maybe before it all went sideways, he gave her a key that she kept."

With resignation, Maria said, "Trust me, Milo, she was not in his apartment the night he died. She'd absolutely have no interest in going anywhere near where Lenny lived."

"How can you be so sure of this?"

Maria hesitated and said, "How? She called him once while I was there, and even though he went into the bedroom to speak to her, I could tell that he was pleading with her about something. Of course, he never told me he was pleading with her or what he was pleading with her about, he *never* would have admitted anything like that, but I know that Lenny was madly in love with this woman, and I could hear it in that phone call that his feelings were not returned.

"But here's what I want to tell you," Maria continued. "Remember the other letters I took from his safe?" Milo nodded. "Well, there are five of them and you need to read them because they were written by a woman who got progressively angrier and angrier with him, and therefore might have had some motivation to do him harm. It's an Albanian woman called Vesuvia." The letters suggested that Lenny had met Vesuvia in Italy. And it appeared that she came to New York at least once to visit him. Maria went on to say that the letters repeatedly implored Lenny to wire money. "Apparently, he'd even promised to marry her."

"Really?" Milo was gobsmacked.

"So she could have citizenship. But at some point he broke his promise to her."

Maria said that there was no surname written anywhere in the letters or on the envelopes. "Which, by the way, have no return address. But the letters are all postmarked from Italy—Prato, to be more precise."

Near Florence. "And they were *in* Italian?" Milo emphasized.

"I have a feeling it was not grammatical Italian. I tried to find her in his address book. I found the name Vesuvia. But again, no surname. There was a telephone number but when I tried it was disconnected."

"So maybe *this* woman might have been in the apartment with him the night he died?"

Maria shrugged. "If the photograph was taken when Mrs. Colicchio said it was."

"And I don't suppose we know what this Albanian woman looks like?"

Maria shook her head and said all she had to go on was the raft of letters housed in the cloudy envelopes. "But let me ask you: does the name Vesuvia sound like a made-up name to you?"

"I think it's an Italian name, actually."

"Oh, okay. Because I looked up common names for Albanian women and I didn't find a Vesuvia among them. Then again, who knows what her name really is or was?" This elicited a laugh from both of them, and the strain of the moment eased a bit.

"My Italian isn't great," Maria went on, "but some of the letters are threatening. I mean, she told him he'd know better than to come back to Italy."

Sitting there opposite her, breathless now, Milo said, "I *need* to see these letters. If they have grammar mistakes, I *need* to see them, too. I need to see the way the words are written. That might help us identify who she is and where she's originally from."

"Okay. The letters are upstairs. Hang on. I'll get them."

Maria rose quickly from the table and left the kitchen. While he waited for her, Aunt Francesca poked her head into the room and threw him a glance of disgust. "Where's Maria?" she demanded.

"Nice to see you, too." Milo was careful not to sound snarky or sarcastic. "She went upstairs to get something."

Aunt Francesca returned his greeting with a bitter smile and a slight nod of the head. "Well I have to go to Queens," she said. "Tell her I'll be back around five. My taxi is waiting outside."

"Okay, I'll tell her."

Milo vaguely wished he could figure out why his presence irked Aunt Francesca so much, but then realized that was one mystery he didn't need to solve.

Maria ended up being gone awhile and the longer she was gone, the higher the wall of anxiety rose in him.

She shuffled back into the kitchen, finally, her robe sweeping against the floor, her eyes focused on a single blue aerogram held between her fingers. She remained standing next to the table, her lips moving as she read the words scrawled on the page. "Okay, this is the most threatening one. And here's what it says. *Se sei intelligente, non tornerai in Italia presto. E sai perché*. 'You won't come back to Italy soon. And you know why.' Nothing ungrammatical about that phrase though, right?"

"No, it's pretty standard Italian. But if she isn't a native, I wonder if she meant to say, *Se sei intelligente, non tornerai in Italia* ***più.***"

"'You won't come back anymore,'" Maria said.

Milo nodded. "Right."

After a few moments of mutual reflection, Maria said, "So, do you want to hear my theory on all of this?"

"Of course," Milo said. "You have one?"

"Let's just say there was a woman who visited Lenny right before he died. I've already told you that woman was not me. And just as unlikely the graduate student. But let's say it was this Vesuvia and there was an argument that Mrs. Colicchio overheard, one of many arguments she overheard. Let's say Vesuvia accused Lenny of doing something or breaking his promise. Maybe she had a method of blackmailing him. Maybe he did something illegal—after all where did all that money come from? Maybe whatever she threatened to do, like report him to the police, played on him so fiercely that he . . . just ended up making a split-second decision. To end it all."

"So what you're suggesting is that he decided to kill himself on the spur of the moment?" Then recalling Detective Rodriguez's recitation of the grim statistics of suicides, Milo said, "Like it's been documented of people who jump off the Golden Gate Bridge?"

Maria nodded. "Yes, that's what I'm saying."

Something else occurred to Milo. "So then he would have died the way Primo Levi died," he said, acknowledging that Levi's sudden, inexplicable suicide had always tantalized Lenny's imagination.

"Perhaps so, and perhaps in some unhealthy way, he was emulating Primo Levi." They stared at each other in silence, Maria's expression stiff and stony. "Let me ask you something," she said at last. "Why is it so hard for you to accept that my brother might have taken his own life? Why do you keep insisting that somebody else had a hand in it?"

"I told you why. Because I saw no evidence of distress or sadness. He seemed normal that last night, he even seemed upbeat. And don't forget he said he had something to tell me. When he said goodbye to me that night, he asked me to call him the next day. If he was contemplating suicide, why would he have asked me to call him in the morning?"

"Maybe he was going to tell you he didn't want to live," Maria said softly yet urgently. Milo was stunned. And then she continued, "Maybe he was going to tell you to look after me . . . and then just got overwrought in a kind of desperation." Her last words provoked a somber silence. And then Maria resumed. "Let's be honest: You have strong reasons for not wanting to believe he could have killed himself."

Milo sprang up from the table, and inches away from her now, insisted, "Of course I have strong reasons! He was my mentor! I modeled myself after him. If he killed himself, it casts doubt on everything—*everything* I ever learned from him."

"I don't see how that is, frankly," Maria told him quietly. "He taught you about literature; he taught you about philosophy; he taught you how to study in order to become an *academic*." The last word was uttered with an unmistakably rancorous tone. "But he never taught you about how to live, about how to survive. Because he didn't know how to do that himself."

A thick silence fell between them. It appeared that Maria was about to say something, but then Milo could see that her face was quivering. A moment later she burst into tears and came over and buried her face in his chest. He soothed her as best he could and tried with little success to repress the feeling in his groin that holding her stirred in him. But then, in the most natural way, as she sobbed, she began to run her fingers through his hair.

22.

Milo was riding the R train up to Forty-second Street. He'd taken a folder of student assignments to correct while he traveled up and downtown; however, he was too distracted to concentrate on the elementary essays riddled with grammatical errors and misusages. Today he hated his job, today he wished he didn't have his unfinished dissertation looming over his head; his lack of progress certainly would have been a sore subject of conversation with Lenny. He was presently too preoccupied with what had unexpectedly happened with Maria, which had left him feeling uncertain and vulnerable and naturally made him wonder what his former mentor would have made of the unforeseen interlude, if Lenny would have condemned it, or welcomed it—probably the former. The ten-year age difference between Maria and himself was not inconsiderable; and yet, he told himself, it was the sort of age difference that would make less and less difference the older one got. Now, however, he worried that having made love to Maria would cause an awkwardness with her. He had to be honest and admit to himself that of course he wanted more of her. And yet, each time Milo had attempted to reach her during the last two days, Aunt Francesca had answered the phone and coldly told him that Maria wasn't at home.

The unexpected intimacy with Maria therefore complicated everything. If she'd become less responsive to his communications, this left him to assume it was due to either regret or some kind of embarrassment. *And* Milo worried that she'd seduced him in order to perhaps distract him from something she was trying to hide or even withhold. Maybe she knew more about Lenny's "secret investments" than she was letting on. Maybe she knew about more of his intimate relationships and just wasn't confiding in him completely.

At Forty-second Street, he switched to the number one subway uptown, and got off at 116th Street. He walked a block over to 1130 Amsterdam Avenue. He rode the elevator to the ninth floor, where the Italian department was located and where he'd spent time visiting fellow graduate students whom he'd met downtown at the Casa Italiana on Twelfth Street, which had opened a few years earlier in 1990 and had become very popular in the academic Italian community. He didn't remember meeting Emma Stein at the Casa Italiana, but he figured that if it were popular among her colleagues, no doubt she'd probably been to at least a few of the lectures there.

It was just after one o'clock in the afternoon. The hallways seemed surprisingly deserted for midday at a university. He'd looked up Emma Stein's office hours and easily located the door with her name posted on it. Luckily, he found nobody waiting to see her.

He knocked. A woman who looked to be in her early thirties with a thick head of dark ringlets and very striking green eyes answered the door; it occurred to him immediately that, from behind, she actually could be the woman in the photograph taken by Mrs. Colicchio. But Maria was right: Despite similar coloring, their faces were entirely different. Emma Stein had prominent cheekbones, and her eyes were deeply set.

"Can I help you?" she asked him politely and officiously.

Milo said in Italian, "I'm a grad student. I teach at NYU. I think we may have met at the Casa Italiana. I was wondering if I could have a word with you."

The woman looked at him with momentary suspicion and said in English, "Sure, okay," opened her door, and, pointing to a chair next to her desk said, "Sit down if you'd like."

Milo had spoken in Italian only because he sensed that speaking in English would have raised more suspicion; surely, she'd be less wary of someone who pitched up at her office speaking Italian, a grad student at another university in Manhattan.

"You actually look familiar to me," she continued in English. "Do you remember which lecture we might have met at, at the Casa?"

Milo shook his head. "I don't. And look, I'm sorry to show up here like this," he said. "But it's because I needed to speak to you. And I had no other way of getting in touch."

Looking surprised and bewildered and glancing at the door nervously, she said, "Well, you could have called the department and asked to be patched through to me . . . but just tell me what this is all about."

He took a deep breath and exhaled. "It's about Lenny D'Ambrosio."

She raised her eyes to the ceiling and shook her head vehemently. “Somehow . . . I knew it was going to be this. I knew . . . That’s why I recognize you. He showed me pictures of you. You were also his student.”

“Protégé, more like.”

She jumped up out of her chair, grabbed the slightly ajar door, and swung it wide open. “I am going to ask you leave, now,” she said with admirable control. He could tell she was genuinely afraid of him, and in light of what she’d been through with Lenny, this certainly made sense.

Milo, however, had the presence of mind to remain seated. “Can you just give me a couple minutes?” he asked in a soft, controlled, docile tone. “I really do need to speak to you.”

She shook her head. “I know he was a close friend of yours. I’m sorry for your loss, but I really don’t want to talk about him.”

“Well, he’s your loss, too,” Milo hazarded to say. “I know once upon a time you were good friends.”

Something in her relented. She cast her eyes down, shook her head, and muttered, “We haven’t been good friends. Not for a long time.”

Milo was banking on the fact that she wouldn’t assume that he knew what had happened between Lenny and her. Lenny being so private, she might have assumed that Milo didn’t know. “Well . . . you can imagine his death has been really rough for me.” His voice noticeably shook, and he could see this seemed to reassure her. At last, much to Milo’s relief, Emma Stein finally sat back down in her chair and tilted her head to the side, signaling that she was in listening mode. "Okay, dica." She employed Italian for just that one word, which required two in English: tell me.

"Well, first I want to let you know: His sister found some letters from you in a safe in his apartment."

He could tell this unnerved her. "What about the letters?"

He'd already decided that to get anything helpful from Emma Stein, it would be necessary to stretch the truth a little bit by saying, "Well, let's say they're of interest because the cause of his death has not yet been firmly established."

"What do you mean 'has not yet been *firmly* established?' The police told me he likely killed himself."

Milo flinched when he heard the phrase "killed himself," which sounded harsh in her iteration of it. "Detective Delzio told *me* that you had a lawyer who wouldn't let them get very far. The reason they came to see you in the first place is at the time they didn't have airtight proof of suicide. All they know is that he was found hanging from a bedsheet. Somebody could have forced him to take his own life."

Emma Stein got up from her chair again and began to pace her office in a scurrying manner. Then she stopped and glared at him. "This is really too much! You shouldn't have come here like this! You really should have called first!" she insisted.

She was right, of course. But Milo knew had he managed to get Emma Stein on the phone, the same conversation would have ended long before now. Now, at least she was his captive audience.

"Please listen to me," he resumed. "I know he treated you inappropriately. I would never try to gloss over that.

But take one step back for a second and try to look at this from my perspective." He paused. "Lenny was everything to me. He was my mentor, he was my close friend, he was my confidant. You studied with him yourself, so you know what a fine teacher he was. His love for the Italian language was infectious." Milo got choked up, couldn't control it, and tears started in his eyes as he spoke to her more haltingly. "I saw him the night before he died . . . he seemed happy . . . he seemed content . . . which, if you knew him, was not so usual. He was reading out loud . . . from 'Paolo and Francesca.'"

"Yes, well, he loved that canto," Emma Stein said with noticeable sadness, clearly moved by Milo's tears. "He was very sentimental about it. Quixotic love always got to him."

Milo managed to smile through his tears. "Precisely. Anyway, the night before he died, the last thing he said to me was, 'call me in the morning.' But I never got a call from him. Instead, I got a call from the police telling me that he hanged himself."

Shaking her head, Emma said, "That must have been really frightful." She reached for a pencil that had rolled to the edge of her desk, picked it up, and started softly bouncing it on the eraser end. "It was really a shock to me when *I* heard about it," she admitted at last.

"But I don't believe it; I just don't believe he killed himself. I think somebody somehow forced him to do it."

She looked alarmed. "And you're saying they suspect *me*?"

Milo shook his head. "The detectives talked to you already. Wouldn't they have indicated if they suspected you?"

"But you said my letters were found."

"*I* haven't read them. His sister did. Would there be something in them that would *make* anyone suspect you?"

She shot him a helpless look. "I honestly don't remember what I wrote. But I don't believe so. Although I can tell you this: He was involved with at least two women when I was his student."

Two women? "He told you this?"

She nodded.

"Were they—"

"Both in Italy."

"I know about one woman, but I don't know her identity."

Emma Stein glanced at her watch. "Just so you know: I have a student appointment in five minutes."

"Okay," Milo said. "Then I'll be quick. I considered myself probably his closest friend. He left me his entire collection of Italian-language books, including a first edition of *Se Questo è Un Uomo*. Which is probably worth a lot."

"The Einaudi?"

"Yes."

"He showed me that book. It probably *is* worth a lot."

"He confided in me and yet he said nothing about his friendship (or relationship, whatever it was) with you or anyone else, or the . . . ultimate confrontation between you."

She shook her head. "Surely you can imagine him not wanting people to know about what happened between us? The only reason that I know about the other women is because I found out about them . . . inadvertently. And when I asked him, it was pretty hard for him to avoid telling me the truth. However, had it been up to him, he would have divulged nothing to me. Or lied. He certainly wasn't above lying when it was required of him." The last phrase was uttered in a mocking tone and Milo wondered if perhaps Emma Stein once did have feelings for Lenny, feelings that were squelched by jealousy. A guarded look now floated across her face. "If you read my letters to him, you'll know what I'm talking about."

Knowing this would probably be impossible, that Maria probably would never share these particular letters with him, Milo allowed silence to percolate through the room before he asked for clarification.

Emma Stein said, "Had he— Did Lenny ever mention what was going on in Italy?"

"Specifically?"

"Why he went there so often."

"Well . . . he loved it—"

"Oh, *please*."

"Cultural reasons?"

"*As if*," Emma Stein said with pained sarcasm.

"Okay, I don't know, so can you please tell me?"

Her expression froze and she looked away. "No, because I have nothing more to say about this. And nothing more to say about Lenny or my letters to Lenny." Her eyes now fixed on his. "Now, if his sister wants to share my letters with you, that's up to her." Emma Stein glanced at her watch. "But like I said, I am expecting someone so I need you to leave my office."

"Okay. I'm going." Milo held out his hand. She took it and gave him a limp handshake in return.

Then she said, "Look, just one thing before you go. Lenny went through a hard time after what happened between us. He lost his footing here at Columbia. He had a lot of trouble getting another teaching job. I don't—and didn't—wish him ill."

"Do you know that his sister was the only person who knew about you?"

"Doesn't surprise me. He worshipped his sister. He always used to say that that there was a strong resemblance."

Staring into the woman's eyes, Milo said softly, "You two look nothing alike."

"From the pictures I saw of her, I never thought so either," Emma Stein agreed.

23.

Reflecting on Emma Stein's sarcastic comment in response to his assumption that Lenny's frequent trips to Italy were for "cultural reasons," Milo, when he got back to his apartment, took out the five letters from Vesuvia that Maria had given him and started rereading them. They requested money for travel expenses, money to pay off a man called Vladimir; they confided her worries about leaving Italy on her Albanian passport and being unable to return. But then it seemed she did actually leave the country—one of the letters referenced New York City where Lenny apparently had brought her. Two of the letters made reference to Lenny's promise to sponsor Vesuvia's becoming a resident of the U.S.—presumably by marrying her. But that was basically the extent of the content, so no reference to Lenny's trips to Italy. Milo therefore couldn't help but wonder about the letters from Emma Stein that Maria had *not* shared with him and which, as the graduate student inferred, might cast light on the purpose of Lenny's frequent trips to Italy.

And yet due to their unexpected intimacy and the simple fact that since they'd slept together, after several attempts, he'd been unable to reach Maria by telephone, Milo was nervous about pressing her.

But he did finally reach her and her brisk way of greeting him was immediately painful, made him think that she'd regretted what had happened between them after Aunt Francesca left for Queens. As difficult as it was to hear her speaking to him so indifferently, Milo knew he had to persevere in order find answers to the question about Lenny's frequent trips to Italy.

"I gave you all of Vesuvia's letters," Maria insisted. "Why would I withhold any of them from you?"

Milo had calculated her response and was therefore ready to say, "You withheld the letters from Emma Stein."

"Because those letters are not relevant. They're personal letters between *them*. Nothing in those letters relates to anything you're trying to find out about who might have been with Lenny the night he died or why."

"That's not quite what I was after." Milo now explained that he'd actually met with Emma Stein who'd reacted with sarcasm when he suggested that Lenny had frequently gone to Italy for cultural reasons.

Maria got angry. "I can't believe you went to see her. You should *never* have done that!"

"And why shouldn't I have?"

She was quiet for a moment and then said, "Out of respect for my brother. You know that was the last thing in the world he would ever want you to do."

This was obviously true and yet obviously manipulative. "Maybe so. But he's not here, and I had questions that I needed to answer."

"What questions?" Maria asked in a less demonstrative tone.

"She made it seem that some of her letters directly referred to why he went to Italy so frequently. When I suggested that it was for 'cultural reasons,' she laughed in my face."

Maria surprised him by also laughing.

"What's so funny about that?" he demanded, now irritated.

"You very likely misconstrued what she told you. Because there is nothing of any nature in those letters about trips to Italy. She hardly needed—"

"But then why would she—"

"Let me finish, Milo!" Maria paused, as if for effect. "You really don't see my brother in a clear light do you?"

"What's *that* supposed to mean?"

"She's right. He didn't go to Italy for cultural reasons. He went to Italy because he was a hound for women. He was *desperate* to have a woman in his life, *permanently.* And it was a lot easier for him to meet available women in Italy. Or perhaps I should say women like Vesuvia who aren't there legally and therefore don't have a lot of options. Which left *him* more in control of things. Gave *him* more power. Which was what he was always after." Maria's rancorous tone was truly disturbing.

Up until now, Milo had no idea about this supposed insatiable quest for power over women. "Well, then if Lenny was so desperate to have a woman, why didn't he marry Vesuvia?"

"Good question. There were probably too many complications. You would need to ask . . . *her*," Maria said, which left Milo with a feeling of dissatisfaction and even suspicion that she didn't want him to find out about any of these complications.

"I have no way of finding her," he reminded her.

"And I promise you that I don't either," Maria told him.

24.

Once again, the three of them sat in the Rossis' living room: Milo and Val perched three feet apart on the sofa, and Rose Marie facing them in an armchair. Milo had offered beer and Val said, "I try not to drink."

"AA?" Rose Marie asked him with an appraising look on her face.

"Well, no . . . but remember I told you about my father? He has a drinking problem." Val went on to admit that, perhaps like his father, he found it difficult to be satisfied with just one beer or cocktail. "So I try and avoid alcohol altogether. If anything, I'll have red wine from time to time."

"We *have* red wine," Milo offered.

Val glanced at his watch. "You trying to get me drunk? Anyway, it's four o'clock in the afternoon. Even if I wanted a glass of red wine, I'd wait until a bit later. I'll take some club soda with lime, though, if you have it."

"I'll get it." Rose Marie jumped up and scurried into the kitchen. Val leaned back against the sofa, and fixing his always-unsettling gaze sideways on Milo, said, "So, on the phone you said you had something to talk to me about. So what's up, *Milo*?"

"What's up is I'm going to Italy. Classes are on break, and I usually go once a year to visit my aunt."

"When does the break start?"

"End of next week."

Rose Marie reentered the room with a tall glass filled to the brim with club soda and a wedge of lime floating on top. She handed the drink to Val, who thanked her cordially. "What did I miss?" she asked them.

"Nothing. I was just telling Val about going to Italy."

Val said, "You told me your aunt lives in Lucca, right?" Milo nodded. "Where, precisely?"

"How well do you know Lucca?" Milo asked with a note of suspicion.

"I've been there a few times."

"Actually, my aunt lives right near the convent where Puccini's sister spent most of her life."

"Oh, wow, she does?" Val looked incredulous. "I actually know . . . I remember reading in some dramaturge's notes somewhere that Suor' Angelica is based on Puccini's committing his sister to a nunnery. A quite common practice during the late nineteenth century."

"He foisted her off on the nuns," Rose Marie remarked. "Nice older brother, huh?"

"I'm not so up on opera history," Milo remarked.

"Well, I am, to a certain extent," Val said with a lopsided grin.

"A man of many distinctions," Milo commented.

Leering at him, Val said, "Do I detect sarcasm?"

"Not at all," Milo assured him.

Val took a sip of his club soda, then squeezed the wedge of lime in his glass, and said to Rose Marie, "This is perfect. Thank you."

She nodded graciously.

Setting down his glass, Val said to them, "Okay, so you're going to Tuscany."

"Right. And I'd like to stop in and see Matteo in Pistoia."

Forgetting himself momentarily, Val pounced on this and said, "I told you everything you could possibly want to know about *my* brother and *your* brother. So, what more do you want?" And even before Milo could answer, he added, "I mean, I can't believe this probing bullshit is starting up all over again."

"Excuse me?" Rose Marie said to him in a menacing tone.

"I'm sorry, Mrs. Rossi." Val turned to face her and sounded genuinely contrite. "I *am* uncouth sometimes."

Tilting his head toward Rose Marie, Milo continued, "Mom is afraid of flying. So on her and my behalf, we have a few more questions for Matteo about the night before the car accident."

Now Val actually looked fearful. "What few questions? I'm sure *I* can answer them."

"No, because you weren't with them that last night. You know only what your brother told you," Rose Marie said.

"We want to ask him what exactly was discussed, how truly upset Carlo was, this kind of thing," Milo said quietly, deliberately, and sadly. Val glanced at Rose Marie.

"We think it might help us," she told him gravely. "Knowing more. Everything you tell us is secondhand. Your brother felt he couldn't even come to the wake for his best friend, the person you say he cared for so much. I—we—want to ask him about that."

"I told you why," Val reminded them.

"But that's the thing," Milo said. "I don't . . ." He glanced at Rose Marie. "We don't agree with you that your brother not attending the wake was what Carlo would have wanted."

"Believe me, this is something *I* know that *you* don't," Val insisted.

"Okay. Understood. But there has to be more that none of us—even you—understand. All due respect, Val, I knew my brother, and Mom knew her son better than you did."

Val held up his hands in a gesture of surrender. "Okay, fine, I won't argue." Frowning and looking back and forth between them, he said, "But I won't, I can't, give out my brother's details unless I clear it with him, okay?"

Milo said, "Of course. And if you don't get back to me before I leave, you can get in touch with Mom and pass along the info and I can always get a hold of Matteo while I'm in Italy."

Val's pale face now reddened with some suppressed emotion. He put down his glass of club soda, leaned forward, placed his hands on his knees, and sat there for a moment, motionless. At last, he said, "Can I tell you something about all of this?" Neither Milo nor Rose Marie replied. They just stared at Val. Milo could immediately sense his mother stiffening in her chair and sitting up taller. "Well, then I can keep my opinion to myself."

"No, *I* want to know. *I* want to hear what you have to say!" Rose Marie challenged him, her voice surprisingly controlled.

With the index finger of one hand Val softly jabbed the palm of the other and said to Milo, "I feel like you're constantly looking for things, digging for information. And always trying to figure me and my brother out. Frankly, it makes me very nervous."

"Well, maybe Milo is trying to figure you out . . . because you're a bit of a mystery to us," Rose Marie said. "You and all your business dealings," she added with what to Milo sounded like an unnerving note of sarcasm, maybe even contempt.

Val turned to her. "Look, I was honest with Milo about our business, because we're all connected, because I figured you already knew about what we were doing, that Carlo had told you. *Because* he was so against it. And *because* he was upset about it."

"Well, that's where you're wrong. He told us almost nothing," Rose Marie said.

"Yeah, well, obviously had I known this beforehand, I would have kept my big trap shut. But now I have to protect myself *and* my brother. Surely, you can understand that. So maybe you can tell me what else you are trying to piece together via my brother."

Milo reminded Val about Lenny D'Ambrosio's death, which had been ruled a suicide, a verdict that was now accepted by nearly everybody.

"Okay, but what does this have to do with either my brother or me?"

"You know exactly what. The video tapes in this man's apartment came from your collection."

Val sighed and said nothing for a moment. Then he blurted out, "But you know it's a mail-order business. We have nothing to do with our customers."

Ignoring this rote explanation, Rose Marie boldly said, "You just sell them to whomever and put the money in the bank."

This comment caused an eruption of rage. Pivoting to Milo, Val hollered, "I don't need this judgment. In fact, I *don't* want you visiting my brother. So no contact information, no phone number for him, okay? You got that?"

And then Rose Marie, diminutive though she was, jumped out of her chair. "Don't you raise your voice!" she hissed, shaking her finger at him. "Not here in my house! If I invite you here, I expect you to behave like a gentleman!"

"Mom!" Milo complained.

"You shut up!" she told him. Turning back to Val, she said, "You don't want to give out the telephone number? Fine. But then finish this conversation . . . like a gentleman. Or"—she pointed to the door—"take a hike back to Whitestone or wherever the hell you live."

Total perturbed silence fell after that, and only then did Milo realize that Rose Marie knew she could take the risk; somehow, she'd divined that her rebuke would be excruciating to Val, who actually got up, walked over to where she was still standing, and knelt before her. In a quieter tone, he said, "Look, I'm sorry I got so worked up. I'll call Matteo, and if he wants to be in touch, I'll give you his contact information. Okay?"

And then Rose Marie got tearful. "Don't you understand?" she implored. "Don't you get that we want to find out as much as we can about Carlo's last few hours? His last few words? Do you have any idea how awful it's been for us not knowing anything, not even knowing his state of mind?"

"I tried—'"

"It's not good enough!" she insisted. "Do you get what I'm saying? It's NOT GOOD ENOUGH!"

What Milo hadn't realized but what Rose Marie already seemed to know was that Val would capitulate to her because, already alienated from his own mother, he was afraid of alienating the mother of the man his brother had once—and probably even still—loved. But perhaps more significant: the night before Carlo died, Val had cajoled his brother into confessing the magnitude of the love he felt for his best friend, a confession that proved to be a disaster.

Part Three

25.

On the train from the airport in Pisa to Lucca, when the conductor came to collect his ticket, Milo asked about the frequency of trains in the opposite direction. The man, not much older than he, started speaking a halting, butchered English.

Jet-lagged and already on edge, Milo said to him, "Where do you think I come from, anyway?"

The conductor said, "I don't know, Sweden?"

"Okay, but if Italian works for both of us, why speak English?"

Deliberately addressing Milo in the second-person familiar, a breach of etiquette easily construed as a rebuke, the conductor said, "Because I don't speak Swedish to you, okay?"

Realizing further conversation was fruitless, Milo gestured skyward with his hands and said, no more.

His aunt Lara was waiting for him on the far side of Lucca's bright orange train station. There was a tunnel that accessed this exit just outside the city's walls that was used mostly by locals. Instead of walking through the tunnel, however, Milo chose to break the rules and cross the tracks. Spying him skipping over the last of the rails, Lara was shaking her head as he climbed into her small, battered Fiat.

"Always bending the rules. Some things never change," she said after kissing him on both cheeks.

"That tunnel is always so choked with cigarette smoke," he told her by way of an explanation.

"Your whole life you've always had an answer for everything," Lara commented.

Rose Marie's older sister was a well-preserved, impeccably tailored woman of seventy, who wore discreet make-up and whose silver-blond hair looked so natural that it was hard to know whether she colored it. She'd always been a rare beauty. She'd moved to Italy just after graduating college to marry one of her classmates, a young dashing man who, though he was the nephew of the renowned Italian author Giorgio Bassani, was a lackluster student whose charms, according to Lara, eclipsed his questionable intellect. They were married in Rome, divorced five years later (when she discovered that he'd been shamelessly cheating on her), and Lara, who'd taken a shine to living in Italy, remained, marrying one more time, divorcing, and finally finding the love of her life: a journalist and true intellectual who abused himself with drink and cigarettes and who'd recently died of emphysema at the age of sixty-seven.

Despite the fact that his aunt was dressed in mourning-dark, expensive-looking clothes, the car was cluttered with detritus. Splayed out on the rear seats were promotional circulars from the supermarkets *Esselunga* and *Conad*, and everything was covered with dog hair and crumbles of dog biscuits. Lara usually kept more or less eight dogs at a time, and at least two or three of them would accompany her while she ran errands. Milo was actually surprised that she'd left all her canines at home.

"You tired?" she asked him.

"Not too terribly. I was able to sleep on the plane. I had an aisle and the spot next to me was open."

"*Caspita!*" said his aunt. ("Good going.")

"But now I have to ask *you* something I don't quite understand."

"What's that?"

"I continually speak Italian in America. I speak to all the natives in the Italian department at NYU, so why is it that whenever I come here, people start answering me in English?"

"Don't take it so personally," she advised him as they entered into one of Lucca's many roundabouts, squeezing into a line of cars, coming so close to colliding with one that Milo shut his eyes and stiffened in his seat. "The same thing happens to me."

He opened his eyes; the immediate danger had passed. "Yes, but you have a very noticeable American accent."

She playfully swatted at him.

"Don't get me wrong, your Italian is impeccable, perfect. Way better than mine, obviously. But you do have a noticeable American accent."

"Well, let me tell you this. When I go back to America and start speaking English, people tend to ask me where I'm from. I think it's from not hearing a lot of English spoken around me—I naturally acquire an accent. Some people call it transatlantic, but that sounds kind of grand to me. The same might be the case for you but in reverse. When you go back to the gym here and hang out with all your soccer-player buddies, you can ask them their opinion of your accent."

"I only have one friend, Paolo. And he won't be honest. Because he loves me," Milo said with a chuckle. He swiveled to face her and said, "You sound pretty chipper for somebody who, pardon my saying this, recently lost her husband." He'd known Lara his entire life and felt he could be frank.

Smiling sadly, she explained that Sylvestro's death was a long time coming, and right at the moment, less than a month after his long illness and passing, she was feeling relief, but she knew that the deep, abiding sadness was soon to follow.

Milo nodded and said, "Of course. That makes sense." And there was a minute or so of reflective silence.

Lara broached the silence. "My friend Ornella said to me, 'The measure of grief over someone you love is equal to the amount you loved them.'"

"*She* said that?"

"You sound surprised?"

"I don't think of her as particularly profound."

"You hardly know her well enough to say that. Don't be an arrogant ass!" Lara snapped. "When you say things like that you really do remind me of how old you are."

She was right: His remark *was* callow. He apologized sincerely with a lame excuse of being jet-lagged and then looked out the window to hide the shameful blush creeping across his face. They were just then driving on an overpass, and he looked down on the speeding traffic of the A11 heading in the direction of Florence.

"Oh, God," he said. "I was going to ask you to stop at Giusti. So I could get their cornmeal focaccia."

Lara glanced at her watch. "It's the midday *chiusura*," she reminded him. "They won't reopen for at least two more hours."

"Damn. Of course," Milo said.

"You can go tomorrow," she told him. "And buy every single sheet of Giusti's cornmeal focaccia." And then a moment later, "I have some nice things planned for us."

"Don't tell me; let me guess. Hanging out with all the expats?" Milo referred to Lara's many Anglophone friends, residents of Lucca whose Italian consisted of necessary phrases needed at the market, the bank, and the post office.

"No, just the Italians," she said. "My Anglo friends think you're a snob anyway."

"It's not that I'm a snob. They just know I don't approve that they've lived here for so many years and never bothered to learn the language. I think that's shameful."

"You make a good point, Milo; however, it's a lot harder to learn a new language when you're an adult."

26.

Lara lived in a residential area called Gattaiola just outside the walls of the city. Her late husband, the renowned intellectual, Sylvestro Calderi, had written frequently for *Corriere della Sera*. From his parents, Sylvestro had inherited a square-shaped sixteenth-century villa that had once belonged to one of Napoleon II's finance ministers. Because Lucca had once flourished as a city state that had accumulated a great deal of wealth due to its silk trade, there were a fair number of grand sixteenth-century villas dotting the countryside. Few of them, however, boasted such large receiving rooms as the Villa Calderi, which made Sylvestro's (and now Lara's, as he'd left it to her) home particularly suitable for large weddings and corporate events, which brought in an annual income that paid the considerable expenses required to keep a sixteenth-century building in good running order.

They drove through a series of tight roads, some of them with tall, two-hundred-year-old stone walls and eventually turned into a driveway with high gates. Lara leaned out the window, engaged the gates with a fob key, and as they sped along the driveway, Milo could see, in the distance, a motley pack of dogs beginning to run toward the car. It amazed him how the dogs knew to get out of the way just at the last minute, parting like a wave and allowing Lara to proceed unimpeded up to the villa. As soon as she pulled into her parking spot, several of the dogs exuberantly jumped up on the car. "There goes your paint job," Milo said.

"Distressed is a good look to have in a car," Lara replied with a disinterested shrug, counting herself among the well-educated class of residents who purposely scorned the newer, fancier cars favored by the nouveau riche, and even had a sense of pride driving around in small, modest vehicles whose tune-ups and oil changes were ignored, the cars themselves becoming more and more battered from being packed tightly into parking lots and eventually just falling apart.

As Milo grabbed his bags, a few of the friendlier dogs approached him timidly, and he patted them. He was making his way up a short flight of stone stairs to the villa's side entrance when Lara's housekeeper, Vittoria, came outside to greet him. He kissed her on both cheeks, something he knew his aunt secretly disapproved of. Vittoria upbraided him for not having visited for a couple of years, but he gently pointed out that he'd actually visited the year before. Of Albanian origin and a tall, sturdy brunette, Vittoria fixed her striking greenish-brown eyes on him and said, "Did I forget?"

He patted her on the shoulder. "I think you did."

For this visit, Lara decided to put Milo in a bedroom off the enormous *trompe-l'oeil* ballroom on the second floor of the five-story building. (The bathroom of the bedroom on the ground floor she normally put him in apparently had a plumbing problem.) Milo didn't at all mind being sequestered on the second floor; this meant that he could escape what seemed like the continuous barking of the dogs downstairs, the noise of dishes clanging in the kitchen, and be able to sit on a sofa that was at least two hundred years old, look up at the sylvan frescoes that had been painstakingly brushed on the high walls and the forty-foot ceilings and dive into the reading he was doing in preparation for his spring semester Italian 4 class.

That first afternoon, however, Milo caught up on some sleep and then went for a long walk up the winding road that led from the villa, past a few local farms with persimmon and olive trees, and ended on a dirt path that, if you followed it far enough, would lead over a small mountain pass and bushwhack its way down toward Pisa. Knowing he'd been sedentary on an airplane for so many hours, Milo pushed himself hard to get his blood flowing and ended up pretty far up the mountainside, with a sweeping view of the city and its numerous brick towers. He was famished and wondered what Lara had planned for dinner.

When he got back to the villa, Lara, with a motley, mixed-breed lapdog on either side of her, was sipping a glass of white wine while sitting in the library that her late husband had had fitted with high bookshelves that held nineteenth- and twentieth-century volumes in several different languages. The crown jewel of his collection was a rather extensive series of Gallimard's *Editions de la Pléiade*, the best of world literature in a French translation collected in one-thousand-plus-page volumes printed on elegantly thin bible paper. Milo moved toward the characteristic green-and-gold leather spines of the *Pléiades*, noticed the William Faulkner series, and started thumbing through the novels until he came upon his favorite, *Light in August*, whose incantatory prose (he would have thought) might make it impossible to find a foreign-language equivalent. And yet, as he read the opening, he could tell how good the translation was, and then it occurred to him that it would perhaps be easier to approximate the lyrical tone of Faulkner's prose in a Romance language. A German translation, surely, would present more of a linguistic challenge.

"Which one have you picked out?" Lara asked him.

Milo told her and said it was his favorite Faulkner, and she beamed and told him *Light in August* was Sylvestro's favorite Faulkner as well. "He adored that writer," she said.

Running his index finger along the spines of the vast *Pléiades* collection that spanned three centuries of literature, Milo said, "Has he read most of these?"

"He read them constantly. So I would assume. I didn't, of course, because my French just isn't good enough."

Milo turned to her. "Why, might I ask, would he want to read something translated into French rather than into his native Italian?"

Lara glanced at the empty space next to her, where Sylvestro used to sit before he took to isolating himself in his room. Fixing a pair of dewy eyes on Milo, she said, "He generally thought French translations were better than the Italian ones, particularly the *Pléiades*. His exception of course was anything Natalia Ginzburg translated into Italian."

"Anything?" Milo repeated. "I didn't know she translated all that much. Beyond *Swann's Way*."

"I really wouldn't know what she translated," Lara said and then looked at him with curiosity. "Speaking of Natalia Ginzburg. How's it going with your dissertation?"

"To be honest, it's not going. It's eluding me."

"Out of laziness?"

"No, out of sheer stupidity. I'm just not smart enough to distill her work into any kind of compelling critical study."

"You're being hard on yourself."

"I wish that were the case."

"Oh come on."

"Anyway, back to Sylvestro. His English was rather good. So why, for example, didn't he just read Faulkner in the original?"

Lara explained that Sylvestro was insecure about his English, never thought it was proficient enough. And that having a command of English was, in Italy, considered to be a mark of good breeding. "His mother spoke it perfectly, and she always criticized his mistakes."

"Ah, so that's why he never wanted to speak English to me. Which of course I appreciated," Milo said. "I wish more Italians were like him."

Milo glanced over at the one feature of the room that always unnerved him. On top of the grand piano that was situated in the corner of the immense room was a small glass display showcasing the white plaster reproduction of a delicate-looking hand. Apparently, this had been cast from the hand of Napoleon II's sister, who'd once been a guest at the villa.

Noticing him noticing the hand, Lara said, "Your mother can't stand that hand."

"It's kind of ghoulish, you have to admit."

"Not when you look at it every day. Like I do," Lara said. "I think it's rather lovely."

27.

Paolo, who was just finishing a biceps set with a pair of twenty-kilogram dumbbells, spotted Milo immediately when he walked in, grinned wildly, and, carefully replacing the weights, headed over to him. He seized Milo by both shoulders, kissed him on both cheeks, and then did something that no American male would ever do: He cupped the side of Milo's face with his open palm. "*Bello*," he said, "you're finally here!"

"Sorry I didn't let you know beforehand. It was a last-minute flight."

"But *I* knew you were coming." And then Paolo revealed to Milo that he'd run into Lara at the *vinaio* in Guamo, a Lucchese suburb where you could buy local wine that was bottled from the establishment's reserve of demijohns. "She told me."

"She never mentioned it," Milo said by way of an apology.

"Who cares? You're here, aren't you?" Paolo said with his charming, ironic grin, and then appraised him. "But why so sad?"

Milo was suspicious. "My aunt said something to you? *Why* I'm here?"

Paolo held up both his hands. "She says nothing. I promise you. Maybe I should say, who is the heartbreaker?"

Milo grimaced at the thought of his bizarre recent erotic encounter with Maria, and how it had made things awkward between them, not to mention leaving him wanting more of what clearly was not forthcoming. He briefly filled Paolo in.

"I can tell she's gotten under your skin. You'll get over it," Paolo told him with a paternal tone. "I'll introduce you to my beautiful cousin, and then you'll get some Italian poison in your blood. And maybe with some Italian poison, you'll forget you're a lovesick American."

"I'm not lovesick."

Paolo threw up his hands. "Fine, I believe you."

Paolo finished his workout before Milo and was waiting for him in the café that was an annex of the gym, his macchiato hardly touched, embedded in conversation with a deeply tanned bodybuilder wreathed in gold neck chains who turned to regard Milo with what were clearly fake, turquoise-colored contact lenses. Milo thought he recognized the guy from previous visits; the man, however, clearly remembered him. "That time of year again, eh?" he said to Milo after placing a heavy hand on his shoulder.

"Actually, I rarely come to Lucca in spring."

"This is true," Paolo told his friend. "Usually, it's November. He brings the rain and he takes—no, I should accurately say he smuggles—white truffles back to America for his mother."

"Ah, yes. At least this time of year I won't have to worry about being arrested at Kennedy airport with contraband." Milo said this (he hoped) very cleverly, and both of the other men burst into laughter.

But then the bodybuilder commented, "That isn't quite how you'd say that, however, I get your point. My name, by the way, is Giacomo. This dickhead"—he referred to Paolo—"forgot to introduce us."

"My apologies," said Paolo with heavy sarcasm.

Giacomo said, "I've noticed you here before and wondered where you came from."

"*Piacere*," Milo said to him.

"Did I tell you not to say *piacere*?" Paolo scolded him. "That's what a lowly person says to a someone of superior breeding."

"I forgot," Milo said sarcastically. "Sorry."

"So, don't give him too much credit," Paolo told Giacomo. "After all, he did grow up here in the summers. He sort of belongs."

Giacomo shrugged, said nothing, and even looked momentarily bored. Glancing at his large, gaudy gold watch, he said, "Okay, got to get back to work, so goodbye, boys," and lumbered off to the parking lot, climbing into a perfectly maintained black Audi A4 and drove away—a car, Milo thought, Lara would not be caught dead in.

"Is that guy on steroids?" he asked.

"Clearly so," Paolo said. "But I never asked him."

"What is his profession?"

"Well, he comes from a long line of plumbers. So, he works in the family business. *Per forza*," Paolo said. "However, he is very well educated." He clapped Milo on the shoulder. "So, what are we going to do while you're here?"

"Well, what's your game schedule?"

"We go to Nice in . . ." He thought for a moment. "Four days. On Sunday."

"By bus?"

"No, by train. A real train that goes appropriate speeds. Not like your mangled American trains . . . good God. We go on the trains because the autostrada gets too crazy closer to the border."

"I hate that road to France," Milo said. "For me, it's nerve-racking. You see all those crumpled-up cars that crashed in the tunnels. And too many of them. Tunnels, I mean."

"Don't be such a baby," Paolo said. "Aren't there places in America where you can drive fast? Where is it called, Montana?"

Milo laughed. "Hey, I want to talk to you about a few things."

Paolo shrugged, looked around the bar as if what Milo was going to ask had to do with something or someone sitting near them. Then fixed his eyes on Milo. "Tell me."

Milo began with his doubts about the nature of Lenny's death, the threatening letters that had been sent by Vesuvia from Italy, and how he was wondering if Maria maybe had even seduced him to distract him from some revelation of truth about her brother that she was perhaps trying to hide. And how he'd be visiting Matteo Cipolla who, Paolo already had heard (when he met Val) was living in Pistoia.

"Oh *Dio*," said Paolo. "This all sounds like one of the English murder mysteries my mother watches on television. Badly dubbed, of course," he added as an afterthought.

"Do you happen to know Pistoia at all?"

"Well, as you know, I was born right next door. But I never have much reason to go to Pistoia."

Out of the front pocket of his backpack, Milo pulled the small, colored snapshot of Carlo and Matteo that Rose Marie had found beneath a stack of Carlo's papers, which were carefully arranged in his closet in the room they both shared. "This is Matteo," Milo said, pointing to the guy on the left.

"Ah, he's a ginger. Doesn't look Italian at all. Maybe he'd stick out in a crowd."

"Well, remember, his brother is blond. They're Polish on the mother's side. Anyway, if you recall, when Val told us about their 'business,' you said you'd heard there were some pornography studios around here?"

"Okay, so I said that. And?"

"Do you have any idea of where they might be located?"

"Well, probably outside the city walls. They would need a big space, I would think."

"But what areas around here would be right for this?"

Paolo frowned at him. "So, you are going to give up your expensive education to become a pornographer?"

"No, not quite yet."

"Let me think about this," Paolo said. "We really should ask Giacomo, the guy who was just here. Remember, I lived until the age of ten in Montecatini. Giacomo grew up here. He is one hundred precent Lucchese. He would know better."

28.

Although Lara was in mourning, she managed to perpetuate the full life she'd always led up until the death of Sylvestro. This meant that she often went within the walls of the city at around noon to meet a friend for lunch, leaving Milo free to do what he liked: to read or make himself meals from the refrigerator that she'd kindly stocked with all his favorite foods like prosciutto di Parma, Tuscan pecorino that was sweeter than Roman or Sardinian pecorino, yogurt, and local fruit. However, she made it clear to him that their long-established tradition of having dinner together at seven p.m. would be maintained. As always, Vittoria cooked the meals.

Dating back to when Milo was a child, Lara always had looked forward to these dinners à deux (or à trois when Carlo was alive and deigned to come to Italy during the summer), even during the life of her idiosyncratic husband, Sylvestro, who, for his last three years, basically dwelled in his book-lined bedroom (a Proustian existence, he once remarked to Milo) and preferred that Vittoria bring him his meals there. Come to think of it, Sylvestro and Lenny had certain similarities, although, in Milo's opinion, at the end of his life, Lenny had been living farther out in the rings of the world.

Lenny and Sylvestro had met just once over a meal in Florence at the only restaurant that Sylvestro would agree to dine in: a place called Il Latini. There, one sat family-style at long, checker-clothed tables; it was famous for steak and sizzling pork chops that Sylvestro's parents used to love. They took him there as a child and, therefore, the place held for him a sentimental attraction. Having both gone to Florence to attend one among the several hundred literary award ceremonies that are given out each year in Italy (this one for translation from a Slavic language), Lenny and Sylvestro had sat opposite each other at Il Latini and quickly disagreed about the monumental importance of the Italian literary greats. But then things really went south when Sylvestro imperiously told Lenny that the Sicilian writer Carlo Levi was better than the Torinese writer Primo Levi. When Sylvestro said this, Lenny graciously bowed out of the conversation, as though retiring from a game of chess with a grand master. He then privately complained to Milo that Sylvestro derided Primo Levi because Sylvestro was a closet antisemite. And Lenny may have had a point there, because Sylvestro had subsequently remarked to Milo that Lenny's Italian accent sounded fake—more specifically: Semitic.

Milo was unsure whether or not Lara knew about the subtext of this meeting between the two men; she hadn't been in Florence that evening. And over dinner on the second day of his visit, he broached it when the subject of Lenny's death came up.

Taking a sip of wine, Milo said to her, "I think there were certain similarities between the two men that you probably wouldn't recognize because you didn't know Lenny very well."

"Well, I could say that you didn't know *Sylvestro* very well either." She sounded oddly defensive, protective almost.

"All due respect Lara, I did spend a fair amount of time with Sylvestro."

"I guess that's true," she conceded. "I do hope you know he liked you very much. *And* he respected you," she said, reminding Milo that Sylvestro had always encouraged him to do his university degree in Italian and had endorsed the idea of writing a dissertation on Natalia Ginzburg.

They were dining on turkey cutlets. Lara had reached a critical point some years ago when she could no longer bear to eat red meat or veal and often substituted turkey. Notoriously bland in America, in Italy, turkey was offered in skinless cutlets that took very little preparation to taste ambrosial. In general, in his opinion, meat in Italy was far superior to what you could get in America.

"There's something about Sylvestro that I've always wanted to ask you," Milo said finally.

Lara frowned. "And what's that?"

"Sometimes I wondered from certain things he said if he might have been an . . ." Milo hesitated, deliberating over whether or not he wanted to use the adjective closet before antisemite and decided not to.

Lara reacted with a wary concern that actually surprised him. "I hate this question."

"I'm sorry."

"I hate it because I wondered it myself. *And* even asked him a couple of times."

"And his answer?"

"He would say how I could ask him such a question. That he loved the writing of Natalia Ginzburg. And *she* was Jewish."

"Oh, come on, that's hardly an answer!" Milo exclaimed. "A taste in literature doesn't account for personal prejudice. A great writer is a great writer—hopefully appreciated by everyone."

"True," Lara agreed, "and he certainly did make antisemitic remarks from time to time."

"Well, because your grandfather (and my great-grandfather) was Jewish, weren't you offended?"

Looking perturbed, Lara thought about this for a moment and finally said, "I told him I was. But then he'd just . . . aggressively deny being antisemitic. So I had to drop it."

"Do you have any theory of why he might have been antisemitic?"

She sighed. "Have you, by any chance, heard the theory that Hitler's grandfather was Jewish?"

"It hasn't been proven, I don't think."

"Perhaps, but many psychologists have said his fear that one of his grandparents was Jewish determined him to try to exterminate anyone who had even a small amount of Jewish blood." She paused, momentarily reflective. "As a way of eradicating it in himself . . . Sylvestro mentioned that theory to me several times during our life together. He seemed to be troubled by it. And then, very late in his life, he confessed to me that his paternal grandfather was also Jewish, one Jewish grandparent was something we had in common."

"But why would he try to hide that?"

"I guess he was ashamed, or embarrassed by it. And maybe in his way tried to eradicate his own history. It makes me sad to think about this."

Lara sat back in her chair and took a hefty swig of her white wine, as if to fortify herself. She was drinking the one-dollar-per-bottle house wine purchased at the merchant in Guamo on the same day she'd run into Paolo. Milo had already drunk nearly an entire bottle of red on his own but barely felt anything because it was twelve percent alcohol, a far cry from the fourteen percent big bouquet California wines that were so popular in the U.S. Refilling his glass and holding it up to Lara in a mock toast, he said, "This stuff is so good. I can drink it like water. Sometimes American wines give me a headache."

"Me, too," Lara agreed. She went quiet and Milo noticed a melancholy glint in her eyes. "This will probably surprise you, but guess who loved California wine?"

"I don't have a clue."

"Sylvestro."

"Really! Did he import it?"

Lara stopped sawing her turkey cutlet and looked at him with what seemed like trepidation. "No, he drank it there. He drank it in the U.S."

"I didn't know he went to the U.S."

"He went frequently, as a matter of fact. Most often to D.C." She hesitated. "You just weren't aware of this."

"And he never bothered to look us up?"

A conflicted look came over Lara's finely lined face. "He didn't look you and your mother up because he didn't want either of you to know he was there."

Of course, by now Milo was intrigued. "And why was that?"

Lara looked indecisive, as though trying to figure out how or what she wanted to say next, but finally continued, "I don't think you really know how Sylvestro made his living."

Milo put down his knife and his fork, whose tines were intertwined with a strand of deep-green rapini, and folded his arms protectively over his chest. "This sounds like a trick question. I assume he made his money writing his columns for the *Corriere*."

"He wrote a bimonthly column for the *Corriere*. How much do you think *that* pays?"

"How should I know?"

"Precisely. How *should* or *would* you know?" she repeated.

"I just figured that he had plenty of family money, and because of family money, he could live in a fair amount of leisure."

"As a matter of fact, he didn't inherit all that much from his parents," Lara now explained. "There were unexpected debts. His father wasn't exactly fiscally responsible."

"But Sylvestro left you enough money, though, didn't he?"

"Of course." She hesitated for what seemed to be an odd length of time. "But it wasn't family money. What he left me was a pension from the Italian government."

Milo was completely bewildered and waited for Lara to clarify.

At last, Lara asked him, "You know how people work for the CIA?"

Milo jumped in. "*He* worked for the CIA?"

"Well, he worked *with* the American CIA, but he was actually an analyst with the AISE, Agenzia Informazioni e Sicurezza Esterna. Basically, the Italian equivalent of the CIA."

"But that office is in Rome, isn't it?" Milo said. "I thought he rarely left the villa."

She raised her eyebrows. "Only for the last three years of his life. Before that, he used to go to Rome every other week. He'd spend three nights at the apartment of a good friend of his. On the Via Julia."

"Of course, on the Via Julia," Milo said with unmistakable sarcasm.

Lara ignored him. "This man also worked for the AISE. Sylvestro had his own room in Rome where he kept clothing and, naturally, lots of books. There was a very lovely housekeeper who took good care of him. She'd once worked for his family back when Sylvestro's parents lived in Rome and when his father worked with the ministry. Rome was always like his home away from home."

"So, he never got in touch with us in America because then he'd have to explain why he was over?"

"Pretty much," Lara said. "Oh, by the way, I have some persimmons for dessert."

She got up from the table and went to an island in the kitchen that had shelves for condiments and homemade vinegars and a few bottles of bright-green, delectable olive oil made by a local farmer from the olives on her land. The gold bangles on her arms clattering, Lara reached toward a red ceramic bowl filled with the orange globes of the persimmons, took two, fetched knives from the drawer in the island, and asked Milo to grab two small plates from the breakfront next to which he was sitting.

Armed with a knife, she reminded him to halve the fruit and, with a spoon, scoop it out from the inside. "I can't tolerate you eating the skin."

"It's not bad. It's chewy."

"Sometimes you're such a peasant."

"And that's a surprise to you?"

"Yes, because you also have your refinements."

In silence, each of them ate, savoring the syrupy fruit.

And then Milo remembered something. "Sylvestro's AISE colleague in Rome— Is that his classmate from the Scuola Normale Superiore?" He was referring to the very exclusive university in Pisa that was modeled after the École Normale Supérieure in France.

Lara looked astonished. "Yes, in fact. How did you guess this?"

"You just said something about the housekeeper. Maybe five years ago, Sylvestro took me on a tour of the Normale. And that friend . . . what's his name?"

"Davide Rotelli."

"Yes, Rotelli was there and seemed out of sorts, and Sylvestro teased him that it was because Rotelli's housekeeper in Rome was fonder of Sylvestro than of him. So I just put two and two together."

Lara nodded. "I actually just spoke to Davide a few days ago. He checks in often to see how I've been doing."

Milo went silent for a moment and Lara seemed to be aware of this. "What's on your mind?" she asked him at last.

"I haven't told you this, but while I'm here, I have to go see this American guy. He lives in Pistoia." Milo went on to explain that Matteo Cipolla had been a close friend of Carlo's at Iona College and that he and Rose Marie had recently found out that Matteo was the last person who saw Carlo right before he was killed.

Lara bowed her head in reverence. She clung to complicated emotions regarding Carlo's death, in particular, circumstances in her life that prevented her from immediately returning to America to console her bereaved sister. Lara ended up arriving two weeks after Carlo's funeral with a vague explanation for her delay, and Rose Marie still harbored some resentment toward her for not making the effort to come immediately. No doubt in some reflection about this, Lara kept her eyes averted and focused on sectioning her persimmon and then delivering it delicately to her lips. At last, she looked up at Milo. "So, why do you need to go see this man in Pistoia?"

Milo explained there were things that happened on the last night of Carlo's life that he and Rose Marie still didn't know about. "For one thing, Matteo and Carlo spent that last night together." He found himself pausing, as if for effect and at last said to Lara, "Apparently, Matteo was in love with Carlo, and probably vice versa and on that last night, Matteo was begging Carlo to bring him home to meet Mom. But Carlo flat-out refused his request."

"*Oh Dio*," Lara exclaimed shaking her head. "Your brother was such a tortured soul."

Milo nodded. "Yes, he was. Although Mom can't really see it that way."

Lara looked at him sadly. "You can't expect this kind of objectivity. She lost a child. The most unnatural thing that could ever happen." She paused reflectively. "What makes me sad is that when I talked to Rosie last week, she mentioned none of this to me," Lara said with hurt in her voice.

Milo advised Lara: Try not to take it too personally. That it was difficult for Rose Marie to talk about it. "She's confused. She's disappointed. If there was something between them, she wishes she could have known, wishes she could have at least welcomed Matteo into our life. Because he'd probably still be there now, in our lives. She would like to know him, but obviously . . . she doesn't fly."

Lara shook her head. "I could say then she should make an effort to get over her fear of flying. But I guess we can't be too hard on her. She did have a very frightening experience over the Atlantic."

At this point, Vittoria poked her head into the kitchen to see if their meal was ready to be cleared. "*Prego*," Lara said, and Vittoria quickly and efficiently removed the dishes, leaving the wine glasses. After exchanging a glance with Lara, she gave the table a quick wipe with a large, flat, orange sponge. Then, before leaving them, she placed her hand on Milo's head and ruffled his hair. He could tell that Lara didn't quite approve of this intimate gesture. But he really didn't care. "Vittoria," he addressed her, "I know you have many Albanian acquaintances who have come to Italy.

Have you heard of any Albanians coming here and working in pornography?"

Vittoria's eyes glazed over with sad concern and she nodded. "Unfortunately, I have, Milo."

"Do you actually know people who are involved in this . . . profession?"

Vittoria looked surprised to be asked such a direct question. She frowned at him and then said, "I believe I might know people who know people. Why do you ask?"

Glancing at Lara who was looking at him with consternation, he turned back to Vittoria. "We can talk about it some other time. No rush."

Vittoria nodded and quickly left the kitchen.

Waiting a few moments, at last Lara said, "Why did you bring that up with her?"

"Because I want to understand this. Let's just say I know people involved in it. In Italy."

Lara looked alarmed. "Are you? Involved in it?"

"Stop! Of course not."

"Well, I think you can see those questions made her very uncomfortable. She's very proper, you know. And by the way, she's one of the lucky ones to get out and find sustaining work. I know she didn't exactly say it, but she probably does know people who have done these kinds of things, but only in order to survive."

29.

Paolo got in touch with Milo to say that Giacomo, the muscled man he'd met at Master Club (the gym), had some pertinent information about a local studio that was making pornographic films. Due to soccer practice, Paolo was unable to meet Milo at Master Club, so they decided to link up during the *passeggiata* on Fillungo, one of the main pedestrian thoroughfares of Lucca that is lined with all sorts of retail shops, small café-bars, and a dizzying number of optical stores that cater to the self-indulgent whims of many Italians who make frequent purchases of eyeglasses.

The *passeggiata* is an Italian tradition still maintained in certain cities where citizens put on their most fashionable getups and walk (often arm in arm) down a designated street. Fillungo was wide and accommodated fairly large crowds.

The rendezvous was outside an easy landmark, a store that sold lingerie for women and silk briefs and boxer shorts for men, the display window animated with mannequins draped in very skimpy, satiny fabrics, suggestive in a way that relegated them more to the category of one of the high-end porn shops found on lower Seventh Avenue back in New York City. And yet such a store window display was, in Italy, standard fare. In general, ads and billboards in Italy showed more skin. In the airport in Milan, while

Milo had been waiting for his connecting flight to Pisa, he saw a poster for Pirelli tires that featured a beautiful naked woman wreathed in bright, metallic, industrial-size chains. He reflected that this sort of larger-than-life display would be shouted down if it were on a billboard in America.

From fairly far away down the street, Milo spotted Paolo standing outside the lingerie store, talking to a rather tall woman whose hair was worn in long, glossy tresses. Paolo was dressed in what looked like a silk shirt that hugged his body and very tight black pants. The woman was leaning back against the wall of the several-hundred-year-old building and Paolo was standing close to her, speaking softly, his left arm outstretched and his body canted forward, his lips only inches from hers. Milo stopped, not wanting to disturb them. Somehow knowing he was there, Paolo looked to his left and spied Milo standing in an attitude of uncertainty. He then waved him on and soon Milo was next to them.

"This is my American friend, Milo," Paolo said to the woman. And to Milo, "This is Antonella Testimoni."

"Hello," Milo said and shook the woman's delicate hand. "Interesting surname. 'Witnesses,'" he added in English.

"Well, it's one of those names that relates to a profession. Like some people are called *Judici*, 'judges,'" she said, the last word in English. "There were professional witnesses in Italy in previous centuries," she told him. "By the way, this store is ours." She pointed to an eyeglass store next to the intimate garment store.

In contrast to the lingerie store, Antonella's family's window display was very tastefully done. It featured what looked like pairs of glasses, some of them metal-frame relics that limned a history of eyewear. In one corner of the window was an even older-looking pair made of crudely bent wire. Pointing to it, Milo asked Antonella how old it was. "Two hundred years old, actually," she said. "Those are from Venice. Where, by the way, the very first pair of eyeglasses in the world was made," she added proudly.

"Really?" Milo said with jocular incredulity. "So *that* explains the Italian fetish for eyeglasses."

"Yes!" Paolo interjected enthusiastically. "Eyeglasses for every day of the week. Or every mood."

"And that probably doesn't even count a person's collection of sunglasses," Milo said.

"Anyway, Milo." Paolo finally got down to business. "Anta here grew up with a woman who now lives in Pistoia. She asked *her* friend and I asked *my* friend. Neither of them remembers ever running into an American guy in his twenties who looks like this ginger you are planning to see."

A moment later, Antonella kissed Paolo gently on both cheeks, gave Milo a warm cordial goodbye, and went back inside her shop.

Knowing that Paolo was a bit of a player and tended to have lots of short-term relationships, Milo asked, "Have you met her family yet?"

Paolo made an equivocal motion with his hand; Milo decided not to press the conversation. "Do you want to walk?" He pointed to the crowded corridor of Fillungo.

"Sure. But let's get off this busy street."

"How about we go up and do a turn around the wall?"

They exited Via Fillungo and made a left on dark, narrow Via Santa Lucia. They passed a small high-end grocery that sold local cheeses and fancily wrapped packages of pasta and was the go-to place for white truffles during the autumn. The owner noticed Paolo and waved cordially. And then he recognized Milo, whom he also knew, and his eyes brightened. On impulse, Milo ducked his head inside the store. "How is the *signora* doing?" the man asked sadly. "So sorry to hear about Signor Calderi," he said of Sylvestro. "Please pass along my condolences. And I have a gift package for her if you'd like to take it." Milo told the man he'd be happy to retrieve the package and would stop by again before the midday closing of the stores in the center of town.

They crossed the Piazza San Michele and headed down San Paolino, a street that was a direct artery to Lucca's surrounding wall and was always thronged with tourists, some of whom Milo could spot by nationality: Germans tended to wear backpacks and Birkenstocks; Americans were often the overweight folks in sneakers with heavy cameras slung around their necks who spoke in loud twangy accents. He cringed when he heard his squawking countrymen and glanced over at Paolo, who didn't seem to notice. But of course he wouldn't.

They took a stone pathway up to the top of the wall, a wide boulevard lined with a straight row of tall linden trees and dotted with pavilions that were either uninhabited or offered restaurants or cafés. Walking the walls allowed a panoramic view of the city, its brick towers with plantings on top of them and the pale-white wedding cake of the cathedral where one could see the famous Della Quercia sculpture of Ilaria del Carretto, which attracted more visitors than any other site in the city. Milo had no doubt that the Americans he recognized on Via San Paolino would, at some point, make their way to the inner chapel and at least for a few moments be transfixed in contemplation of the serene-looking noblewoman who died at an early age. Her death had not only been an inspiration to the great sculptor but also to the Cipollas, who presumably created the yellow insignia of Ilaria Films, a distribution business dedicated to pornography that employed undocumented workers.

Milo filled Paolo in on what he didn't know, including the fact that the Cipolla brothers named their company after Ilaria. "So, what did Giacomo find out about the film studios?"

Paolo nodded and raised a finger. "From a friend of his, he heard about one such place. Near Master Club, actually. Giacomo is going to get the address, so maybe we can check it out by the time I get back from France?"

"Giacomo can always call me directly at the villa, if he'd like."

"I'll tell him that," Paolo said. "He already has the telephone of the villa because his family are the villa's plumbers and have been for two hundred years. And he was actually there recently fixing a toilet."

They had reached a long straightaway on the top of the wall that afforded a striking view of a pointy row of blackish-green cypress trees and the distant blue outline of the Apennines.

"So, when are you going to visit this Pistoia brother of the man I met?"

"I haven't been able to make contact with him. If I don't reach him by this evening, I'll just go to the address and knock on the door."

"Well, whatever you do, be careful. There are some not-so-nice places in Pistoia and despite your Italian, you'll stick out. You have the look of an American and the *zingari* will see that, and they are very good at robbing people. They jostle against you, and the next thing you know, they've run off with your wallet."

Milo assured Paolo that he'd been jostled by street people before (in Rome) and knew how to handle them.

30.

Yet another person felt compelled to trot out their English. The problem in this case was that Milo wanted to speak coherently to Davide Rotelli, Sylvestro's colleague from the AISE. Milo assumed that a good deal of English was required for intelligence analysis and that Rotelli, who had a less-than-confident command, would hopefully grow weary of the task and at last lapse into Italian.

Rotelli was Pisano by birth. He and Sylvestro had met at an exclusive private school, and then both had gone on to attend the Normale before being conscripted into the service of Italian intelligence. Rotelli had to come up to Pisa from Rome to give a lecture at the Normale.

Lara was clearly in frequent contact with Rotelli, and Milo was suspicious. Now that his aunt had lost her husband, he wondered if Rotelli actually might be courting her. At any rate, without telling Milo, she'd gone to Rotelli and told him that Milo knew some people—quite possibly Americans—involved in the Italian pornography trade made with undocumented workers (although he'd never mentioned Matteo's involvement in this, she somehow thought to make the connection), and Rotelli had asked if Milo would meet up with him. Although he was annoyed with his aunt for blabbering, Milo thought perhaps Rotelli might help him understand the troubling landscape of this illegal profession. And so he'd agreed to the meeting.

Rotelli suggested Camposanto, a twelfth-century cemetery that was originally meant to be a church. With its Gothic arches and windows, its flooring inlaid with inscribed tombs, and a broad courtyard manicured with stretches of bright green grass, Camposanto was a pleasure to stroll through. Rotelli, whom Milo had met on two other occasions, was a tall, bony man who looked to be in his early sixties and wore his hair in a ponytail. Dressed in a fashionable though ill-fitting suit, he somehow gave off the appearance of an aging rocker. Like many men with his level of education, Rotelli felt he needed to give the younger man a more comprehensive sense of Camposanto. Clearly, this was a preamble to whatever Rotelli wanted to speak to him about, and Milo thought it was best to keep walking, to say little, and just wait.

"I assume you know what happens in Pisa during the second war of the world," Rotelli continued in his uncertain, unidiomatic English as they began strolling along one of the long colonnades, treading over the slabs of ancient, inlaid tombs.

"I do somewhat," Milo said in Italian.

"Well, the bombs *fells*. From the Allies. Before Italy left the Axis. To this building, came lots of damages and destructions of artwork."

Just then Milo spotted a man up on a ladder examining a fresco that, on closer inspection, looked as though something had stained it.

"I can see that something happened to *that* fresco," Milo said, stubbornly adhering to Italian. Then he stopped, turned to Rotelli, and said, "I know for your analysis, you need to have English. But take it from me, with certain exceptions, Italian is much more beautiful. And as I've been away from Italy for almost a year, I was hoping that perhaps we might continue in it."

The shameless flattery worked like a charm, and the man reverted to the cultured Italian that Milo expected from him.

At last, Rotelli said, "So, shall we talk about the people you know involved in this pornography trade?"

Milo was brought up short by Rotelli's question. But then realized if he wanted to get an understanding of what was going on, it behooved him to explain that it was actually just one person who'd been a friend of his late brother.

Rotelli nodded. "I see," and said with feeling, "May I assume then that you have some understanding of the dire situation (at the moment) of refugees who are desperate to live here, to survive here, and how many of them get involved in illegal trades?"

"Some understanding, yes," Milo said.

Rotelli went on to explain that the shameless exploitation of innocent people in global sex trafficking was a natural feeder of untrained actors into the porn industry. "What surprises me in this particular case is that the person you are here to see, the person involved in this industry, is an American. A colleague of mine who specializes in this area said he's never before come across an American involved in or distributing pornography made here, illegal or otherwise. "So may I ask: who is this person?"

Milo felt idiotic, not to mentioned cornered. He'd certainly had no desire to bring Matteo to the attention of anybody in Rotelli's circle of intelligence colleagues. For one thing, he needed unimpeded access to Matteo; he needed to speak to him about Carlo. He could hardly express any of this vexation to Rotelli and began worrying about just how punishable (in Italy) the crime of distributing illegal pornography was.

Without waiting for his answer, Rotelli continued, "As it is in the U.S., in Italy it's illegal to make pornography with undocumented workers. Italy has many problems and because it has many problems, there has been a bit less focus on these various pornography studios." He raised a finger. "Although we do crack down on them.

"Anyway, when Lara mentioned that you might be knowing some people or person involved in this pornography, I felt I needed to tell you that these people can be dangerous and you need to stay away from them. I must insist on this. I am very fond of your aunt. She is worrying about you, and I don't want her to worry."

Perhaps Milo was being cynical, but to him, Rotelli's concern for Lara was out of self-interest. Clearly the man had designs on her. "Okay, I hear you," he said at last.

Rotelli patted him on the back. "Good. *Dunque.* So let's begin here."

Begin? Milo thought with annoyance.

Rotelli continued, "When your aunt told me about this American, I asked one of my colleagues in Rome who tracks the banking system in Italy for money laundering. There is one American man on our radar. He comes from a town in the area of New York where you grew up. And he is the same age as your late brother. His name is Matteo Cipolla."

Milo wilted into himself.

Rotelli raised his eyebrows and persisted. "Lara told me his name. I checked."

Milo looked down at his feet and nodded.

"This man is already on a list. He's already been surveilled. In fact, my colleague even before I spoke to him had scrutinized deposits and withdrawals into various bank accounts of this man. In the Cassa di Risparmio di Veneto in Europe there have been large deposits from an untraceable bank account in Central America. We have our ways of identifying those accounts, and we discovered an account in the country of Belize that belongs to . . . I asked Lara if she thought you might recognize the name, but she actually recognized it; according to her, it is the name of . . ." Rotelli fetched a small notebook out of the pocket of his suit jacket, opened it quickly, and then read out, "Leonard D'Ambrosio."

Milo stopped walking. He felt a rush of blood going up his neck and into his head and was breathless. Strangely, he couldn't feel his legs and was afraid of tripping on the uneven tomb-strewn walkway. Noticing this, Rotelli offered him a steadying arm and said, "Keep walking, it's better for you."

"Okay," Milo weakly agreed and they continued.

Allowing him a minute or so to recover his composure, Rotelli continued, "Many deposits. And many withdrawals. Large numbers in both directions, and in the hundreds of thousands of dollars. These, I assure you, are not payments for a personal library of pornography."

In the midst of his momentary fragmented thinking, it occurred to Milo that something like this sort of connection had always been Delzio's hunch and therefore something he'd secretly feared all along. He remained in bewildered silence. At last, he asked, "So, what about the money transfers?"

His eyes focused distantly, Rotelli replied, "It seems clear that Leonard D'Ambrosio and this Matteo Cipolla are co-investors in a film production and distribution company."

But how, *how* could Val have so blatantly lied about and covered up their connection to Lenny? Val had seemed sincere when he denied knowing him. Beyond this, he'd been painfully candid about his acquaintance with Carlo, about Carlo and Matteo's relationship, about Carlo's final hours.

"Now, this D'Ambrosio has a sister in America, correct?"

Milo managed to nod and explained that shortly before his death, Lenny had transferred 1.5 million dollars into their joint bank account.

Rotelli nodded. "Yes, but does *she* know where the money came from?"

"To be honest, I have no idea."

"Did she report the transfusion of money to any authority?"

"I don't believe so."

"Then she may already know about this business."

Milo shook his head and sighed. "I would have thought she might have told me if she did."

"She might be too embarrassed to tell you. Or maybe she was, or is, part of it."

"I really doubt that," Milo said emphatically, although he realized he couldn't know this for sure.

Just then, a young man with carefully combed blond hair and his perfectly turned-out mother came around a corner of a low, rambling building at Camposanto; noticing Rotelli, their faces beamed with recognition and delight.

"Ah, Signor Rotelli!" they exclaimed, and approached him with obvious respect and reverence—like suppli-cants. "We are really looking forward to your lecture." Rotelli, in turn, greeted them cordially and waving good-bye, continued walking. Turning back to Milo, squinting through his glasses against the surprisingly potent sun-light of the early-April afternoon, Rotelli said, "I must tell you that in my world, you often see the most ordinary people taking these kinds of unfathomable and extraor-dinary risks."

31.

Disoriented and demoralized by his unforeseen conversation with Rotelli, Milo wandered around Pisa, looking for an empty public pay phone, which wasn't easy to find due to the number of students wedging themselves into the small spaces and making leisurely phone calls, smoking continuously. At last, he found an empty cabin that reeked of tobacco fumes and cheap-smelling cologne, and using his international calling card, managed to get through to Delzio.

The detective listened without comment as Milo detailed what he'd learned about the money transfers between an account belonging to Lenny in Belize and Matteo Cipolla's account at the Cassa di Risparmio di Veneto.

Delzio said, "I must say I'm impressed that you were able to dig all this up, Milo."

Milo explained that it was pure luck, that his aunt happened to have a direct connection to Italian Intelligence.

Delzio said, "FYI: I think *our* pension plan might be better than what they give college professors."

"I'll take my chances and stick to academia," Milo told him. There was silence on the line. And then he asked Delzio, "Do you have any theory of why Val might have told me such an elaborate lie? Why he would hide his affiliation with Lenny?"

"Self-protection of course. Not to mention that he probably realized you'd be gutted by the truth? I've always told you that you gave that guy way too much credit. You were so impressed by where he went to school and all that."

"I'm not forgetting what you said, believe me," Milo interrupted him.

Before the call ended, the last thing Delzio told him was, "That there was an involved business relationship between them all is, I know, upsetting to hear. But we don't have the whole picture yet. Let me see if I can find out more from this end, from here."

"But are you going to question Val?"

"Of course not. I'd get nowhere. And I have no jurisdiction. You're in Italy, after all."

Nursing her glass of wine, Lara said, "So how did it go at Campo Santo?"

"How did it go at Campo Santo? I'm surprised Rotelli didn't tell you how it went . . . at Campo Santo?"

Looking chastened, she shook her head. "I asked him. He said it was a private conversation between the two of you and that if I wanted to know something, I should ask you." She paused, tilting her head to the side in an inquisitive attitude. "As I am doing now."

It was late afternoon and they were sitting at the kitchen table, sharing a bottle of local white wine that they kept passing to one another using the lazy Susan. Filling his second glass to the brim, Milo grunted. Of course, he was annoyed that without his permission, Lara had shared intel with Rotelli and yet he also knew that had she not said anything to Rotelli, he never would have learned about Lenny's connection to the Cipollas.

Milo was still struggling with the fact that Val had lied so boldly about knowing Lenny, particularly because he'd told Milo that if someone mentioned to him that they'd taught Italian at a local college he'd certainly remember them. It was artfully deceptive, which was galling. Not to mention that Val had been relatively candid about his and Matteo's business dealings—he easily could have kept all that to himself. But then again, when he'd first encountered Val at the diner on that Saturday night, Val probably had no idea that Lenny and Milo knew one another. Milo had brought Lenny up *after* Val had already leveled with him about the porn distribution business and Carlo's objections to it.

Now he said to Lara, "Basically he doesn't think I should go visit Matteo in Pistoia. *Or* go anywhere near anyone involved in making these films."

"Because it's risky?"

"He says there are a lot of sketchy people working in the porn industry, and some of them, according to him, are dangerous."

"Well, that's a known fact. About eastern European foreigners coming here engaging in illegal activities. They're the ones, by the way, who bring guns into the country."

Hesitating a moment, trying to contain his vexation, Milo said, "I told you that I have to speak to Matteo who now, thanks to me, is being doubly watched. There are things I need to talk to him about. I just hope to God he doesn't get arrested before I get to him."

"Why would he get arrested?"

"If the movies he distributes are made illegally, can't he be arrested for them?"

Lara remained quiet thinking about this and at last said perhaps the people who procured the actors, managed them, and gave them places to live were more likely to be held responsible.

"I obviously don't know what his involvement is. But do me a favor?" Milo said at last. "Can you please not discuss my next moves with Rotelli? When I go to Pistoia, for example, I insist that you not tell him."

Agitated now, Lara said, "I don't know if I can promise that. You're my nephew as well as my guest and I feel responsible for you. What would I tell your mother if something happened to you?"

"My mother?" Milo retorted. "My mother is the main reason why I'm going to Pistoia." He reminded Lara that Rose Marie was hardly satisfied with what Val had explained to them about Carlo and needed him to speak to Matteo himself. "And now that I know that Val is a liar . . . there's even more of an imperative. Who knows what the truth about Carlo's death really is?"

"I understand what you're saying here, but obviously I still think it's a bad idea."

"Okay, then you call her and tell her you're standing in my way." Milo knew he didn't have to bring up the fact that Rose Marie still resented Lara for not attending Carlo's funeral.

Just then, the telephone rang. When Lara answered it, she looked momentarily confused but then, smiling at Milo, said, "*Ah, certo, certo. Ti passo à Milo,*" handed him the phone, and whispered, *"Paolo chiamanda da Francia."* Paolo was calling from France.

"Really?" Milo said as Lara handed him the receiver.

"*Ragazzo*," Paolo said to him.

"Everything okay?"

"You decide. I just called Mama, who told me Giacomo called. He has the address of the warehouse where this *questionable* pornography is made. He says he will take us there in two days. I'll be home tomorrow. So, we can go before you leave back for America."

Glancing at Lara, wishing she wasn't in the room with him, Milo didn't quite know what to say in response. He needed to move the conversation along, so he said, "Wow, that's great! Good for you! Tell me: how often do you call your mother from the road?"

"Too often is the answer to your question, you *stronzo*. But it's different in Italy, you know. Men like me call their mothers often. Unlike in America where many children live thousands of miles from their families. Anyway, when those phones you carry with you become affordable and common, my life will be over."

"Unless you marry Antonella."

"Then they—Antonella and my mother—both will be calling me! Constantly!" Paolo exclaimed.

32.

Despite her disapproval of his trip to Pistoia, Lara insisted on dropping Milo at Porto San Donato in Lucca an hour before his train's departure for Pistoia; he wanted to stop in at the Cathedrale San Martino.

Whenever he went inside a church, Milo always struggled with his ambivalence toward genuflecting. In the company of his mother, he managed the flourish of the gesture because he knew she took comfort in it, took comfort in his momentary embrace of the religion he was born into but sadly no longer had faith in, the religion she practiced on a daily basis and that, she claimed, helped to ease her constant pain of having lost a son.

Once inside the nave, he stood opposite a seventh-century wooden crucifix, the carved face of Christ looking downcast. Local legend attested that this hewn crucifix was discovered in the Middle East, placed on an uninhabited boat that sailed across the Mediterranean, and directed by a divine hand until it landed on the shores of the Ligurian Sea. Regarding the statue, considered by many to be as holy as the Shroud of Turin, inspired Milo to dip his fingers in the fount of sanctified water and make the sign of the cross.

The custodian in a small booth preceding the inner sanctum that housed the Della Quercia sculpture immediately recognized Milo from his many previous visits and, with a brown-toothed smile, remarked, "Ah, you're back. Good to have you with us again. But don't you usually come later in the year?"

"Usually, but not always," Milo replied, not really surprised that he was recognized. He extracted his billfold to pay the entrance fee: fifty thousand lira.

Waving at him dismissively, with an attitude of authority, the man said, "No, no, you don't pay this time. You've given a lot of money to the city for this sculpture and at least deserve one free view. *And* you're lucky," the man added. "There is only one other person in there."

The only other person turned out to be a diminutive, well-dressed Japanese woman who stood a few feet from the head of the funerary sculpture in a kind of mesmerized rapture that made it obvious she had some sort of personal rapport with the marble figure lying in her attitude of death. Milo didn't want to intrude upon whatever it was that held the woman so spellbound. But then she noticed him and, nodding her head, made her way into the next room, leaving Milo in solitary contemplation of the noblewoman in her flowing garment, with its stiff collar and pendant sleeves, lying not on a cushion that might have been afforded her by a coffin, but rather a slab that lent her an eternal marmoreal repose. Milo had always been struck by the mysterious sadness her face exuded. Transfixed, he leaned over the railing that protected her from the throngs of visitors and put his face inches from hers, trying to imagine her final moments, as countless times he'd tried to imagine his brother's final moments, tried to imagine what Carlo's unfulfilled life would have been like, would have become. Like Carlo,

Ilaria perhaps faced death as a painful anachronism, foisted upon her before she really understood or experienced love. She was, after all, a young girl whose marriage had been arranged. For somebody in her position, sex was perhaps more of a duty than a pleasure. Once again, he thought of her image imported to the label of the pornographic video cassettes, indignant that her likeness had been tarnished.

An hour later, on the train in Altopascio, two heavily mascaraed teenaged girls with large, knockoff designer purses came barreling through the car, cackling and taunting each other. They glanced at Milo and raised their heavily penciled-in eyebrows. They were speaking in rapid Lucchese, and he felt frustrated in his momentary incapacity to make out *precisely* what they were saying, but it had something to do with two boys they knew and whose was "bigger." After saying this, one of them actually winked at Milo. She probably assumed that he was an Anglo foreigner and didn't understand.

The Pistoia station was crowded, as was the labyrinth of streets surrounding it, but as Milo walked into the depths of the small city, the crowds slowly thinned out. Constantly referring to the map of the city that Lara had given him, he passed a narrow warren of shops, many of them still closed and draped in early morning shade. One of the shuttered businesses he passed looked like a gun store, an astonishing discovery in a country where handguns were illegal. Fascinated and also bewildered, he approached the display window, which was literally filled with all kinds of pistols, many of them antique-looking. A printed sign in the window proclaimed that pistols were invented in Pistoia. And then it occurred to him that the Italian word *pistola* was as close to the name Pistoia as it was the English word *pistol*.

Matteo Cipolla lived in a modern-looking, five-story building that looked as though it had been built in the last ten or fifteen years, a building that, compared to the several-hundred-year-old Mediterranean-style buildings on either side of it, looked brand new. The façade was constructed of gleaming rose-colored granite, and the five steps leading up to the vestibule were black-and-white-veined travertine. Milo glanced at his watch and saw that he was fifteen minutes early and was deciding where to go to wait when the window of a bright-red Fiat parked around ten yards up the street rolled down. A swarthy, hefty-looking man with a thick, dark beard called out, "*Awwoo, ragazzo*," before sucking on what appeared to be a Marlboro that was dangling from his lips. The man was motioning to him.

"Me? You're talking to me?" Milo asked as he headed toward the car.

"Yes, I am talking to you. I work with Rotelli," the guy said with a heavy Roman accent.

"*Davide* Rotelli?" Milo asked, incredulous.

"Certainly, *Rotelli*."

"*And?*" he said.

"*And?*" the man repeated with rancor. "*And* you can stop playing detective and let us handle this."

Although Milo was taken aback, he managed to reply, "I'm visiting a friend, okay. Nothing more. So, no problem."

In a gesture of disgust, the man threw his half-smoked cigarette into the street. "I'll tell you . . . what the problem is. The problem is privileged pricks like you sticking yours into—" He indicated the building and then rolled up his window.

To put some distance between himself and the angry man, Milo decided to take a short walk down the street. The terse, unpleasant exchange kept replaying itself. Rotelli must have told the man who he was, but then how would the guy have recognized him? Had Lara ignored his request and informed Rotelli that he was going to Pistoia? Was Matteo now under renewed surveillance as a result of the conversation at Campo Santo? Preoccupied with all of this, Milo almost bumped into Matteo, who with his shock of bright-red, unruly hair and well-over-six-foot-tall frame, was, nevertheless, hard to miss. He was accompanied by a much shorter woman, who looked to be in her early-to-mid-twenties.

Matteo stopped short and looked surprised. "Oh!" He glanced at his watch. "You're fifteen minutes early." He reached out and vigorously shook Milo's hand. Then he introduced Milo to the woman whose name was Sonia and whose dyed white-blond hair was cropped close so that it fell on and highlighted her prominent cheekbones. Visibly nervous, Sonia glanced at Matteo, but then her eyes met Milo's, and her stare lingered. In heavily accented Italian, she told Matteo she needed to get back to her own apartment; however, she'd left something of hers at his. "You know the code," he told her. "The door is open."

She hurried ahead of them into the building. Matteo held the door open for Milo, who couldn't help noticing the bulge in his breast pocket. "Is that a gun?"

Matteo said it was.

"How come you need a gun?"

His tone heavy with sarcasm, Matteo said, "I mean, you know what we export? They are some people I have to deal with who are . . . let's say, questionable."

"Like who?"

"Oh, like people who help us get the actors. They say they are from places like Albania and Romania but sometimes they're not. Sometimes I ask for ID because I want to know who I'm dealing with. And it often doesn't match what they've originally told me. Also, we pay in cash, so I have to carry around a lot of it." He patted his other slightly bulging pocket. "So this protects me."

Milo asked, "Did you buy this at that gun store? The one near the train station?"

Matteo chuckled. "That place? That place isn't a gun store. It's more like a rinky-dink gun museum. Because pistols were supposedly invented here in Pistoia." Pointing to the protrusion under his jacket, Matteo said, "I got this baby in Amsterdam."

He led the way to his building and opened both the outer and inner doors with a keypad. Inside, the building was even more expensive looking, with arched ceilings and gold-leaf moldings. Without further word, they took the elevator to the top floor. Matteo opened the door to his apartment and led the way in.

It was a sparsely furnished one-bedroom flat with a sizeable balcony inhabited by a bottle palm tree and two metal chairs placed haphazardly around it. There was a single piece of furniture in the living area: a cheap-looking, contoured, yellow sofa that looked as though it had known a better life in a Scandinavian hotel. The sofa was on castors that were set on a dark sisal rug that was worn in places. An enormous, clunky-looking television perched on a pedestal. Just visible beyond the living room was the bedroom with a mattress lying directly on the floor. Around the television there seemed to be no trace of "product"—not that Milo really expected to find a repository of the crudely labeled videos in Matteo's possession. From where he stood, he could see into the small kitchen and noticed a fairly large Gaggia espresso maker that probably cost at least a thousand dollars. With her back to them, Sonia was standing near it, presumably brewing coffee; its redolence pervaded the flat.

"That's a manly coffee machine you got yourself there," Milo remarked.

"Speaking of . . ." was Matteo's reply.

"*Here* is coffee," Sonia said as she emerged from the kitchen with two small white cups of espresso.

Looking at her more closely now, Milo was struck by a kind of familiarity and couldn't quite place it. And then realized that Sonia somewhat resembled the pale-haired actress in the porn movie that he had partially watched. It was the perfect, sensual bow of her lips that he thought he remembered, a body girlishly lanky and yet graced with the curves of a mature woman. His heart began pounding as he tried to scrutinize her without being too obvious, but then he quickly arrived at the not-quite-certain conclusion that she couldn't be the same person he'd watched in the film. He did notice, however, that she kept avoiding his glance. After delivering the coffee, Sonia disappeared and moments later emerged from the bedroom wearing a long, expensive-looking wool coat and a Gucci purse (which Milo assumed was imitation and probably made in one of those knockoff factories in Calabria or Sicily that produced remarkably good product).

"Headed home?" Matteo asked her.

"I have to pick something up first," she replied tersely. Nodding to Milo, she said "goodbye" in English and left the apartment.

Noting that Sonia had gone uninvited into the bedroom, which indicated to him that they had a close relationship, Milo asked, "Is she your girlfriend?"

Blushing to the roots of his bright-red hair, Matteo said, "No, not at all." He went on to say that he and Sonia were good friends and that she understood him (whatever that meant). "Why do you ask?" And yet the tone in his voice telegraphed he knew precisely why the question was being asked. He turned back to Milo now. "*Dica*," he said. "So tell me."

"Val mentioned why I wanted to see you."

Nodding, Matteo said, "Yes, but I'd rather hear it directly from you."

"Okay, then. I never knew . . . or maybe I should say my mother and I wish we'd known about how close you were to Carlo, specifically about the argument you had with him the night before he died." As the words hit him, Matteo's head slumped slightly. "And though Val told us, we'd like to hear from you directly why, after the accident, you never came to find us."

Matteo made an equivocating gesture with his hands. "Very simple. First, I would not have been able to do this, I just couldn't bring myself forward without explaining what my feelings toward him were. And as my brother has already told you, *this* was something that Carlo *absolutely* did not want either of you to know."

"Yes, I understand this," Milo said. "But I guess . . . well, one thing we'd like to understand, what we've been wondering is: Don't you believe Carlo was in love with you, too?"

Matteo's head jolted upward with the impact of the question. He turned his hands over, studied them, glanced up at the ceiling, and then his eyes once again met Milo's. "Honestly I can't say. I always hoped or thought that he was and just couldn't admit it . . . to himself. Much less to me."

"Well, he was," Milo told him. "I read letters he wrote to a . . ." (he wasn't going to bring up Lenny D'Ambrosio just yet) "friend about it. He just couldn't come to terms with it. He struggled with a lot of things. I mean, I was his brother and most of the time I found him incredibly hard to reach."

Nodding, Matteo said, "I can tell you this: I spent a lot of time with him, we were very close, and I *was* able to reach him. I just couldn't bring the relationship to the place where I wanted it to be." He shrugged. "So, I settled for what he could give me. Which wasn't enough and, obviously, was a great mistake."

Milo said he understood.

"And yet," Matteo went on, "even though he knew how I felt about him, he never tried to pull away. Until that last night. Something set him off. And he started by attacking our business."

"So, why then, do you think?"

"I've thought about it a lot obviously. After listening to him going on about it, I finally told him that he was using the complaint as an excuse, avoiding the real conversation . . . I think Val mentioned that he was on me to confront Carlo directly about it all." Matteo hesitated. "Carlo also knew how financially involved Val and I were by then and that we couldn't just bail and give up the business. He knew we'd lose all our money."

Milo considered this and then asked, "Why do you think Carlo cared so much that we'd find out about how . . . both of you felt about one another?"

Shaking his head, Matteo said, "It was like he was afraid that . . . you and your mother would come to the wrong conclusion about him."

"Wrong conclusion?"

Matteo shifted uncomfortably in his chair. "I can't explain it. But those were the exact words he used."

"But it wouldn't have mattered to us," Milo agonized. "Why didn't—why couldn't he realize this?"

"Precisely. Why?" Matteo asked miserably. In his agitation, he kept tapping one of his feet up and down on the tile floor and rubbing both hands on his knees, as though to ward away some kind of physical pain. Studying him in this attitude of agitation, Milo realized that Matteo and Carlo had a similar look: both were tall and skinny and pale and comported themselves with nervous restraint.

"He kept so much from me, from us," Milo remarked.

The conversation lapsed momentarily and, finally, Milo said, "How did you get involved in your . . . distribution business, if you don't mind my asking?"

Matteo frowned and, with reluctance, said, "I spent the summer of my freshman year over here. I met two guys from the Ukraine who were bringing people in and making deals with filmmakers. They needed someone to get involved in the distribution side and made it seem like there was a great opportunity to make some serious money. Before that I was planning on going into accounting. So I got involved, and things started going well and I eventually convinced Val to get involved also."

"But what about the actors?" Milo asked. "They're undocumented." Matteo nodded. "Aren't they being exploited?"

Matteo frowned. "How so, exploited? They get paid well. I obviously know how much they get paid. It's way more than they could make in Italy doing menial work like gardening or being cleaners. The challenge is that they're here illegally, so their life is naturally limited."

"But where do they live?"

"Apartments are provided to them. They share."

"But how many people to an apartment?"

Matteo stared him with a look of sad frustration. "I can't really get into this with you . . . for many reasons. And it's better that you don't know."

"But I *want* to know!" Milo insisted.

Matteo was shaking his head. "I need to protect myself and my brother and the business. I really can't divulge anything more."

Feeling almost breathless, Milo continued, "Okay, but then you will tell me about Lenny D'Ambrosio."

Matteo looked beleaguered. "What about Lenny D'Ambrosio?"

"Val lied to me and said that you guys didn't know him."

Matteo said, "But I think you suspected all along that we did know him, right?"

"Wrong!" Milo insisted. "I literally just found out about it. I knew Lenny came to Italy often, but he always told me he was coming over to visit his sick aunts in Perugia."

Nodding, Matteo said, "He did that, too, visited his sick aunts. But yes, Val lied to you. And there's a simple reason why he lied to you and that has nothing to do with us and has everything to do with Lenny. Lenny *made* us swear no matter what not to tell anyone he got involved in the business. In life or death were his exact words. I'm sure you can imagine him saying something like that."

Milo nodded. Yes, he could. "But his involvement in your *business*, it seems like such a coincidence."

"It's not. I'd met him several times through Carlo. You probably didn't know that Lenny became Carlo's . . . I don't know, confessor. So he obviously learned about me. And actually looked me up here. Carlo told him where I was and he came to see me. I happened to be with one of the actors, and he took one look at her and was completely gone. He lost his mind over her.

"She owed a lot of money to people who'd brought her into the country from Albania and after he got to know her, he was determined to pay them off. But then when he was dealing with some of the guys, *on his own* he saw an opportunity to become an investor, and he asked me if he could become involved. We actually needed money at the time, so I agreed."

"Is this woman around now?" Milo asked.

"I don't go to the film sets anymore. I don't deal with the actors anymore. I have someone right now I trust who takes the money to them."

Milo pointed out that Matteo hadn't answered his question.

"That's right, I didn't. Because there are things and people that I will not discuss with you. He was involved with several women, most I didn't really know. But you're really here to talk about your brother, aren't you?"

Milo persisted. "Did you know about a woman named Vesuvia who went to the U.S. to visit Lenny?"

"Are you listening to me, Milo?" Matteo asked with impatience. "Look, I understand all this Lenny business is a surprise to you. And I *can* tell you what I know about him, which isn't a lot more than I've already said." Milo doubted this. "But there's something you need to know, which is more important than any of this."

"And what's that?" Milo asked.

And then Matteo told him that the morning of the car accident, after he and Carlo had spent a sleepless night in the misery of what seemed like endless argument, knowing Carlo was heading home for the day, Matteo explained, "I went and sat in his car. I told him that I wanted to ride with him back to Harrison—I promised to get out before we got to your neighborhood. I was . . . well, I was desperate . . . I told him it was okay if I didn't meet your mother,

I just wanted a few more minutes with him. And finally, he agreed. And we started driving."

"Wait! So you were *in* the car with him when the accident happened?" Milo could barely get the words out.

Matteo nodded. "Yes, I was in the car with him."

For several moments Milo didn't have the wherewithal to speak. But then he managed to ask, "Why didn't we know this? Why didn't you inform the police?"

Matteo continued, "I realize this is not easy to hear . . . to learn, and I specifically asked my brother not to tell you this part. Because I wanted to tell you myself." He nervously ran his fingers through his bright, bristly hair and his eyes had a gloss of desperation. "I thought that I'd have at least eight miles between New Rochelle and Harrison to convince Carlo to change his mind and bring me in to meet your mother. But I never even got the chance. We were on the Boston Post Road in Larchmont." Matteo paused and shut his eyes, and then Milo could see his whole body shudder; and indeed, Matteo's subsequent sigh seemed like a deflation of his entire being. He opened his eyes again and continued, "It was so quiet as we drove. It was truly, terribly quiet. I guess we'd already said everything we were going to say. And then suddenly, out of nowhere, Carlo starts banging the steering wheel. I'd never seen him so angry. Why was he so angry? Our business? My feelings for him? His feelings for me? But he never said a word to clarify. And then when we came to a red light, he just floored it. Floored it right through the red light, into the intersection."

Matteo was looking directly and unwaveringly at Milo as he spoke the last few words. "He did?" Milo murmured at last.

"I wish I could tell you something different," Matteo said. "I wish . . . but we were the ones who ran the red light, not the other driver. The light was green for them. So it wasn't the other driver's fault, although they still fled the scene of the accident."

"But after the other car struck you, the other driver—"

"I never saw the other driver. The car barely stopped. I just happened to notice it was a blue sedan. The person threw it into reverse and sped away. I guess they were afraid of something. Maybe they were driving illegally."

"No, they probably were drinking," Milo said, clinging to the original conclusion. "And that's why they kept going. That's why they didn't want to stop." Despite what he'd just learned about the accident, Milo realized this explanation was something that he still needed to believe.

Nodding, Matteo said, "Carlo's car was pretty smashed in, but he was still able to drive to the side of the road. We were both . . . kind of out of it. He was leaning toward me . . . like he was compensating. I kept asking if he was okay, and he kept saying he was fine, that his back hurt but he could move alright. He was sort of breathless. Thinking about it afterward, I know I should have suspected he was more injured than he was letting on. But I was shaken. I just didn't put it together that he was bleeding on the side of him that I couldn't see." Matteo stopped and had to collect himself for a moment. "And when he asked me to go call the ambulance, then I knew it was worse. And after I called the ambulance

I was told not to come back to the car. Something about me being questioned about why I was in the car?"

"Why you were in the car? But that makes no sense."

"I told him precisely that. But then the rest of what he said was kind of garbled. Something about how I wasn't expected to show up at your house. That neither of you knew me. And why would I have driven all the way with him without having a way of getting back. He was just so paranoid. And so I did what he asked." Matteo raised his hands. "I know it's hard to believe that I would leave him there like that, but because it was so early in the morning, because it was still so dark, because there were still so few cars on the road, I figured that no matter what, I would need to find a pay phone and call in the emergency. And so I did, but to find a pay phone, I had to run around a quarter of a mile. And then I decided not to listen to him. I rushed back to the car, and just as I got there, the ambulance was coming. Carlo already made it clear that he didn't want me there, so I just stood and watched . . . like a bystander," Matteo said bitterly. "They got him on a stretcher pretty quickly and took him to the hospital. And then I went back to the same pay phone and called Val, who came and got me."

Just as Matteo was finishing his story, a bird flew into the large glass sliding door leading to the apartment's balcony. From where Milo sat, he could see the injured creature rolling around on the red tiles before it finally went still. He could see that the bird had a yellow throat. "Birds keep flying into that door," Matteo informed him. "I don't know why."

Not quite hearing him, Milo said, "I don't know how I'll be able to tell my mother . . . that the accident was really Carlo's fault."

"No, it was really *my* fault," Matteo said. "Because I was distracting him. Because I made him so angry that he floored the gas pedal."

Milo shook his head. "It was *not* your fault! Carlo had a temper. He had my father's temper."

They both bowed their heads. At last, Milo said, "Do you happen to remember the last thing Carlo said to you?"

Matteo shrugged and said cynically, "Yeah. He said, 'Go call 911 and don't come back.'"

Go call 911 and don't come back. What a cruel thing to say to the person who loved you.

Matteo continued, "So after he died, I just couldn't come forward and tell you and your mother what had really happened. Val and I went to the funeral service at the church, and afterward, I went up to your mother and gave her my condolences. I told her my name, that I was Carlo's close friend from Iona, but I didn't explain anything else.

"I actually feel differently now," Matteo pointed out. "I actually regret *not* saying something more."

On a whim, almost like a gesture of solidarity, Milo turned his forearm over to show Matteo his memorial tattoo. Matteo moved closer and, just like Val had done, softly ran his fingers over the letters of Carlo's name, over the dates that tattooed Carlo's lifespan. A single tear dropped on '88, the year of his death.

Milo now told him, "I'll say this: A big part of my grief for my brother has always been that, as far as I knew, he'd never been in love or had never been loved by anyone. Except by us, by my mother and me . . . and I guess my father, who died quite a few years before Carlo did."

Shaking his head and shutting his eyes, Matteo said, "Carlo may have said something else to me as I was getting out of the car, but I don't remember what it was. But I do remember the last thing I said to him when *I* was getting out of the car. I told him that I loved him."

33.

After the conversation about Carlo, rubbed raw by the exchange, Milo then told Matteo that a man in a red Fiat had parked outside his building and seemed to be surveilling it. Matteo waved off the information with a smirk on his face. "That guy has been watching me on and off for a few days now. But it's not the first time I've noticed someone outside the building. There are many people out there doing worse illegal things, like selling drugs. And I happen to know that the government doesn't have the—Let's put it this way, the means to bust everyone."

It then occurred to Milo that while his most pressing purpose, to find out every last detail of what happened to his brother on the day he died, had been accomplished, Matteo's revelation had also led them astray from a discussion of Lenny's relationship to the making of hardcore pornography and his love affair with Vesuvia.

"And so what about this woman Vesuvia that Lenny was involved with?"

Matteo shook his head and looked impatient. "Didn't I say—"

"Can I talk to her?"

Matteo shook his head. "She wouldn't talk to you. And she wouldn't want me to identify her to you. I *have* to respect her wishes."

"I guess you also probably know *where* in Lucca these films are made?"

Matteo looked at him awry. "Like I said before, *that's* not what I'm prepared to talk about. But I will talk to you about Lenny. About how he got involved in filmmaking. Beyond investing."

"Okay," Milo said.

"As time went on, he started watching the filming, and then he got involved in the story ideas, the scripting. He began encouraging and critiquing the actors' performances. Kind of like a producer who also was fond of giving suggestions to the director. Truth be told, he was really into it because of the women, the fact that they were doing porn, that's what got him going. He just couldn't get enough of it."

"That's kind of what his sister said," Milo told him. "But I don't know if she has any idea of what he actually did over here."

"I think he kept *that* to himself," Matteo said. "Just like most people would keep their sex lives to themselves."

"Well, I think she knew more about him than he thought she did," Milo said.

34.

Milo could tell that Aunt Francesca certainly relished her role as Maria's gatekeeper. The first two times he tried to reach Maria, the stubborn aunt summarily dismissed him with, "She's not here. She's in the city. I don't know when she's coming back." Or, "I gave her your last message. That's all I can do."

Milo couldn't decide whether or not to pass along the news that he was in Italy, thinking it might actually deter Maria from speaking to him. So after his third attempt to reach her, he told Aunt Francesca, "It's really urgent that I speak to her," and was surprised when he was told, "Then call back in five minutes."

He waited, watching the minutes on his watch drag by. "What is it, Milo?" was how Maria answered the phone.

Stunned and wounded by her tone, he said, "What do you have against *me*?"

"What do I have against you? You don't leave anything alone. You're relentless. As relentless as my brother," she added with a bit of a softer tone.

"Well, it's no wonder," Milo said, "since I did model myself after him." But only to a point, he wanted to say, but didn't for obvious reasons.

"Well I had to deal with his relentlessness my whole life. So I don't want to deal with yours. Anyway, so what do you need? What's so urgent? Or not."

The last sarcastic comment made Milo quite angry. "Oh, it's an urgent matter," he told her. "At least to me it is, and I think it will be to you."

"Try me," she challenged him.

"Okay. I am in Italy. And I am going to assume you know about what Lenny was up to over here. His business dealings. The reason why he was able to deposit a million and a half dollars into your joint back account."

"Let's say I had my suspicions, but that's as far as it went," Maria said in a more conversational tone.

"So he never discussed anything with you?"

"Milo, you knew him almost as well as I did. Do you really think he would discuss his . . . let's call it 'side business' with me?"

"Then how did you find out?"

"How do you think? The letters from Emma Stein. Clearly, for some reason, he discussed it with her."

"And *clearly* this is why you didn't want me to read the letters."

"It's precisely why."

"Then why didn't you read them right away?"

She reminded him that Lenny had not been dead all that long and while she'd had a vague impression that there was a collected correspondence between him and Emma Stein, she'd never had any intention of exploring it, certainly while her brother was alive.

"Fair point," Milo told her.

She asked him how he'd found out and he explained.

"Wow," she exclaimed. "So I guess then they'll be coming after the money in the bank account?"

"I suspect that might happen."

"Well, at least I have other means to live on," she told him. And then to his relief, her tone turned conciliatory. "Look, I'm sorry you had to learn all this the way you did."

He now confessed how rotten he was feeling about all of it, not to mention her distant attitude toward him.

She apologized and said, "Just come and see me when you come back. And we'll talk."

As hopeful as he was tempted to feel, Milo knew that her intentions toward him were merely cordial.

35.

As it turned out, Giacomo had gotten a free pass to visit the film set from his family acquaintance who he always knew was involved in garden-variety pornography production. Like many secular Italians, Giacomo kept a lackadaisical attitude toward the making of pornography. Live and let live—if the participants were willing and there was a market.

As Paolo had indicated, the studio was located outside the city walls in a warehouse district in the general vicinity of Master Club. Milo figured that, in all the summers he'd spent in Lucca, he had probably driven by the place dozens of times on his way to and from the gym.

"Obviously they don't harm anybody at these film productions, do they?" Paolo asked.

They were driving in Giacomo's Audi A4, Paolo in the front seat, Milo in the rear. Looking at Giacomo's wide, rough-hewn face in the rearview mirror, Milo could see the bodybuilder's eyebrows raise.

"Harm?" Giacomo asked. "Does sadomasochism harm? You tell me, lover boy, if that's what you get into."

"Hardly!" Paolo shot back. "By the way," he went on, "I think this warehouse we're going to is actually owned by Delfini," referring to a multinational fabric company whose world headquarters was located in Lucca.

Giacomo drove surprisingly slowly along Via San Concordio. *He drives like a grandmother,* Milo thought to himself, this muscled man behind the steering wheel, with his gold chains and his tight black nylon shirt that showed every ripple of his body. Also notable about the bodybuilder was his indeterminate age. Milo pegged him for around thirty, but Giacomo's air of self-confidence made him seem older, more like forty.

When Giacomo made a right turn at the wide street that passed the huge, Esselunga grocery store, Milo said to Paolo, "I can't forget to buy Parmesan for my mom. I need to bring back six kilos."

"*Madonna,*" said Giacomo, "why six kilos?"

"Because it's young Parmesan, really good and so cheap. You can't get young Parmesan like that in America. All you can get is aged, crumbling Parmesan."

Then, surprising Milo, Giacomo said in very clear English, "So, Mama likes her Italian Parmesan young." And then he laughed. "And you bring it home to her in quantity. You must be a very good son."

"*Cosa*? What did you say?" Paolo asked Giacomo.

Giacomo and Milo locked eyes in the rearview mirror, Giacomo's bright eyes behind his turquoise-colored contact lenses. "So, you *do* know English," Milo said.

"Who said I didn't know it?" Giacomo replied. Then deliberately changing back to Italian, he said to Paolo, "Why don't *you* learn a little more English? So that next time you land in America you won't feel so isolated." The actual phrase he used in Italian translated literally as "walled in."

"If I learn English, it will only get me in trouble," Paolo said. "I'll get to meet American women. And now, especially with Antonella, not such a good idea."

"You're a legend in your own mind," Milo said in English. Giacomo frowned, not quite getting this. Milo dutifully explained the idiom and then both agreed that idioms were the most difficult to translate from one language to another.

The road was now passing under the rounded arches of an old Roman stone aqueduct that led to another roundabout and came out abruptly upon a completely industrialized area of long two-story buildings and warehouses, as well as spits of unoccupied burnt-looking land. As they veered past Delfini's modern, low-slung building with enormous glass windows and veered into a parking lot, Giacomo said, "We keep going all the way to the back, and then we should see a yellow prefabricated building."

The structure was easy to find.

Parked in front were several trucks lined up next to one another, their rear doors completely open and chock-full of large black wires and bright metal dollies that identified them as belonging to the film industry. Off to one side was a small, battered, turquoise-colored trailer that reminded Milo of the sun-faded dwellings in the American Southwest, punctuating desert landscapes. A very busty blond woman wearing a corset-like garment was exiting the trailer. "Oh my God, look at her. Now, she's perfect, isn't she?" Paolo said in a lascivious tone. "So sexy, *cazzo!*"

Giacomo smirked and said dismissively, "Calm down, *porco*."

The woman was heavily made up, her hair piled on top of her head. With all the makeup, it was hard to know what she really looked like. Milo said nothing, although he watched her carefully. "Now what?" he asked, noting that Giacomo seemed on edge.

"I will go in and meet my friend." Then he turned around in his seat and said to Milo, "You can come with me. But Paolo stays here."

"What?" Paolo protested, affronted. "*I* want to see this pornography-making. Why did I come otherwise?"

Giacomo said, "I don't think my friend will mind if I take in one other person. Especially if it's *him*." He pointed to Milo, who immediately asked Giacomo to clarify what that meant.

"Wait a moment, and I'll explain." Then to Paolo, "He's the one who's interested, for God's sake. You couldn't care less. So it's not worth trying to get you in—my friend won't allow three of us, I just know it. Two will already be asking a lot. Anyway, we shouldn't be more than a half hour."

Disgruntled, Paolo, using the polite verb form, told Giacomo to go castrate pigs.

Once they were away from the car, Giacomo said, "Under normal circumstances, you would not have a chance of coming in here with me." But then he explained that his childhood friend, the assistant producer, would "like" Milo, going on to say that, steeped in this world of heterosexual, pornographic moviemaking, against his better instinct, the man would probably agree to allow what basically translated as "eye candy" to accompany Giacomo.

Stationed at the door to the warehouse was a very tall, extremely broad Eurasian-looking man regarding them with angry suspicion. As they approached, Giacomo calmly gave his friend's name, and the man told him to wait there. He returned with another man who looked to be in his thirties, dressed entirely in black and with very pale skin and closely cropped, prematurely gray hair. He was rail thin to the point of looking undernourished, and his black clothes draped on him. He regarded Milo with a discerning gaze and then turned to Giacomo. "Did I *say* you could bring someone?"

"You didn't say don't bring anybody," Giacomo replied. "Besides, I *had* to bring him. Milo is my first cousin from Milan. He's staying with us. We had to leave the house. There is restructuring being done there. Right now, the water is turned off." Tapping Milo gently on the shoulder, Giacomo said, "He can be trusted."

Giacomo clearly had prepared this explanation. And if so, why hadn't he alerted Milo in advance, so that at least Milo could have braced himself to be designated "the Milanese cousin?" Did that mean he'd now have to speak without an (or at worst, with a slight) American accent? Had Giacomo assumed this would be no problem for him?

The producer's gaze lingered on Milo; then he shrugged and led both of them into a dark corridor that opened to a large space with at least twenty-foot-high ceilings and brightly lighted with arc lamps. The set was simple: constructed out of gypsum were four eight-foot-high walls painted a pale olive green. The walls enclosed a king-sized bed with a carved, flimsy-looking gold-leaf headboard. On either side of the bed were two square end tables, and on one of them was a pint-size container with a pump that looked to Milo like personal lubricant.

Giacomo's friend and neighbor took him aside, said something, and Giacomo nodded. He came back over to Milo. "He says our presence will disturb the crew and the actors and suggested we go upstairs. He says there is a viewing room with a big window. We can look down from there and not be seen by anyone."

Giacomo lumbered slowly up the winding flight of metal stairs with Milo close behind. At the top of the stairs, a door led into a room with a brown sofa and a couple of portable wooden chairs. Looking around, Milo's attention was caught by something. On a low coffee table perched atop a pile of glossy magazines was Primo Levi's *Il sistema periodico* (*The Periodic Table*). An eerie feeling came over him. He picked up the familiar book and started thumbing through it.

The door opened, and in came the pale-skinned assistant producer, who saw Milo perusing the book. "That belongs to someone here."

"Yours?" Milo asked.

"The director's. Was a gift." Milo naturally wondered if Lenny had given the book to the director. Had Lenny and the director struck up a friendship?

The producer pointed down to the set where a tall, lanky man with a frenetic air was hurrying between a few technicians and several young, attractive Eastern European-looking men and women, their faces pancaked with makeup—the actors. The director looked impatient and annoyed. The male actors were shirtless, their bodies hairless and sculpted. One woman had impressive cleavage; the other was flat-chested. The women dressed in tube tops and short shorts. The director was spewing orders at all of them.

The assistant producer looked at his watch and said, "Ten minutes and they're starting." And then to Milo, "Your accent sounds a bit strange. Where are you from? Originally."

"I think what you're hearing is my mother's American accent," Milo said, careful not to glance at Giacomo. "People often say they can hear the influence of her English. I speak both. In fact, I spoke English first."

The producer looked skeptical. "So then *how* are you two related?"

"On my father's side of the family," Giacomo told him with remarkable assurance.

To distract further, Milo asked, "I wonder if the director has read this book."

The assistant producer glowered at him. "Most educated people in Italy have read this book."

"We never did. In Milano," Milo risked saying.

"Well, *we* did at the Normale," Giacomo said.

"Of course you did at the Normale," the assistant director said snidely.

The *Normale*? Milo was incredulous. "The Pisa Normale?" he blurted out. Then quickly realized that as Giacomo's cousin, this is something he already should have known. Giacomo glanced up at the ceiling with a shake of his head.

The producer smiled, showing a row of very yellow teeth, and said, "I know Giacomo's a plumber who looks like he spends the entire day at the gym, but his brain, proportionally, is actually bigger than his body."

"I only spend ninety minutes a day at the gym."

"Only ninety minutes?" Milo asked with irony, and they all laughed.

"I need to get back downstairs," the producer informed them.

After the man retreated, Giacomo said, "As my cousin, the Normale is obviously something you would know."

"I'm sorry. But you also should have warned me about all of this."

"I decided not to. I thought you might get too nervous in anticipation."

"So you really went to the Normale?"

Giacomo said, "Are you skeptical about my education because I do plumbing?"

"No—"

"Paolo told you that it's a two-hundred-year-old family business. Keeping it going is my obligation. You bring your mother Parmesan to keep her happy. I keep carrying on the plumbing business to keep *my* mother happy."

"Your English is very confident."

"I studied it my whole life!" Giacomo said emphatically. Then he said, "And now I need to explain something to you, something that Paolo does not know because, let's face it, we are really just gym acquaintances. My brother is a Carabinïeri."

"Why are you mentioning this?"

"I told my brother we were coming here to see what goes on. Naturally, he's interested in something like this. I told him I'd call him if I see anything he should worry about."

Milo looked down at the set and spied a dark, Middle Eastern–looking man wearing a black silk bathrobe entering from the left side. And then the blond woman they saw exiting the turquoise trailer emerged from another corner of the makeshift stage. A man armed with a handheld camera approached them. The arc lamps were turned up, everything blindingly bright, and Milo heard the smack of the clapboard.

It was a relatively short sequence between two people who began to kiss passionately and realistically. The robes fell off to reveal stunning physiques. Milo felt sad that these two actors, probably surviving in Italy without steady employment, were allowing themselves to be exploited for the hungry eyes of viewers all over the world. Two other handheld cameras emerged from the shadows. Soon, the woman was lying in a submissive position on the bed, the man standing over her, his robe tented with his excitement. The frenetic director cut the scene, but she remained on the bed until another woman dressed in black, goth-like clothing (a uniform that eerily matched what the assistant director was wearing) approached her with the pint-size vessel of lubricant. The actress stood up and held out her hands to receive a dollop of the glistening fluid. She hurried offstage and into a dark corridor, presumably to apply it to herself.

Milo suddenly identified the woman in black: Sonia, who'd been in Matteo Cipolla's company two days before. He immediately shrunk back in order not to be recognized.

Matteo hadn't mentioned that she worked on the film set; perhaps she was the one who now brought the cash to the actors.

The actress returned to the blinding glare and once again lay on the bed. The clapboard clacked. There was some minimal caressing between the couple before the man climbed on top of her. One camera was trained on his back as he entered her and began thrusting, but only for a minute. Suddenly, her hands were around his neck and, with all the force she seemed to possess, she throttled him. Still inside her, he grabbed her wrists and tried to pry them away. Her grip was steely and seemingly unbreakable and soon you could see him beginning to choke. Milo noticed a camera trained on the woman's face, as if to record her look of determination as she persisted in subduing her partner. By now, the man's movements grew desperate. He kept trying to fend her off. "Will they stop her at some point?" Milo pleaded aloud. Giacomo didn't answer; at once either perturbed or mesmerized, he didn't seem to hear or register the question.

To Milo's great relief, the director cut the scene, and the woman released the man from her life-threatening grip. Even from their considerable distance, they could clearly identify red fingermark contusions around his neck.

Giacomo turned to Milo. "Okay, you can see his neck from here—he's clearly been compromised. I personally don't want to watch any more of this. I think we should leave *now* before they start filming another scene."

Milo just then happened to notice Sonia approaching the assistant director and saying something that caused him to look up to where they were watching; and then the man began walking quickly and purposefully toward the staircase. So she *had* noticed him come in. He informed Giacomo who said, "Ah, well then I think we might have a little problem," and yanked his phone out of his hip pocket and engaged it. "Ciao Giovanni, I think you probably do need to come here." A moment later, the door cracked open, the assistant director popped his head in and asked Giacomo to come out into the hallway to have a word with him.

It seemed as though Milo waited a very long time before the door flew open and the Eurasian bouncer from downstairs came barreling in holding a thick metal chain.

"Stop! Hold on! Hold on!" Milo cried as the man started coming toward him. The next thing he knew, the chain swung and slammed against the side of his face. The pain was terrific; hazed with disbelief, he crumpled to the floor.

36.

"*Dio mio,* that is quite the bruise you have on your face," Rotelli was telling Milo with grave concern. "That brute of a man easily could've killed you." Turning to Lara, he said, "Your nephew didn't take my warning very seriously—I advised him to stay away from this pornography business."

The Carabinieri who'd arrived at the film set had brought Milo to the emergency room, where it was determined that the terrific blow from the chain swung by the bouncer had luckily only given him a mild concussion. The entire right side of his face was now swollen in a jaundiced, purple bruise, and he was told to expect headaches, like the one he had presently, for the next few days, or maybe even a week.

They were in the ballroom. Milo, lightheaded with the dull, persistent throbbing in his temples, reclining against the hard cushions of the ancient sofa, gazing up at the five-hundred-year-old trompe l'oeil scenes of shepherds and their obedient flocks of sheep. When Lara had knocked on his bedroom door to tell him that Rotelli had come to see him, he'd shambled out into the enormous room in order to receive the man, who now stood next to Lara, staring down at him.

Rotelli went on to explain that Giacomo's brother and the Carabinieri shut down the film set and rounded up the actors and crew to determine which of them were in the country working illegally. Giacomo had told them that Sonia had recognized Milo and when questioned, she didn't deny it. "She recognized you, not from having met you in Pistoia, but from photographs she saw of you."

"Photographs? What photographs?"

"When they searched her, they found an address in Pistoia near to where Matteo Cipolla lives. They went to her apartment, searched it, and came up with some letters written to her by . . ." Rotelli paused and then sighed. "Your professor, D'Ambrosio."

So she *must be Vesuvia,* Milo thought, stunned.

"Clearly they were very well-acquainted."

"Is she Albanian?"Milo asked.

Rotelli nodded. "Yes. And Sonia is not her real name. It's—"

"It's Vesuvia?" Milo broke in.

Rotelli was taken aback. "Bravo! But how did you know?"

Milo explained about reading the letters that Vesuvia had written to Lenny.

"Well, Vesuvia has been using the name Sonia Elezi for life as well as travel. We took the Albanian passport along with other documents." He paused for a moment, his face looking even more grave. "The passport reveals that she went to New York."

Rotelli went on to explain what Milo already knew: Vesuvia claimed that Lenny had promised to marry her and give her enough money so she could eventually become an American citizen. But once she arrived in New York, all he really wanted to do was make videos of her; in her apartment the Carabinieri found videos of her dominating and roughing up a young man who spoke American English—"We don't know who he is, presumably some American boy the professor found and hired. The videos were looked at and then she had to answer our questions about them."

Silence echoed throughout the ballroom and through his persistent headache, Milo could hear the distant din of the A11 autostrada that began at Viareggio and ended in Florence.

Rotelli continued, "At first, Sonia Elezi denied having anything to do with D'Ambrosio's death." Rotelli raised his index finger. "But that was before she knew that we went into her apartment, got hold of six videos, and studied them."

Surely those must be the videos that Lenny had been keeping in his apartment safe, the ones that Maria claimed had disappeared mysteriously.

Rotelli continued, "There was one video in particular, when we told her we'd seen it and described what was in it, she had no choice but to confess."

"Confess to what?" Milo asked.

"Confess to holding him at gunpoint and making him climb up on a chair and end his life by hanging himself."

Milo felt breathless. Rotelli was peering at him, blinking rapidly. Lara was shaking her head, with her eyes cast down on the terra cotta flooring of the ballroom. "Do we need to go into this anymore?" she asked Rotelli. "Can you give him a little bit of time to recuperate before—"

"But I don't have more time," Milo told her angrily just as he felt an electrical plume of pain flash across his forehead. "My plane back to New York leaves tomorrow."

Lara said, "Oh no. With an injury like this, you must delay your return until you're feeling better."

"The hospital told me I would be okay to fly. And if we call my mother and tell her I'm delayed, she'll want to know why."

"We can think of something," Lara replied. "You'll just tell her everything when you get back."

Milo shook his head. "I'm not going to lie to her about something like this."

"He's right," Rotelli said, turning to Lara. "Don't try to keep him here. You will just complicate things. He's young and strong. I'm sure in his condition he can withstand a plane ride."

Lara turned her palms up in a gesture of surrender.

Rotelli held up his hand. "Anyway, did you know that your dear departed friend participated in the making of these films?"

Milo repeated what Matteo had told him.

"Apparently it was a bit more than that," Rotelli replied with a pinched expression on his face. "According to Sonia Elezi, he cheered the actors, he cheered the sex, he cheered the violence like a football fan. *Then* he sometimes berated the actors with a mouth that sounded like he came from the street. It was a complete transformation of character, apparently. And after all his verbal abuse, he then got access to some of the women on his own private time."

Milo thought of Emma Stein sneering when he told her Lenny had gone to Italy for "cultural reasons." Desperately trying to digest the idea of Lenny jeering and taunting the actors in their varying sexually violent roles, an attitude that seemed to have bled into his own sex life, Milo recalled the story Lenny told him of how he'd lost his faith in God, the African refugee who came to Italy and suffered in loneliness and despair and who surely was exploited the way some of the refugees who took part in the films Lenny had funded and participated in were, despite being compensated, arguably exploited. To think that Lenny always railed against this kind of exploitation of the weak, exploitation of the innocent. How could he have acted against his own principles? His own beliefs? How could he have gone against his own nature?

Lying back on the sofa and looking up at the Tiepolo-like clouds painted on the ceiling of the ballroom, Milo said, "Can I watch this final video?"

"What?" Lara interjected with vehemence. "You want to watch it?"

Rotelli interjected, "You *want* to witness your professor naked and standing on a chair and putting a noose around his own neck?"

"No! But . . . maybe I'll see something, some gesture, maybe I'll hear something he said that will help me understand . . . how it all ended up the way it did."

Shaking his head, Rotelli said, "All the films have gone to Rome for further evaluation. There's no access to them."

"Can I see them eventually?"

"I'm afraid not." Turning to Lara, Rotelli said, "I think I will tell him what is in this final film. But you'll not want to hear this, I imagine, so I suggest you go downstairs."

"I don't want to know anything more," Lara said and quickly walked out of the ballroom. Both men waited until they could hear her footsteps echoing as she descended the stone stairway that led to the lower level of the Villa Calderi.

37.

A closeup of a hand holding a black eyeshade, the voice of a woman telling the owner of the hand to put the eyeshade on. It must be the same eyeshade Milo discovered in the apartment, the one left on top of Diary of a Country Priest. *A rail-thin torso climbing uncertainly onto a chair, the woman's hand now in the frame helping him climb up* (she must be holding the camera), *the bedsheet hanging from one of the rafters of the vaulted ceiling—of course he doesn't want to put it around his neck, but she insists, how is she able to make him do this?*

"Come on, just like Marco and I did it." She tells him unless he wants to get down from the chair and do what he promised her and he tells her why he can't do what he promised her, why he can't marry her, and she tells him, "Well, then now, it's going to be beautiful."

And he actually agrees with her. "Yes," he says, "it's going to be beautiful."

The chair pulled away, the weight of his body bending his neck into an unnatural angle. What kind of cruelty could he have inflicted on this woman that would make her film him frantically scrabbling at the noose, his legs kicking desperately, trying to find an impossible purchase in midair until at last, his body entering the throes of violent, lifeless twitching?

In the midst of hearing and imagining this macabre scene, Milo conjured up the photograph of a dark-haired woman scurrying away from Lenny's building, the one taken by feeble Mrs. Colicchio. "But Sonia is blond," he managed to point out to Rotelli. And then mentioned the photograph taken by the downstairs neighbor.

Rotelli replied, "One of the other actors told us she previously had curly, dark hair, her natural hair." *Like Maria's hair,* Milo thought. *Like Emma Stein's hair.* "More recently, she apparently cut her hair short and dyed it platinum. She *does* work in films, after all. But it doesn't really matter in the end, because we have the video itself with her hands and the audio that implicates her."

Milo managed to nod as he shut his eyes against another jab of head pain.

"I'm going to leave now and let you get some rest," Rotelli said. He reached out to shake Milo's hand. "Do have a safe trip home."

38.

Val and Milo were sitting in armchairs at the FBI office in Federal Plaza, where they'd both been questioned in conjunction with the overseas shutdown of the illegal film studio and Matteo being detained by the A.I.S.E in Florence. The FBI now had records of the deposits and withdrawals between Lenny D'Ambrosio's bank account in Belize and the Cipollas' bank account at the Cassa di Risparmio del Veneto in Pistoia.

Holding his head in his hands, Val's long tresses had swung forward and were mostly obscuring what Milo presumed was his splenetic expression. "I knew it would be bad news if I got you and Matteo together," he said dismally. "And all that *patronizing* crap about what a shame it was that I wasn't in a more legit profession. You know what, go *fuck* yourself!"

Knowing that Val had originally told him more than he should have because he'd assumed Milo knew way more than he did, Milo's instinct was that if the conversation were to proceed to where he wanted it, he'd have to maintain his composure and by definition, try and keep from rattling Val any more than necessary. "You were very far away from what was going on. It was easy not to be concerned about any of it."

Val continued, "And since you knew Lenny way better than we did, maybe you'll get it that under no circumstances would he have wanted us to divulge to *you* that he had anything to do with our business. In fact you're probably the last person he'd want to know what he was up to."

"I get it," Milo told him.

Val leaned back in his chair and pushed his hair back. A bar of sunlight was just then pouring through the window of the glass building, illuminating his eyes, which made their look of distress sparkle. Squinting at Milo, he remarked, "Wow, you really got slammed by that bouncer guy, didn't you?" Milo explained that the doctors at the hospital in Lucca had told him he was lucky not to have been more injured. "Does it hurt a lot?"

"Six, on a scale of one to ten," Milo replied. "I still have these pretty persistent headaches."

Val nodded, and right before Milo was going to veer them back to the conversation, Val resumed it on his own, "Okay, so now I am going to tell you everything I know about your dear, departed Professor Leonard D'Ambrosio . . . right up until his death, about which until today I had no clue except for . . . my educated hunch.

"As you now know, business-wise, we were entwined. And like my brother told you, Lenny was the one who supervised and visited and, when he was in Italy, bothered to give input to the movie sets. Yes, he liked to watch the actual filming. He was into it big time. And you already know that he had a few involvements with some of the women who acted in the films. To what extent he was involved with these women is not something Matteo or I ever knew very much about. Like I said, he was very tight-lipped about everything he did outside of film production. I would guess they were all short-term relationships. However, the one with Sonia obviously ended very badly. Somehow it doesn't surprise me to learn he offered to marry her for the sake of American citizenship. He could be very generous with people. Why he didn't follow through is . . . well, maybe you could answer that question better than I. Again, he wasn't our friend, he was our business partner. He invested; then he got involved in filmmaking because he wanted to."

Val leaned forward with clasped hands, which looked like the hands of a tradesman and certainly belied his acute mind and his worldly sophistication. And then it occurred to Milo that Val was like the American equivalent of Giacomo. "When Lenny died the way he did, Matteo and I, of course we had our suspicions. We tried to look into it ourselves. We'd known Sonia had had some kind of involvement with him. But when Matteo asked her point blank about his death, she said she knew nothing about it and that their relationship had ended a while back." Val shrugged. "*And* we had no reason to disbelieve her. We did ask some of the other people Lenny had worked with on the film set, but nobody knew anything. So, we had to drop it. Our only explanation was that maybe he offed himself because he felt so guilty about what he was doing. Catholic guilt."

"He was an atheist," Milo pointed out.

Val shook his head. "Once a Catholic, always a Catholic.

"We only started to suspect more when you started to suspect more. But again, we were bound . . . bound to the original promise we'd made to him."

"Okay, but I do need to understand one other thing unrelated. Why you told my mother and me only part of the story of what happened between our brothers. And not—"

"Matteo felt it was *his* responsibility to tell you about the part that involved him. You can understand that, can't you?"

"No, because you'd already decided to tell me about it well before you even knew I was going to Italy."

Val shook his head. "Right, but early on, once I mentioned that I told you about the argument with Carlo that last night, Matteo asked me not to discuss it any further."

"And so if I hadn't gone to Italy I never would have learned the rest of it?"

"But you did go to Italy, so what's the point of conjecturing otherwise?" Val held up a finger. "And by the way, I have to wonder if you and your mother might have been better off not knowing the full extent of what really happened."

"Well," Milo conceded, "now the wound has reopened. And she's miserable again."

"Exactly my point. Why add to people's misery?"

"Why, indeed," Milo said.

Val said, "Just think: If only your brother could have handled it, maybe the two of them could have had a life together."

Milo tried to imagine this, his brother in a loving relationship, and felt a terrible, harrowing emptiness.

"The real truth is an awful truth, isn't it?" Val said after a brief silence.

Milo considered this, and then said, "It is. But what would have been more awful is if you'd lost your brother in that accident, too."

Val groaned and shook his head. "Don't think I haven't thought of *that* a million times," he told Milo.

39.

They were sitting in the kitchen. His mother's candle was burning brightly as Milo relayed the conversation he'd had with Val at the FBI office.

"I can't concentrate on what you're saying. With that *faccia brutta*," she said about his face. "But, maybe I want to be distracted from listening to you." She sighed. "No, I really needed to know." Then, she muttered something under her breath.

"What did you say, Mom?"

"It's about your brother. I never really felt he wanted to look after me. I felt he wanted me to feed him, do his laundry, keep the room tidy. That I didn't really matter so much to him. Sometimes, I felt like I wasn't even there. It's always been very painful for me to think about."

"Mom," Milo countered, "it wasn't because he didn't care about you. He was too far inside his own head. He was fighting against what he knew he truly was. Maybe that's why he was so angry all the time."

Nodding, Rose Marie said, "I guess that could be true." She reached across the table, touching the tattoo on Milo's pale forearm. "But you always took care of me, Milo. Even when you were a little kid. Even before your father died."

"Well, if you say so. I guess you'd know."

"I do know."

He saw she wanted him to agree with her, that she needed him to agree with her. And so he agreed. For at least a short time, it would make her feel better, and maybe, even for a few moments, a bit happier.

She sat back and took the round cover to her burning candle and was about to put it over the top to staunch the flame, when Milo exclaimed, "No, no! Please don't put it out that way. Blow it out instead."

She turned to him bewildered. "Why?"

"Whenever anyone puts a candle out that way, the flame fades from no oxygen until it dies. It's like watching a life go out. I don't like seeing that. It. . . makes me think of Carlo."

"I understand," Rose Marie said, and they sat there for a while. And then she blew the candle out.